# ROYAL MAYHEM

SAMANTHA JAYNE GRUBEY

Cover Design © https://www.theprettylittledesignco.co.uk

Editing © https://www.jadechurchauthor.com/editorial & https://editingbyjessicasydney.com/

Formatted with Vellum

*Never give up. Keep fighting always. You've got this.*

*"You're braver than you believe, stronger than you seem, and smarter than you think." — Winnie the Pooh*

## TRIGGER AND CONTENT WARNINGS:

Mention of abortion (Views)
Mention of weight
Abandonment of a parent
Alchohol
Sexual content
Chronic illness
Slight mention of attempted murder
Brief mention of stalking and rape
Mention of dyslexia, ADHD etc

# Chapter One

## MELINDA

The lights flickered before shutting off completely.

I let out a groan and flipped the blanket off as I got up off the sofa and headed into the hallway under the stairs, pulling the door open looking at the breaker. All the switches were on, which only meant one thing, we were out of electricity again.

I reached for my phone and pressed the screen. Nothing happened. I pressed down on the power button and the battery image flashed on my screen. Of course, my phone would be dead, that meant a trip to the corner shop, but I needed to find the electric card first.

*Now, where would it be?*

Looking around the kitchen, I opened the junk drawer, papers spilled on the floor. I sighed, leaning down as I reached for the papers. My hand felt something hard. It had to be the card. Placing the rest of the papers in the drawer, I shoved the card into my pocket.

Now where did I put my purse?

I needed to get better at remembering where I was leaving things. Tapping my foot I tried to think back when I came home from work, kicked shoes off heading to the fridge. I headed into the kitchen looking around the sides opening the fridge. I saw my purse on the empty shelf.

*What the fuck was I thinking? Man, I needed a nap.*

I opened up the purse and saw I had no money.

*Fuck. Could this day get any worse?*

I probably shouldn't jinx the rest of my evening; everything could always get worse. No phone and no money, first world problems. I peered out of the kitchen window into darkness, usually an overgrown garden would stare back at me, I didn't know what was worst, the garden or the darkness. I looked along the corner and noticed some coins on the counter and swiping them into my hand walking out the house heading towards the streetlamp. I looked down in my hand seeing a few pound coins, I could at least put five pounds on I guess. At this rate, I would be late for work today. No alarm, no phone, no electricity, at this point I'd just give up and go to bed if it wasn't so early in the morning.

I walked back into the house, shutting the door behind me. I slumped down on the sofa.

I was too young to deal with this bullshit.

The front door creaked open, I watched as mum walked in and hit the light switch. "The electricity is gone."

Mum jumped holding her chest. "Jesus Christ, Melinda," she gasped. "Why on earth would you be sitting in the dark?"

"Did you not listen when I just said the electricity is gone?" I raised an eyebrow.

Mum shook her head and let out a yawn.

"Well, I have to go to work, here's five pounds," I said, putting the money in her hand. "Also, the cupboards are empty. We need food shopping, and I don't get paid until next week."

"What happened to your student loan?" Mum asked, raising an eyebrow. "You just got it."

"Course materials mum, I had to buy a laptop for my assignments and stuff," I said pointedly. "Also, you just got paid. Where's your money?"

Mum folded her arms over her chest. "I'm the parent here, not you."

"The parent who can't remember to keep our cupboards full and electric on," I said flatly.

"Melinda—"

I interrupted her, shaking my head and standing up. "I don't have time for this argument. I need to go to work."

"You work too hard. "If you would just accept—"

"No," I cut her off immediately. "I will not accept Roman's guilt money. You may have forgiven him and fallen straight back into love and bed with him; he stopped being my father the moment he walked out the door at eight-years-old."

"Mel—"

"I don't want to hear it, mum," I shook my head walking away.

Nothing she could say would make up for the fact he left and didn't return for almost ten years. At times like these, I wish I had chosen to stay in university housing, but unfortunately, it was cheaper to stay home and that was the case for both me and my best friend, Megan.

"It's more complicated than that, Melinda."

"I don't have time for this, I have to work," I said, grabbing my bag from the kitchen. I poked my head into the living room and looked at my mum. "Please just put some electricity on and buy some actual food for us both to eat."

I left the house heading straight to the bus stop scanning the bus pass I got onto the bus which thankfully wasn't too busy.

Forty minutes later, I had finally arrived at campus. I'd like to say it was quiet when I walked into the diner, but it wasn't. The diner was currently getting redecorated, so the American decoration didn't really fit the vibe of what Daisy wanted this diner to be. The American flags had been taken down, and the wallpaper was in the middle of being scraped off ready for the new one that she had picked.

Cindy was at the till making herself look busy whilst some of the other girls were running up and down the diner serving and delivering food and drinks to them. I wasn't surprised that's usually how shifts went when Cindy was on, I wasn't sure how she got the manager position because she was allergic to work from what I had seen.

I walked behind the counter heading straight for the staff room putting my bag and coat in the locker, getting my apron on and tying it around my waist and heading towards the kitchen where Dave stood there, cooking away.

"Good morning, Melinda," he grinned as he saw me approaching.

"Is it a good morning though?" I asked, raising an eyebrow. "How was the night shift?"

He shook his head. "I am so glad freshers are over. Two weeks of hell, hell I tell you."

I let out a snicker, Dave could always be a little bit of a drama queen, but I had to agree with him.

I understood why the idea of a twenty-four hour diner on a university campus was a good idea and realistically a gold mine. But damn did it drive those of us who worked at the diner crazy. They were drunk all the time, and I wasn't sure any of the freshers attended lectures for the first two weeks, I was confident most of them just drank themselves dumb.

"I don't think it fazes me anymore after working here for two years, I'm immune to the idiots."

"Mel, you count as one of those idiots, you're a university student this year," he said. "I would have thought you would apply to a university further away than Derby. I didn't expect you to apply to the one straight on your doorstep."

"It's home." I shrugged. "A shit hole but home. Anyway, I best go clock in."

"Yeah, you don't want to be late on the floor. The dragon is in." Dave chuckled. "She looks ready to blow."

I giggled. "All I can think of is the dragon from *Shrek*."

"Didn't the dragon have babies with Donkey?" Dave asked, raising an eyebrow.

I nodded, walking away to the machine pressing my finger on the scanner to clock in. I headed back into the main part of the diner and took a scan of the room. There were a few people scattered across the counter and a few groups in the booths. Cindy was currently taking an order.

The doorbell chimed, I watched as a group stumbled over to the booth, I grabbed my notepad heading over to the table. "Hi, welcome to Daisy's diner, what can I get you?" I asked.

A hand landed on mine as the man tried to pull me into the booth. "How about you?"

"I'm not on the menu," I said, firmly pulling away.

*Drunk university students for the win.*

"Jake, stop." A girl frowned as she moved her blonde hair from her face. "Sorry, can we just get four large Cokes please?"

"Of course, I'll be right back with your drinks," I said politely.

I grabbed four glasses reaching for the soft drink pump pouring it into their glasses. I popped straws into them, placing them on a serving plate before taking them back to the table. I placed them on the table in front of the group.

"So, I have a question," another one of the guys in the group said.

"Guys seriously, this is why we don't let you do a two-day bender," the girl said, shaking her head.

"No, for real, like...are the diner decorations American?" He asked, looking at me.

I smiled a little knowing exactly where this question was going, whilst we had rebranded the menu, the diner had not been refurbished just yet. "Yes," I confirmed.

"Why is it an English breakfast? Like, that's tripping me out, man."

"That could just be the alcohol," I said flatly.

"Or the weed," the girl snorted with a laugh.

"But Daisy's is currently undergoing a rebrand, do you guys know what you're ordering or should I leave you for a few more minutes?"

"Girl, I'll save you the trouble," she said. "Three full English breakfasts for the piss heads, and I'll have a breakfast bagel."

"Thank you," I said, scribbling down the order. I headed to the kitchen handing the ticket to Dave who called it out into the kitchen. "We got this."

After two and half hours of hell I can confirm we didn't have this. I clocked out, grabbing my bag and headed into the university. My first lecture started at 9:00 a.m. and thankfully this was one I had with my best friend, Megan.

I headed straight to our seats sitting down and getting my things out. Megan's dirty blonde hair fell around her head as she looked at her phone.

"This seat is ta" Her words cut off as she finally looked up. "How was work?"

"Drunk people," I told her.

She went back to typing on her phone, and I raised an eyebrow.

She wasn't usually this attached to her phone. "Say no more, girl." She chuckled. "Do you have any more lectures today? I really can't get to grips with the schedule."

"Nope, just digital storytelling today. Wednesday, it is writing skills for Media & Communication, and then Audio podcasting on Thursday."

"Damn, I kind of wish I had your schedule. Add in a

lot of library extra help skills and we match except obviously we have two different modules," Megan said. "Are you working after?"

"Yep, got another shift at the diner I finish at 7:00 p.m." I told her.

Megan angled her body to face me and crossed her arms over her chest, "have you eaten today?"

"What are you, my mother?"

"Melinda, you can't keep skipping meals. It's not healthy." She frowned. I rolled my eyes, Megan reached over, slapping my arm. "I'm serious Mel."

"I know I'm just not very hungry at the minute," I lied.

It was half the truth; I had got used to not eating constantly.

The conversation stopped as our lecturer came in. Thankfully, the lecture and my shift at the diner went by just as quick.

And before I knew it, I was walking through the front door at home. The house was in darkness. I reached for the light switch, and nothing happened. I walked to the meter pressing the button and saw it said no credit.

"For fuck's sake," I muttered walking into the kitchen seeing the five pounds that I gave mum on the side. She didn't bother going to get electric which meant any food in the freezer if we had any would have gone off.

I scraped the money off the side and headed to the corner shop, walking in I headed straight to the counter. "Hello, could I put five pounds on electricity?" I asked, handing him the electric key. He put the key into the machine, and I placed the five-pound coins on the counter.

"Here you are," he said as he passed the key back.

"Thanks," I said. "Have a good evening."

I headed straight home into the garden finding the electric box and put the card in following the instructions on the screen.

As soon as the electricity loaded on the kitchen and hallway light flickered on immediately. Now, it was time to see the damage that was the freezer. I just hoped that there wasn't much food in there. I wouldn't be able to cope if a freezer full of food went to waste.

# *Chapter Two*

# ALEXANDER

"Alexander, are you even listening?"

I couldn't help but roll my eyes at him. "Yes, sir," I lied as I continued to look out the window.

My father was in one of his usual ranting moods. The man said nothing of use, just too bad the rest of our country couldn't see that. He had done a great job at raising a Prince. It was too bad that he didn't care what he did to his son during it all.

I need to get out of here; the cage just seemed to get tighter. I wanted freedom. I wanted to be able to do my own thing and right now that wasn't being here with him.

"What did I just say?"

I turned to look at my father and flashed him a smile. "I'm going to guess it was something about how you're disappointed that your son after his gap year that you didn't approve of in the first place has now chosen to go to a non-prestigious university," I mocked.

"You mock Alexander, but this is years worth of history." My father slammed his hand on the table. Once upon a time, that action alone would have frightened me. Now I just thought it was dramatic. "You are spitting on our traditions."

I stood up because I've had enough of the lecture. "Some traditions are worth breaking."

"Alexander."

"Are we done here?" I asked, clearly expressing my boredom. "I have places to be."

My father tapped his foot pressing his lips into a thin line.

Was I pushing my luck? Yes. Did I care? No.

"Alexander."

"If we're done here, I have an induction at university," I said standing up from the seat. That may have been a little white lie. My induction wasn't until 3:00 p.m. I had chosen a quiet time to speak to my new course leaders, and the university eased my way into it. I knew I wouldn't be able to keep my identity a secret, but I could hope people would just ignore the fact I was a Prince and treat me like a normal person.

"I don't approve, Alexander."

"Father, you said that when I told you earlier in the summer, none of your lectures or ranting have changed my mind. I am being the leader I want to be. God forbid I ever have to take your position within the next few years. I want to be able to say I made a difference. I'm figuring out my path, please respect that," I said. "Mother supports me."

"That's because you're her favourite child," my father

muttered, rolling his eyes. "One step out of line and you will return home."

"Yes sir." I saluted him.

My father narrowed his eyes. "Alexander," he said sharply. "I will have Penelope connected to your calendar. You must attend all our events."

"Whatever you say." I headed for the bedroom letting out a laugh as Elizabeth was riding our brother like a horse. "El, you do realise we have horses, right?" I asked my baby sister.

Her head spun around. "Ander!" She squealed excitedly, sliding off our brother Henry and jumping into my arms.

"Oh, thank God," Henry muttered, standing up as he stretched his back out. "She is not as light as she used to be."

I laughed. "You are dumb enough to let El do that to you, Henry."

"It's not my fault," Henry grumbled out. "She just suckers you into agreeing with everything, my baby sister owns me." He stumbled to the floor, landing on his knees and dramatically looking up at the white ceiling.

"I'm not a baby! I'm four!" Elizabeth shouted, slapping her hand on my chest. I put her back on the floor as she stamped over to Henry.

I couldn't help but grin that my little four-year-old sister thought she was that intimidating.

"Oops, my bad," Henry mocked her. "Alex, are you sure you can't take me with you?"

"Henry, you're ten, you aren't ready for university." I chuckled.

"Charles and Arthur, they gang up on me for everything. As soon as I haven't done something they go straight to dad," Henry complained. "I feel trapped. I can't breathe without them reporting back."

I felt pity for him. More than anything I could relate to him.

Charles and Arthur could be a nightmare when they were together. Once they found a common target, everyone was fair game. I'm talking from my own personal experience. I couldn't understand why I had managed to have a good relationship with Elizabeth and Henry. We had never seen eye to eye with Arthur and Charles as our relationship was always strained.

"Just stay with Elizabeth and keep your head down," I told him, patting his shoulder. "She's crazy enough to distract them from you."

"Why can't I come with you?" Henry pouted.

"You aren't old enough for university," I told him pointedly. "Anyway, I really do have to go. I love you both."

I headed to the front of the Palace and saw my bodyguard Jones waiting with some other men. "Are you ready, your highness?" Jones asked politely.

"Jones, please tell me those men are with you because you were having a nice catch up?" I asked, hopeful.

"King's orders."

I groaned, "the man really is ruining my life," I grumbled opening the door.

"Sir, he is just trying to keep you safe," Jones defended.

I rolled my eyes. I loved my bodyguard. I truly did, but

when he defended my father, it made me want to punch him in the face.

"Keep me safe, I call bullshit on that," I muttered to myself.

Jones led me towards the car. I huffed, sitting inside crossing my arms over my chest frowning.

"Sir, you're acting like a child, if I didn't know better I'd say I have Princess Elizabeth in the car," Jones said.

I stuck my middle finger up at him.

"I rest my case."

"Seriously, Jones, can we not leave them here? I'll be safer with you," I protested. "Nobody is going to attack me at the university. All the extra security is just going to bring more attention to the fact I'm there."

Jones shut the door, walking around the other side sitting next to me as another guard got in to drive, I looked back out the car to see at least two more cars full of security.

My father was a dickhead, going totally overboard as usual. This would bring more attention than anything, the press loved to see multiple cars leaving the premises because it meant one thing, a royal was on the move.

"Sir, your father would have never let you go to university if not for all the security," Jones said.

"Jones, how am I meant to have a normal university experience with a squad of goons? Let's face it, if I had gone to Cambridge or Oxford or whatever other elite university, he wouldn't have done it. He's done this because I went against what he wanted. A punishment."

Jones smiled. "Well let me tell you, sir, the other

guards are going to be at the entrance of the university. You will only have me inside."

I stared at him with a surprised look on my face. "My father approved that?"

"Yes, sir, when I made the point of security attracting attention. Alexander—"

"Alex," I grumbled.

"Alexander," Jones said pointedly. "I know how important this is for you. I will always try and fight your side."

"Thank you."

Jones had been with me since I was ten. The poor man had been dealing with my shit for nine years. He deserved a medal. I definitely didn't make it easy on him during my early teenage years. Although, I could blame that on Jeremy. What good was having a best friend if you couldn't blame the dumb shit you did on them?

"Jones, can you make sure we don't share my calendar with Penelope?" I asked. "I mean she can have the university schedule but I would rather she didn't know about the personal part of university."

"You're expecting to have a personal life?" Jones chuckled.

"I could make friends," I protested.

"Sure you could." Jones shook his head.

I narrowed my eyes.

*What a dickhead.*

I turned my body to look out the window; this was going to be a long journey.

Was I ready to commit to a two hour and ten-minute trip from home to university? I wonder if it was possible to get a place closer to university. I shook my head. That was a silly idea, and I know my father would never go for it. I wonder if I could persuade my mother. I can say my father was right about one thing. She did have a soft spot for her first-born son. I used to use this to my advantage a lot.

The car journey thankfully went smoothly with there being no accidents on the road or not much traffic either. As we arrived at the campus, I couldn't be surprised how busy it seemed. Although, I guess I had arrived two hours before my appointment time.

We drove up the path and my eyes stayed glued to the window. The campus looked stunning. It was clear that autumn had begun. The leaves had begun to fall on the floor. The campus was huge. I could see tennis courts, football pitches placed around the greens, and a diner straight next door to the campus.

"A twenty-four hour diner? I see that could cause some interesting experiences," Jones muttered.

"You mean like a bar on campus?" I grinned. "I could technically do shots at the bar and head to a lecture."

Jones let out a groan. "Am I going to be dragging you out of there drunk every day, Alexander?"

I grinned. "Is that disapproval I hear?"

"Yes," he said flatly.

We drove up to right outside the university, there were three different bus stops outside, everybody seemed to be just going about doing their own thing. I just hoped with me on campus it would stay the same. I doubted it though, everybody always wanted something.

"Are you ready for this, sir?"

I looked at Jones biting my lip.

I could do this. It was only going to university. I had managed crowds of people before.

I nodded at him, and he got out the car coming around to my side of the car, he opened the door. I stepped out of the car, glancing at Jones as we headed inside the university.

People were starting to stare, but I pushed through and ignored the looks. As I walked further into the atrium, a small shop was on the left and the library was further away on the right. I don't know what I expected but the whole campus looked very modern, floor length windows letting so much light into the building. I walked up the ramp and saw a small coffee shop, a subway, and a Starbucks.

*How much shit could they fit into this place?*

Another set of lifts took my attention which was next to the student centre.

We spent the next hour walking around the campus inside and outside exploring what was around. Luckily, nobody had approached me yet. There have been small whispers and pointing. We headed back inside the campus as I made my way over to the east tower and hit the button on the lift.

Eventually, we arrived at E917. Jones peered through the window on the door and pushed it open.

I entered the room sitting at the table. It was at least another ten minutes before the meeting was due to start. I pulled out my phone, shooting a text to Jeremy about meeting up with him after.

The door opened once more, and two people piled in to join me at the table.

"Hi, my name is Julia. I will be your course leader." She points to the guy sitting next to her. "This is George. He will be your university tutor and your point of contact if you need anything," she said. "Prince Alexander, do you have any questions for us?"

"Please call me, Alexander," I said. "I know as a university you can't control the actions of your students, but all I ask is for your staff to treat the same as they do with everybody else. I do not want any favours."

"Alexander, I assure you our staff will be professional in terms of your studies and everything else," Julia said.

"Thank you, Julia," I flashed her a smile. "I know I've missed the first two weeks of the course, is there a way for me to catch up?"

"In all honesty, Alexander, the first two weeks are just giving out the module handbooks discussing assignments," George said. "I have your module handbooks here." He reached down, pulling them out and handing them over to me. I opened them up and began to flip through them to see what my modules would entail. "All of your courses are assignment-based. I'll give you a chance to read through them if you have any questions."

"Thank you."

## Chapter Three

# MELINDA

Ugh, I hate people.

I did such a people-y job for someone that hated people. I was glad when my shift was finally over.

The campus was buzzing with a weird energy, but I was too tired to even care what it was about. It usually ended up being about some kind of party, and I just wasn't in the mood for the party scene. I could do with getting drunk and forgetting all my life problems that sounded like a really good shout. The sad fact was after all this; the routine would begin again.

I took a bite of my noodles as I read through the reading for the next lecture. I wanted to try and keep on top of my university work before I got bogged down with work.

The front door opened and closed. "Roman you're overreacting," I heard mum's voice float through the hallway.

*Oh, great.*

"You're under-reacting."

"How was work?" I looked to see mum standing against the counter directing her question at me. Roman was standing next to her.

"Fine. I suddenly lost my appetite." I stood up putting the bowl in the sink.

"Melinda, please," mum said.

I reached for my university work and pushed past both of them. I had no time for either of them. A hand grabbed onto my wrist. I turned to find Roman holding onto it. "Let go of my wrist," I snapped.

"You need to stop being such a bitch to your mother," Roman ordered. "She did what she could to survive."

I laughed. "Father of the year, huh? Calling your daughter a bitch isn't an award I'd want in my trophy case." I couldn't help but shake my head. "It isn't your credit she ruined. It isn't your life that she's put on pause because you left. I'm glad we live in England where they don't punish you for getting higher education and provide tuition money, grants, and loans. I'm still working my arse off. I'm not going to accept your money because you feel guilty about leaving her." I pointed to my mum.

"It wasn't all that rosey where I was," Roman snapped.

I spun around looking at him with disgust. "Because, as always, it's all about you!" I squeezed my eyes shut as the memories of my mum on the floor flooded my mind.

"Melinda don't," mum said. She stepped in between us as always being the middle man, trying to make sure that we were all trying to get along.

"You know what? It's not even worth it," I shook my head.

"Yes, so forget it," Roman said flatly.

"Forget it?" I laughed. "Yeah, okay. Forget that your eight-year-old daughter had to pick their drunken mother off the floor? Your eight-year-old who had to sit by their mother's side worried she may choke on her vomit. So don't tell me to forget it because I never will."

I stormed off from them not wanting to hear either of their excuses.

*Did I need therapy? Most definitely.*

I headed straight into the bedroom, shutting the door. I shook my head, falling back on the bed with a huff.

We always ended up in the same fight. A part of me wanted to be the bigger person and forgive both of them for what they had done, but the eight-year-old version of me wanted to be heard and protected.

The memories flooded back almost instantly and I shook my head. "No Melinda, shove that trauma back into the box," I mumbled to myself.

I reached for my headphones, putting music on and concentrating on trying to get my reading done for the next lot of lectures in a few days. If I could get ahead, it would help. For the rest of the night, I concentrated on getting my required reading done and making notes. And that was how I fell asleep.

---

Too soon I was back at work. It wasn't that I hated my job. It was more about how I hated people.

The service bell dinged with an order. "Mel, order up!" Dave called out from the open hatch.

I headed towards the hatch grabbing the two plates looking at the ticket, I headed to table four and stopped in front of them. "I have Eggs Benedict with ham," I said.

"Me," the woman said.

I placed it down in front of her and placed the other plate in front of the person opposite her. "Do you need a refill of your drinks?"

"No, thank you."

"Lovely, enjoy your meal," I said with a nod.

I headed back to the counter reaching for the spray bottle and cloth and began to wipe down some empty tables. All of a sudden, I heard a crash. I turned to see smashed glasses and plates on the floor.

"Melinda, clean that."

I glared at Cindy who was standing over the mess.

"Now! I'm going on break."

"Whatever happened to please or thank you, dick-head," I mumbled.

I walked into the store room to grab the cleaning trolley wheeling it in, I got the dustpan and brush cleaning up the spray of shattered glass before depositing it into the black bag attached to the trolley. I swept up the remaining glass before grabbing the mop and bucket off the trolley and began to mop.

Something crashed into me pushing me forward into the mop bucket and falling to the ground. I felt something heavy land on top of me. "Ow!" I snapped. I felt the heavy presence lift off me and turned to see a man wiping himself down.

"You idiot!"

"Alexander!" I heard someone shout.

"Excuse me!" I stood up ignoring the soaking wet apron I was now wearing spinning around to glare at the man. "You ran into me, maybe you should watch where you're going and use your walking feet inside like a normal person."

Anger flashed through his brown eyes as he clenched his fist. "Who do you think you're talking to?"

I stayed silent trying to keep my temper in check. I wasn't sure how Daisy would feel with me yelling back at a customer. I clenched my hand into a fist using my nails to keep me centred.

"Are you deaf? I'm talking to you." His nostrils flared. "Who do you think you're talking to?"

I stopped closer to him. "Did I not make it clear?" I raised an eyebrow. "You."

"Do you have any idea who you are talking to you stupid—"

"Alexander," a voice cut through. "Don't be rude. Apologise."

"Why? She's just a cleaner."

"Okay, number one, I am not a cleaner. I am actually a waitress where cleaning is a part of my job. Number two, even if I was, you don't get to look down at me like shit on the floor."

He stared at me, his mouth falling open as he stepped back.

"Now, if you don't mind, could you please leave this area, so I can mop the floor to stop it from being a hazard?"

"Alexander, go to the car," the other man said.

I couldn't help but raise an eyebrow, a grown man having to be told what to do.

"Jones—"

"Now Alexander, you can not be late for this meeting." Alexander rolled his eyes but followed this Jones man's direction. "I am truly sorry for his behaviour."

I shrugged picking the mop and bucket up and began to mop the water up. I was just glad I hadn't filled the bucket all the way up.

"What's your name?"

"Melinda Brown. Why?"

"Very nice to meet you, Miss Brown, again I apologise for his behaviour," the man said. I watched as he walked out the door and I couldn't help but frown, what interesting people. At least one of them was nice.

I focused on mopping all the water back up before putting it away in the store room. I walked into the kitchen peeling the wet apron off. "I fucking hate people!"

"Girl," Dave said, appearing from behind the cooker. "Do you have any idea who you just yelled at?"

"Some arrogant dickhead," I said, clenching my fist slightly.

"He's the—"

"Nope," I cut him off. "I don't want to hear it. I don't want to think about that stupid man for a second more."

Dave just stared at me shaking his head. "Alright, your next order is up."

I took the order looking at the ticket, seeing it was a booth. "Hi, I've got chicken burger and chips," I said, placing it in front of the woman.

"Thank you so much. Would it be possible to have another Coke Zero please?"

"Absolutely, I'll just get that for you now," I said, taking her glass. I placed it on the cubby window getting a fresh glass filling it with Coke Zero before taking it over to the lady. "Here you are."

"Thank you."

For the next few hours, I focused on waiting tables and cleaning the booths as we had customers and they left any time anyone tried to talk about the incident I would just walk away. I didn't want to hear about it. The man had already ruined my good mood. The last thing I wanted was to think about it even more. It would be a situation of the more I thought the angrier I'd get about the whole thing.

"Mel."

I looked up seeing Megan walking towards me. She sat at the counter and flopped her head down on it.

"Oh, babe, what's wrong?" I asked leaning my arms next to her.

"I have a bunch of lecture notes I need to decipher."

"Why did you write them in code?" I asked, confused.

She bit her lip and shrugged. "I wrote them in something. I don't know. I feel like I'm spiralling a little bit."

I reached over and patted her arm. "You can talk to me, you know that, right?"

She nodded. "Life is just a little hard right now." Megan flashed a smile in my direction, "I'll get there."

I patted her arm gently. "You got this."

She lifted her head and pouted, reaching into her bag before placing a piece of paper in front of me. "Do I?"

I picked up the paper and stared. Okay, maybe she doesn't got this. She had written all of her notes in a spiral but by the time she got to the middle they had begun to overlap on each line. I tried to keep my face neutral as I looked at her.

"You're doing a terrible job at hiding your thoughts, Mel."

I smiled sheepishly. "Sorry, but damn that's impressive even if it is a mess."

"Why did I decide to continue in education? I could have just gotten a job, been earning some dough," she muttered.

"Because you had a dream—"

Megan chuckled, "You are not Dr. Martin Luther King, do not give me the I have a dream speech."

I grinned. "That wasn't where I was going with that but..." I shrugged. "All these hurdles are just little blips in the road for you to get the career you would like." I gasped. "We should make a mood inspiration kind of board thing."

She groaned. "Nah, that sounds like effort." Her phone buzzed and she looked down before flipping her phone over. "Tell me about your day."

"Oh jeez, Megan, you're going to get her going again," I turned to see Dave leaning through the window watching the both of us.

"Excuse me," a voice cut in.

I looked over to see one of the customers waving their hand in the air. I moved away from Megan making my way over to the table. "Sorry for shouting," she said sheepishly. "I tried waving for a good five minutes."

"It's okay, what can I get you?" I said with a smile.

"Erm, could I have a large Coke and some fries?" the woman asked.

"Absolutely," I said.

I walked over, grabbing the Coke and bringing it straight over to her. I walked over to the window where Dave and Megan were chatting. "Time to stop the chatting, Chef. You have an order of fries."

"You think Cindy ever plans to come off break?"

I snorted. "Probably not."

I don't know how Cindy became manager because the woman takes more breaks than she does orders. I truly couldn't wait for Daisy to be back from her honeymoon. It was turning into the longest month of my life. Cindy behaved a tiny bit better when Daisy was around.

"Right. I'm getting back to work, and you, Miss Megan, sit there and try to decipher your notes."

"Yes captain," she saluted.

I shook my head, I loved my best friend. She really could make a bad day good again.

# Chapter Four

## ALEXANDER

Another day of stupid shit and when I said stupid shit, I meant dealing with yet another lecture from my father.

I looked at the buzzing phone in front of me as more and more meetings came through that my father believed were vital to attend. It meant that it would bore me to death, he just needed a new punishment because this one was getting old and boring fast.

The whispers still hadn't calmed down after two weeks. If anything, they had gotten even worse, especially after my run-in at Daisy's with that girl. Everybody seemed to have been waiting for my next outburst, not that I could blame them. The first one was spectacularly bad. Stories had already been leaked to the press as well as some lovely photo stills. I couldn't help but feel slightly bad from my outburst from earlier today. The girl didn't deserve it. She just ended up being the one I took my anger and annoyance out on.

I sat in the back of my writing skills lecture, doodling on the piece of paper that I was writing lecture notes on. As much as it was easier to type them, I didn't want to get distracted by all the things my father would be demanding me to spend my time doing rather than getting my degree in Media and Communications.

I couldn't quite get that girl out of my mind. The way she stood up and called me out on my bullshit was so attractive. Her long brown hair and her beautiful brown eyes captivated me. It was like she could see right through me.

The door opened, and the girl that had been on my mind since the encounter walked inside. She sat down at a table near the front and pulled out her work stuff. This girl was totally in her own world. I wish I could have gotten her name. It would make finding out about her easier. I mean, I had one bit of information about her I suppose. She worked at Daisy's.

*Would it be weird to try and approach her?*

I shook my head.

*That was a stupid idea.*

I needed to focus. I had to make this work, and I couldn't get distracted by a girl. Not when I needed to show my father that this was the right path for me.

I looked away from her and back to my lecturer as he continued to speak about what made a good piece of writing, what drew people to what you were saying whether that was speeches or written words. It started to feel like I was well within an English class the way he kept going.

My phone buzzed once more and I took a deep breath in trying to not get pissed off with my father, Jeremy's name quickly flashed on the screen, I closed my eyes as a small smile appeared on my face.

Dude, I'm bored.

I let out a snort.

*Of course he was.*

In lecture. Meant to be concentrating.

The reply was almost immediate.

Doing a bad job

Fuck off, dickhead. If you want, come meet me. I need to do some recon.

Recon?

I wasn't usually a person that found education boring, but damn, this lecture was dragging. I couldn't even pretend to be interested in what he was saying and to be honest most of it was common sense. Well, I suppose it was common sense for me, but if someone was at university I'm going to guess they passed English and would know how to write correctly and know about grammar as well as all the other things you needed to know.

Not too soon after the lecture finally ended, I watched as the girl packed up her stuff. She did it with such care, putting her laptop and notes away. She walked out of the lecture classroom.

I shoved my notes into my bag, slinging the black backpack over my shoulder and followed her out. She squeezed into the corner of the lift as we all filled it, she brushed her hair out the way of her face as she scrolled through on her phone. The phone buzzed in her hand and she quickly placed it to her ear.

"Hey, Daisy," she said, pausing. "Thank you for coming back to me. I was worried."

I wonder what she could have been worried about? The doors opened, and it was a good job she was focused on getting to wherever she was going because it would seem unintentionally like I was stalking her. Was I over-thinking this? I followed the crowd out of the door, not being able to take my eyes off her. She was a puzzle I couldn't figure out yet, but I wanted to.

"Alex." I pulled my gaze from her to see my best friend, Jeremy, leaning against the railing outside. "You didn't tell me there were so many fit girls here."

"It would turn into your new hunting ground," I said, rolling my eyes at him.

"How many did you hit on?"

He gasped. "Wow, I'm offended."

"Bullshit." I scoffed.

"Three or four, and I got their numbers, too." He grinned. "Now forget about my future conquests. Who is she, and why are you staring at her?"

"Who?"

"Don't play dumb. Oh wait, there's no playing, you are dumb."

I reached out punching him in the arm. "Okay, dick-head. We're going to Daisy's."

"Why? Is she hot?"

I stared at him flatly.

Jones joined us as we headed towards the building, as he pushed open the door the bell jingled. I couldn't see her, which meant I had to sneak in and observe without her realising I was here.

The booth in the corner was the perfect view of the diner as a whole, sitting down on the red leather cushion with Jones and Jeremy sitting across from me. It was hidden enough that hopefully no other students or staff would realise I'm here. I hated the attention that being a Prince brought sometimes. Just once, I would love to fly under the radar and meet someone who has no idea who I was or could ignore the fact I was part of the royal family.

Jeremy flipped open the menu and began looking at the options.

I did the same, keeping my eyes peeled for another view of her. I didn't have to wait long before she came out from the back and headed over to us.

"Good afternoon welcome to Daisy's, what drinks can —" She finally looked up from her notepad.

"Ugh, it's you." Her eyes narrowed at me straight away.

Jeremy raised his eyebrows, tilting his head slightly.

"Hi," I said, flashing her a grin.

"I'm surprised to see you sitting down and not knocking over poor innocent girls who are just doing their job," she said. She looked away from me and to Jeremy. "What can I get you to drink?"

"A coke please," he said.

"Do I dare ask you? Or will I get that thrown at me, too?"

*Damn, the sass on this girl.*

"Coke Zero, please," I said.

She nodded walking away as soon as she left Jeremy turned to face me instantly. "Who is she?" He asked.

"Nobody," I lied.

"Yeah, and I'm the King." He scoffed. "She looks familiar."

I said nothing, but I could see the wheels working in his head. It wouldn't be too long before he put two and two together and figured out this was the girl I ended up having my argument splashed over the papers.

He gasped. "I figured it out. What was your plan here? Were you going to apologise to her? I hate to break it to you man, but I think she hates your guts. Also, I'm surprised the way she talks to you, usually everyone fucking sucks up to you. And tries to get something from you."

I grinned. "I know. I like it. She seems different. I want to know more about her. So, yes, this has turned into a little research and not just grabbing a little lunch."

"I thought this whole university experience was for you to find yourself not get distracted by a—" Jeremy cut off as he saw her approaching again and laid our drinks down in front of us. "Thanks."

"What can I get you?"

Jeremy flashed her his usual seductive grin making me frown, I moved my foot kicking him. He didn't even flinch. "Sorry, I didn't catch your name."

"I didn't give it," she said flatly. "Do you know what you're ordering or would you like some more time to look over the menu?"

"I'll tell you my order if you tell me your name," he said.

"What makes you think I want your order?" She counted.

He tilted his head looking her up and down and I bit my lip to keep from laughing. She had gotten him, she shifted slightly and Jeremy finally gave in. "I'll have chicken burger and chips with a side of onion rings."

Her gaze shifted to Jones, and she smiled. "And for you, sir?"

"Just some fries, thank you," Jones said with a nod.

Her gaze finally turned to me, she plastered a fake smile and I couldn't help but be slightly amused.

Was it killing her to be this nice to me?

"And you?" She trailed off mumbling something I couldn't quite hear.

"What was that?" I asked.

"Nothing."

"Oh no, please share with the class."

"And for you, Mr. Dickhead?"

"My name's Alex."

"My version is better."

"Pulled pork burger with fries, please," I said. "Please don't spit in my food." She walked away mumbling something to herself, and I looked at Jeremy in concern, "Should I worry?"

"I mean you pissed her off," Jeremy said with a shrug. "Anyway, forget the girl who hates you. Races are tonight. Which car are you racing in?"

I grinned. I loved the races. It was the one place where nobody cared who I was, well they only cared when they beat me and could brag about it within our circle but otherwise it was normal life. "I think it's time we take the Bugatti for a spin, see what that baby can do. Will we be at the tracks like normal?"

"Yeah," Jeremy pulled out his phone, tapping away and setting everything up. How he ended up with being the King of the races I will never know, but I didn't complain. "It's set."

"Which flavour of the day are you bringing?" I asked.

He pursed his lips thinking. "Maybe Phoebe."

"Dude, you don't shit the bed," I said, shaking my head.

"That's not the saying Alex," Jeremy shook his head. "Phoebe isn't that bad, I heard she gives good head."

"Phoebe isn't a fuck around girl, Jer. She likes you," I said.

Phoebe made her feelings for him clear; she was waiting for her opportunity where he would finally choose her. Unlucky for her it would only end in heartache. "She's not a good time girl. She's a long-time girl."

Jeremy rolled his eyes. "She's a fun-time girl."

I sighed, flopping back into the booth. "I don't know why I bother warning you. One day you are going to meet someone who is not going to take your shit."

He laughed, "nah, no girl could conquer me."

"I'm not sure why one would want to." I let out a laugh as the girl appeared with our burgers. She placed them down in front of us.

I looked at the plate hesitantly. "Did you spit in it?"

She let out a laugh.

"Dude, she wouldn't tell you if she did." Jeremy shook his head.

"He's right. I didn't though."

I looked at her and then back at my burger. "Did you?"

"I didn't," she said. "I'd never do that. It's not a line I would want to cross. I hope you enjoy your meals."

"Thank you," I said. She went to walk away and I quickly grabbed her hand. "I just wanted to say I'm sorry."

"Sorry?"

"About the other day. You didn't deserve that," I told her.

"Melinda! Stop chatting and get back to work," a woman said loudly as she passed by us.

I grinned.

I had a name.

It would make finding out about her that much easier.

"Thank you, Melinda."

Jeremy and I started eating our food, not really talking in between whenever I could watch Melinda's every move.

*Was I moving to stalker territory?*

"Dude, you're hooked," Jeremy said, shaking his head. "You've had two conversations, and you're a goner."

"I'm just curious about her. That's all," I defended.

# Chapter Five

## MELINDA

He was here again.

Well that was an understatement. He seemed to be everywhere. He would be at the back of some of my lectures, I'd see him if I was working in the library and he would be in Daisy's on most days. Sometimes he would be eating, sometimes he would be working but I could always feel his eyes on me. It was like I had my own little stalker.

Should I be concerned? Probably.

Was I? Not really.

The only places he tended to be was the diner or at university, when he appeared near my house then I would worry. He could waste his time if that's what he wanted to do.

"Melinda." I turned to see Megan walking in, and she sat at the counter. "I found a new show for us to binge watch."

I looked at her, raising an eyebrow. "I don't know if I trust your recommendations."

Her mouth dropped open, offended. "Excuse me, my recommendations were good. What was wrong with *Julie and the Phantoms* or *Winx*?"

I folded my arms over my chest, "the fact that they haven't been renewed for another season."

"Dude, I can't control Netflix, they just don't know decent television if it smacks them in the face," she said. "Anyway, this is a new reality television show. It's called *Below Deck*, and it keeps stalking me on TikTok because there is the scene—"

"Hi, sorry to interrupt. Could I pay now?"

I turned around to see him.

I narrowed my eyes at him, I thought I was over it, but clearly I still held a tiny grudge. What could I say? Sometimes a girl just needed to be petty.

I walked over to the till pulling up his order.

He had been here well before my shift had started.

"That will be £24.99 please," I said politely.

He handed me a ten and twenty pound note. "Keep the change, Melinda," he said.

I bit my lip from saying something sarcastic. I walked over to the till processing it and made my way back over with the change.

"I told you to keep it," he said.

"You already apologised to me. You don't need to buy my forgiveness," I told him.

"What do I need to earn your forgiveness, Melinda?" The man said, running a hand through his hair.

"Nothing," I said flatly. "I'm sorry. I have to go back to

work." I added the money into the tip jar and pretended to wipe the counters trying to not pay attention.

"Mel, do you know him?"

I looked up as I heard the bell ring and looked back at Megan. "He's the idiot that knocked me over," I said with a shrug.

"You really don't know who he is?" Megan asked again.

I looked at her, confused. "I just told you who he was." I knocked on her head with my knuckles. "Are you okay up there?"

She slapped my hand away from her head, "You know what I'm going to let you figure this little situation out. But honestly, flabbergasted. Hurry up and clock out. I have a show to share."

I smiled a little, this is where I knew her ADHD was spiralling other than her very interesting notes, her brain was moving miles a minute. "Are you okay?"

She looked up at me. "Of course I am. The sun is shining—"

"Babe, it's October, and it's cloudy as shit outside," I told her, shaking my head. I patted her head as I walked to the staff room reaching for my things we headed outside to the bus stop and waited. "Maybe one of us should learn to drive."

Megan grimaced. "I don't know if that's a good idea. I don't know my left from my right." She paused. "Neither do you."

I protested. "I do, too."

She raised an eyebrow. "Melinda, what's in your left hand?"

I looked down at my hand. "My phone."

"Babe, that's your right hand." She laughed. I looked down at my hand realising she was correct. Well that was that idea out of the way. "The only other option is one of us marrying a billionaire and promising to keep the other as a live-in bestie."

"Or we live in a throuple," I suggested. "A very platonic throuple."

"Platonic, that's a big word," Megan teased.

I elbowed her, gently rolling my eyes.

I wasn't that thick. Not all the time anyway. I had my moments. It thankfully didn't take long for the bus to come and traffic was good.

An hour later, we arrived at Megan's. Her parents weren't home, so we headed straight into the living room and got settled for a binge watch.

Three hours later we hadn't moved an inch. Megan had decent choices in television shows. I just hoped this one wasn't cancelled because that would be just our luck. I stood up, heading into the kitchen getting two cans of Coke Zero out and brought them back into the living room. I handed one to Megan.

I opened the can sitting next to her, and her phone vibrated. She picked it up and then put it back down. "You know you can talk to me, right?"

She flashed me a smile, "I know, I appreciate it. There's nothing going on that needs talking about. Now hush. I'm watching TV."

She turned away from me, focusing on the television.

I looked at her. I was worried because her ADHD spiralled when she was stressed or overwhelmed. And as much as she complained about the work from university, she was on top of it. Her phone buzzed multiple times, and she pushed it further and further away, usually she was attached to it.

"Megan."

"Shhh!" Her eyes didn't leave the television screen.

I let out a little sigh. I would play her game and pretend there was nothing wrong. If that's what she needed, then that is what I would do for her. I heard the front door open.

"Have you two been attached to this sofa since you came home?"

Megan paused the television and turned to look at both of her parents. "No. Melinda got up to get a drink."

"Really, Megan?" Oliver said, shaking his head.

"It's an achievement." She chuckled. "So, what are you cooking for us for dinner?"

"Shouldn't you be offering to cook us dinner?" Lily said pointedly.

Megan looked at her parents, annoyed. "Last time I checked, you're the parents?"

"Last time I checked, you're an adult." Oliver countered.

I laughed. "They have you on that, Megan. We are adults."

"There is a reason I didn't move out you know," Megan said. "It was so I didn't have to fend for myself."

I looked at my phone and saw it was almost 7:00 p.m. "Anyway, I got to go. I'll see you tomorrow in our lecture. I've got a shift at Daisy's in the morning."

Megan nodded.

“I’ll text you,” I told her. I got off the sofa, slipping my shoes on. “Wait, can I watch this without you?”

“Yeah, I just needed to get you hooked, so I have someone to talk to when the new season comes out,” Megan said.

“Of course.” I rolled my eyes. “I’ll see you later, bye Lily and Oliver.” I waved goodbye to them heading straight out the house.

Parked cars littered one side of the road as the traffic lights stayed green, I looked both ways before crossing the road.

Our roads were so quiet sometimes I wondered why we had lights instead of a zebra crossing.

The bins were outside the houses ready for bin collection tomorrow morning, the street lights shone light on the bags that were next to some of the bins. The cold breeze of the wind moved some of the rubbish along the road.

I walked into the garden avoiding the broken step reaching the front door pulling the keys out unlocking it.

I entered the house, locking it straight away behind me before heading straight to bed.

---

I was going to kill Cindy.

It wasn’t many people that could piss me off this bad, but she did it easy, it wasn’t just the way she spoke to me and slacked off doing her job. It was the way she was rude to the customers, I think she forgets that without customers we’d be out of a job.

Leah walked over to the counter where I was standing. "Girl, have you seen who is in the far booth?"

I looked over to where she was nodding her head. "Yeah, that's the idiot who knocked me over the other week," I said. "I should really probably most definitely still stop holding a grudge."

Leah frowned, cocking her head to the side, "I feel like I missed something. Anyway, he would like you to serve his table."

"Since when did we take requests?" I scoffed. "Tell him to fuck off, customer friendly way of course."

"I did."

I narrowed my eyes. "I'm sensing a but."

"He gave me a tip to not be his waitress," she said. "Believe me, I didn't think I could be bought but apparently I can." She walked away laughing and I couldn't help but smile a little. As annoyed as I was at him, I loved that it made Leah happy. We all loved a good tip, so I couldn't blame her.

I walked over to his booth. "You may be willing to pay off the other waitress to have me, but most normal people tend to just walk over and talk to the people they would like to take care of," I told him, crossing my arms over my chest.

He scoffed. "Don't kid yourself, Melinda. If I tried to talk to you, you would've told me to fuck off."

I smiled a little. "Don't be silly I would never use such foul language," I fluttered my eyelashes at him.

"You called me a dickhead the other day," he said, scrunching his face up in disbelief.

"Slip of the tongue," I lied.

"Can you sit please?" He asked, gesturing to the seat in front of him.

I sat down in the booth across from him, he bit his lip looking nervous. His brown eyes looked away from mine as he looked around the diner before his eyes landed outside for a moment. "Alex—"

"No, no." He shook his head, turning back to me. "I need to get this out."

I sat back on the seat getting comfortable. I could wait until he found his voice. I tapped my fingers on the table as I looked out into the quad. Students were milling around, and I knew it wouldn't be too long until it started to get busy in the diner.

"The day I knocked you down," he started. "I know I already said sorry, but I feel like I owe you a little explanation. I was in a terrible mood, which isn't any excuse for the way I treated you."

"Alex, it's fine. I understand. We all have shit days," I said with a shrug.

It was hard to stay petty at the man when he was being nice.

"Does this mean you'll stop stalking me?"

"I call it research." He shrugged. "I needed to know more about you."

"Oh, and that doesn't sound creepy at all," I said pointedly. "Should I be worried about you? Do I need to call the police and tell them I have a stalker?"

Alex shook his head. "Lucky for you, Melinda, I'm far too lazy to be an actual stalker."

I let out a little laugh, that I could relate to and also

why I was not some big far fetched criminal. I was far too lazy for that. "So, why the babysitter?" I asked curiously.

"Who? Jones?"

I nodded.

"He's my personal assistant. My mother and father like to know my days are filled with all the boring and important things that need to be done. I prefer not to be bored all day."

I smiled. "Sometimes boredom is necessary."

"My parents would like you," Alex said with a little grin. "A woman who knows that boredom is necessary and doesn't take any shit."

"Thanks, I guess. Anyway, I have to get back to work," I stood up from the booth.

I didn't get far before I felt his hand grab mine, I looked back at him confused. "What?"

"What time do you finish work?"

I looked behind me at the clock. "In about an hour," I said.

"Don't you have a lecture at 9:00 a.m.?"

I cocked my head to the side. "Stalker. I should be waving a million red flags at you right now."

"Do you even own any flags?"

"Nope."

"So, can I see you again please?"

I grinned. "You seem to know where I am. Goodbye, Alex."

# Chapter Six

## ALEXANDER

I was a goner. Jeremy was right. I was hooked. As much as I wanted to stay away from her, something was drawing me to her. I just hoped she was joking about the police comment, I don't think my parents would like the knowledge that their son had taken to slightly stalking as she said. I preferred research. I needed to focus. Whenever she was near my focus was on her, the way she moved, her body, she had a light about her.

I walked into the lecture and I saw Melinda and her friend sitting at one of the tables, I walked over to sit with them.

"Two visits in one day. Wow, I must be the luckiest person in the world," Melinda said teasingly. "Do you not have anyone else to stalk?"

Stalking was such an ugly word. Although, the truth was even if it did blur the line there was nobody else I wanted to know more.

I sat down, raising an eyebrow. "It would be a little random if I was here in your lecture," I said.

"And yet, here you are."

"Girl, you realise he's in this lecture right?" The friend asked, raising an eyebrow.

Melinda looked at her sheepishly. "Definitely."

"Liar."

Melinda put her hands up. "Alright, I didn't know. I don't pay attention. I'm just trying to get my degree and work, you don't see me paying attention to everyone around me."

I had to smile a little, I liked her mindset there, just focus on whatever she was doing and don't bother about anybody else. I needed to take her advice.

My eyes didn't leave her. The way her shoulder had peeked out from her top. I bit my lip. I craved to leave a mark on her. She turned to her friend, and I took in every inch of her. Her outfits were simple and showed off every curve she had. Her bum hugged her leggings that made me just want to grip her with my hands.

I adjusted in my seat, feeling myself getting hard.

*Shit.*

I needed to stop looking at her.

A door opening snapped me out of the trance I was in. I opened my bag pulling out my notepad and module information with a pen placing it on the table.

"You don't have a laptop?" I looked to see that it was Melinda's friend who was asking that question.

"I didn't catch your name," I said.

"Megan."

"Well, Megan, I don't bring my laptop because I find I

get distracted easily. I would just be working or answering emails and like Melinda, I'd rather focus on my degree than be distracted," I said.

"What are you getting your degree in?" Melinda asked curiously.

"Media and communication. It will fit into what my future role will be in life," I explained.

I hated explaining to people what my role within the Royal Family actually was.

A lot of people just thought it was a lot of money, fancy parties and travelling. In all fairness some of it was that but a lot of it that wasn't shown was charity work, liaising with different countries, heads of state, and different companies. They were just a few of the responsibilities that we had.

"You think I have time to run to the loo before the lecture?" Melinda asked curiously, looking around the room.

"Definitely," Megan said.

Melinda stood up and left the room. "You, Mr. Prince."

My eyes widened, not one person had used my title whilst I had been at university.

"Yes, I know who you are. I'm not as thick as her."

"What do you mean by you're not as thick as her? She's not thick. I'm not surprised you know me. Most people do," I said. "Why doesn't Melinda care that I'm a Prince? She is a force to be reckoned with."

Megan scoffed. "She's my bestie. I can call her what I like. Your whole family could walk into that diner and she would still have no clue who you are. To be fair, I think celebrities could walk past her, and the girl still wouldn't have a clue."

My eyes widened as my mind went blank. "Eh?" I rubbed my forehead slumping back in the chair. "She has no clue that I'm part of the Royal Family?"

"Not a clue. Are you telling me that you had no idea?" Megan said. "Are you dumb?"

"Wow."

I was speechless. I couldn't actually form a coherent thought. It hadn't even crossed my mind that she had no idea. I just assumed she didn't give a shit about it. I thought for once I had found one person who didn't care about my status or my title.

"Whatever you're planning for revenge. Get it out of your head."

"You think that's my goal here? Revenge?"

"Honestly, yes. You don't have a good reputation," Megan said pointedly. "If you hurt her, prince or not, I will hurt you."

Could I keep my royal life away from her? One thing was certain if she googled my name she wouldn't find good stories. The gap year I insisted on having was mostly Jeremy and I getting drunk. "I promise I don't want to hurt her."

Megan nodded and slid back into her chair, typing something on her phone.

She had my respect that was for sure anyone who was willing to defend their best friend was good in my book.

"Megan," I said. She looked up from her phone and raised an eyebrow. "Can you not tell her I'm a prince please?"

"Why? Honest answers only or I will tell her."

"To her, I'm normal. I'm not a prince. She doesn't want me for money or fame or what I can do for her," I admitted. "I like that she puts me in my place and isn't scared to tell me what she thinks."

Megan looked at the door and then back to me. "Fine. I won't tell her, but if she asks me, I will not lie."

"Thank you." This girl clearly deserved a good Christmas gift, she was going to be on my Christmas card list, well she would be if I sent personal Christmas cards.

The lecture was dragging on. And from the look on everyone else's faces, I'd like to think that they agreed with me.

"Alright, I can see some of you have checked out, let's have a twenty minute break and resume after," the lecturer said.

Almost immediately, people started getting up to leave the room. I watched as Megan and Melinda flopped their heads down onto the table with a groan.

I could relate.

"I think watching paint dry would be more interesting than this."

"Amen, sister," Melinda agreed.

"Not even planning the Halloween pub crawl stopped my boredom, and you know I love planning pub crawls," Megan said shaking her head.

"Halloween pub crawl?" I questioned. "What is that?"

"Exactly what it says on the tin," Melinda said, shaking her head as if I was stupid. "If it had a tin that is."

"Take pity on the sheltered man," Megan defended with a chuckle. "He could live in a really small country side that has no pubs, or he could be a recluse and live in a basement."

I stared at her in disbelief. She was really having too much fun with this. Technically, she could tell any story, and I probably wouldn't deny it. Well, as long as it didn't get close to the truth.

"Oh, you mean like that girl who was kept in the basement by her dad," Melinda said. "What was it called?" She scratched her head. "You know the one where she fakes the kid being sick to go to the hospital and she finally tells someone and escapes."

Megan shook her head. "I have no idea what you're talking about. Why were you watching that? Does not sound like something you would watch."

Melinda looked at her sheepishly. "It's not, but I got sucked into TikTok and part thirty-four. Later, I had nearly watched the whole film. Something about needing to go to the next part really gets you and hooks you."

"I clearly need to download this app."

Both of their mouths dropped open in shock, "do you live under a rock? How do you not have TikTok?" Megan asked, shocked. "It's like a staple. Maybe you were really raised in a basement. Mel, I think we need to save him from the basement."

I crossed my arms over my chest. "We have gotten so off track with this, what is a Halloween pub crawl?"

"It's basically on Halloween, hence the name, and every year Megan plots a map for different pubs and clubs for us to visit and if we see a costume we take a shot," Melinda explained. "If someone says something we take a shot. The aim is to get as drunk as possible."

I frowned. "You're both eighteen, right?"

They nodded.

"So, how did you get into pubs?"

"Fake ID's," Megan admitted.

"Naughty girls." I laughed.

"It's the one time of the year Mel can't say no to me," Megan said. "She refuses to go clubbing or drinking any other time. My one time is Halloween, so you bet I go all out for it. We dress up in costumes. You know, the whole shebang."

"Do you not like drinking or something?" I asked curiously.

"Between work and university it doesn't leave much time for anything else," she admitted.

I couldn't help but pity her slightly. That was no life work and school. Every once in a while, people needed to have some freedom and let go of everything. I fought like hell to have that freedom, the races, coming to this university, and defying my father by doing the course I wanted to do.

"Is that the life you want?" I asked curiously.

Melinda stared at me before turning to look out the window, I had a feeling she wouldn't be answering me.

"Anyway, you can come if you like. The more people the better. It would be even better if you're going to buy us some drinks," she said with a wink, making me laugh.

*Damn, this girl wasn't subtle at all.*

"I'll buy you some drinks." I laughed. "As long as you don't give me silly costumes to wear."

Megan tilted her head.

Melinda laughed. "You shouldn't have said that." She

shook her head turning to face me with a grin. "She doesn't choose the costumes. Although you've given her an idea now."

She best not come up with some stupid ideas now. I had a feeling it would make Melinda hate me even more if she had to wear a stupid costume.

Megan smiled a wide grin. "Oh, the possibilities, Alex! What could I turn you into?" An evil laugh escapes her mouth.

I looked at her flatly. "I'm shutting down whatever idea you are having right now. If you put me in a stupid costume, you can say goodbye to me buying you drinks."

"Poof," Megan said, clapping her hands once. "Idea gone. What idea? Mel, did you hear me have an idea? Nope. I don't know what you're talking about."

Melinda smiled, and I couldn't help but smile with her. I wanted to see that smile of hers everyday if it was possible.

## Chapter Seven

# MELINDA

Same shit, different day. Just once I'd like the day to be different, not the same work, university, work, university, sleep routine I had going on. That's what I told myself when I had to deal with working with Cindy. I just hoped she would leave soon.

I looked at Leah as we hid in the kitchen with Dave, Cindy was on a rampage. "How long do you think we can hide here for?" I whispered to Leah.

"How long is left of the shift?" Leah asked, looking around the kitchen for the clock.

"Half an hour," I mumbled.

"I mean if we stay not busy then yeah we can hide," Dave said. "Also what are we hiding for?"

I looked at Dave and chuckled a little.

I loved the fact that he had no idea why we were hiding but he was willing to hide with us. "So, her favourite customer came in. You know, the one she has a crush on and is slightly obsessed with? He didn't want

Cindy to serve him, so we hid him in the booth on the opposite end of the diner where Cindy doesn't go."

"Ah," Dave said with a nod. "So, that's what the slam on the counter was for. Poor guy getting her attention."

"Where are you, dickheads?" I heard Cindy ask as she entered the kitchen. "One of you needs to go and unblock the toilet."

Dave looked at us and stood up. "Whatever happened to hello?" He asked, pulling out some cans next to us. "As much as I would love to clean and unblock the loos, I'm cooking."

"I wasn't talking to you," she said. "Where did the useless girls go?"

"Were they not serving customers?" Dave asked with a frown.

"If I had seen them I'd be talking to them right now and not you," she said, sounding irritated. "If you see them, tell them Melinda needs to unblock the toilet. It's all she's good for."

I rolled my eyes.

I'd love to know why Cindy hated me so much. I let out a yawn covering my mouth. I was wilting away. It was not a good idea to pull an all-nighter. So for the next half an hour Leah and I stayed hiding under the counter talking quietly until our shift was over. As soon as it was, Leah and I crawled out underneath and walked to the staff room as we pushed open the door. Cindy stood there with her hands folded over her chest.

"Where have you been?" She snapped.

"We were sorting the bins out." Leah lied looking at Cindy. "It looked like some drunk students decided to go dumpster diving. I figured Daisy would prefer to not have to pay for a rat or mouse exterminator."

"Oh," Cindy said. "Thank you for that. I didn't even think of checking outside."

"You're welcome. Anyway, we've got a class to get to," Leah said.

We grabbed our stuff together and walked out of Daisy's and headed up the short path towards the university. "The way you lied was so effortless. I'm impressed."

"Aw, that's sweet," Leah chuckled. "I can't believe she brought that bullshit."

I laughed a little. "When are you back on shift?"

"Erm, in two days I think. What about you?" Leah asked.

"Tomorrow," I said. "I have a twelve-hour shift."

"Girl, I don't know how you keep on top of everything. Well, I have to go or I'm going to be late. Again."

I chuckled a little before I headed to my lecture and went straight into the classroom sitting down. I rested my head on the desk, dragging myself into work and university on zero to no sleep was not my brightest idea, but alas I didn't want to fall behind with my work at university because once you fell behind it was like walking up a down escalator when trying to catch up. I was fighting a losing battle, so I didn't want to add catching up on university work to my already hectic schedule.

The question was: could I keep my eyes open for the remainder of this lecture?

I felt a tap on my hand lifting my head. I saw Alex and Megan looked at me concerned.

"You don't look good, are you okay?" Alex asked softly.

"I'm tired," I mumbled, rubbing my eyes.

"Mel, you are wearing yourself thin," Megan said. "You need to slow down and take a break. The world isn't going to go to hell if you don't go to work."

The world might not go to hell but the debt in my name won't stop gaining interest.

A number flashed onto my phone that I didn't recognise, reaching for my phone answering it as I left the classroom. "Hello."

"Is this Melinda Brown?" A woman asked.

"Yes, can I ask who is calling?"

"Ma'am, I'm calling from the hospital. Your mother is here. She passed out hitting her head. You are listed as next of kin," she said.

My heart dropped. "Is my mother okay?" My finger itched the inside of my thumb as I waited for a response.

"The doctor will update you when you arrive at the hospital, Miss Brown," she said.

"I'll be there soon, thanks," I said. I ended the call walking back into the classroom. I picked up my books, throwing them into my bag.

"You okay?"

"My mum has been taken to hospital," I said. I looked around the table making sure I had everything I needed. "I need to go."I left the classroom hitting the button for the lift, looking up at the floor numbers it seemed to be taking forever.

I hit the button again. "Come on. Come on."

The doors finally opened. I stepped in hitting the close button a few times, before they shut Alex stepped in just as the door closed behind him. "What are you doing?" I asked. "Shouldn't you be in the lecture?"

"Do you want a lift to the hospital?" He asked, ignoring my question.

I looked at him hesitantly, it was easier to get a lift to the hospital that was for sure. I bit my lip looking at him and nodded slowly. "Okay. Thank you."

The doors dung open, and I followed him out the university heading over to a black BMW.

He unlocked the car, opening up the passenger door. I climbed in and put my seatbelt on, immediately placing my bags on the floor next to my feet. Alex got into the car putting his belt on and he drove us to the hospital. I tapped my feet impatiently, as I tapped the side of the passenger door. It felt like we were driving at 10 miles per hour, not the speed limit which I was pretty sure Alex was pushing right now.

I looked to see Alex watching me out of the corner of my eye. "What?"

"You work too hard," he said.

"I don't have a choice," I admitted.

We pulled up at the hospital.

I climbed out of the car, grabbing my bag. I ducked down to look at Alex again. "Thank you for giving me the lift. It means a lot."

"You're welcome, Melinda. Call me if you need me to pick you up."

"I don't have your number," I said.

He held his hand out. I placed my phone in the palm of his hand and he inputted his number, and I heard his phone beep not a moment later and knew he must have texted himself, so he had my number. "There, now you do. Make sure you use it. I hope your mum is okay."

"Thanks."

I shut the car door making my way through the hospital to reception, once I got the information for what ward she was on I made my way there. "Excuse me, can you tell me what room my mother, Elena Brown, is in?" I asked the nurse.

"Follow me lovely," she said.

I followed her into a bay with three other people and my mother in. I walked over to my mum kissing her head, "Oh, mum," I mumbled. I sat down in the chair next to her just watching as she slept.

"Miss Brown?" I looked up to see the doctor, I stood up looking at him. "My name is Doctor Blaze. I'm your mother's consultant."

"What happened? Is she okay?" I tried to take a breath to calm down.

"She was brought in as she passed out at work and hit her head. She has a mild concussion and is very dehydrated."

"Concussion?"

"Yes, so we would like to keep her overnight to keep an eye on her for the time being. Do you know if your mother is experiencing any stress?" He asked.

I stared at him trying to think of anything she had mentioned. The one thing I could think of was the arguments in the house. I didn't think that would have anything to do with it. "I don't think so."

"I suspect your mother is going to spend a lot of time

sleeping. If you want to leave your number with the nurse, we'll call you with any updates or changes," he said softly.

I looked at him. "I don't want to leave her," I said.

"She's going to be sleeping," he said.

I nodded.

I walked over to the bed looking at the machine. All of her stats seemed good. I guess that was one good thing.

I brushed her hair away from her face, she looked so peaceful like this. I bent down pressing a kiss to her head. "I love you."

I sat in the chair next to her just watching, I know the doctor said I should go, but I needed to see her. She was okay. She was alive.

A metal IV stood next to the bed with saline bags hooked to it as the wire led into her hand. The smell of anti-bacterial filled my nose. All I could hear was the hospital intercom buzzing with doctors and nurses being paged and the beeping of the machines.

I let out a sob as tears fell, closing my eyes as light headedness surged through me. I gasped for air holding my arm. I needed to get out of here.

I rushed out of the hospital sitting on the bench pulling my coat tighter as the cold air hit me. I took a breath, enjoying the coolness and watching the cars go by, it felt peaceful. Far more peaceful than I felt.

"You okay?" I looked to see Alex sitting down next to me.

I looked at him, lowering my eyebrows. "What are you doing here?"

"I never left," he admitted.

My heart stopped a little when he said he had stayed.

nobody had really stayed. I was so used to people walking away.

"I was worried about you. I wanted to make sure you were okay."

I pressed my lips together and shook my head trying to keep my tears from falling. "I'm not okay," I whispered.

He reached over, squeezing my hand and I felt a tear slide down my cheek.

I hated crying. It made me feel weak that I couldn't control my emotions. "You weren't in the hospital very long. Is she okay? Is she—"

"Alive? Yeah." I nodded. "They said she has a concussion so they want to keep her overnight."

"That's good, though. The hospital is the best place for your mum."

I nodded. I knew that. A blast of cold air caused a shiver.

"Let's get you out of the cold. Let me take you home."

"I need to give the receptionist my number, so they can update me when she's awake," I said.

"I'll go," he said softly. He left me on the bench, and I continued to watch the cars drive past. Something about it was calming.

"Let's get you home," he said.

I took his hand, and he led me to his car. I noticed he had parked in a loading zone.

I stared at him. "You're going to get fined for parking here."

He shook his head. "No, I won't."

He opened the passenger door.

I got in, putting my seatbelt on and placing my bag at my feet.

He got in the car putting his belt on and began to drive. "Where's home?"

I reeled off my address, and he inputted it into the satnav. I reached for the seatbelt, clipping myself in. And the drive began. My hand found my hair and began to twist it out of nervousness.

*She would be okay. She had to be right? The doctors didn't sound too concerned. That meant it was good, right?*

"Melinda."

I shook my head snapping out of my thoughts turning to look at Alex. "She is in the best place for her health."

"I know," I mumbled.

"Connect your phone to the car," he said.

I tilted my head to the side as my eyebrows scrunched together. "Why?"

"You need a distraction, and I want to see what your music taste is like," he said with a shrug.

I nodded and went to work on connecting my phone to the car, almost immediately *Kelsea Ballerini* blared through the speakers. I reached over, turning the volume down. "How loud?"

He laughed. "It's a two-person karaoke party. So, country music is your favourite?"

I shook my head. "Nope. It's basically whatever pickles my fancy at the time. I have a mixture of Disney, pop, rap, R&B, anything really. My music is on shuffle, so you will get a wide variety of randomness."

"What's your favourite song?"

I bit my lip. "Okay, so, it has to be *What Dreams Are Made of* by Hilary Duff, what's yours?"

"*Not Afraid* by Eminem," he said. "Death row meal."

"Death row?" I raised an eyebrow. "What crime did I commit?"

"I don't know. Whatever you want to have committed." He laughed.

"Wait, we don't even have death row in this country, so unless I'm going home, well back to America," I said. "I think I'd like to have gone on a robbery spree."

"So, banks?"

"No. Bingo halls."

"Huh?"

"Bingo halls have a lot of money in them. Think about how much people pay, and how much the bingo halls pay out. You have the little tabletop games, they probably bring in so much money too," I said pointedly. "So, I'd rob bingo halls. They don't have a lot of security"

"You've thought about it a lot. I guess I know who I will be keeping an eye on if there are any reports of bingo hall theft."

I laughed. "Death row meal would be samosas, chicken curry and rice, with a side of mashed potatoes. Ugh, I love mashed potatoes. Oh, and stuffing!"

"What a mix."

"Yours?"

"McDonald's, just something about that Big Mac sauce." He laughed.

I smiled. "Thank you."

"For what?"

"This. I mean, I don't even know you that well, and you're helping me," I said.

"My parents always told me that if you can help people then you should. It's our duty to help people," he said.

"You're helping me out of duty?"

"No. I'm doing it because I like you."

"Your mum sounds like a smart woman," I said, finally putting him out of his misery instead of slightly teasing him.

"Many say so." He smiled. "Did I say how sorry I am for the way I treated you?"

"Nobody has ever scolded you, have they?" I couldn't keep the grin off my face.

"Do my parents count?"

"No, everyone gets scolded by their parents," I rolled my eyes.

I looked out the window, the roads weren't terribly busy although I guess it wasn't too bad when it was mid afternoon. I wasn't sure if I would like to drive. For the rest of the drive we spent playing a version of twenty questions and for once I was glad Alex was there because it was the perfect distraction from worrying about my mum.

## Chapter Eight

# ALEXANDER

"Do you want to come in?" I looked at Melinda's house and back at her.

"I just don't really want to be alone right now." She let out a yawn and smiled sheepishly.

"Okay," I told her.

Locking the car I followed her into the house she sat on the sofa as her head leant back. She closed her eyes, and I couldn't help but admire her.

She was stunning. Her hair flowed down her face. Her tight top did nothing to hide her curves because her boobs were practically begging to be let free of her bra.

*Fuck, I wanted to bury my face in them.*

I shook my head. I didn't need to be getting an erection right now by looking at her this way.

I heard a soft snore. "Melinda?" I reached for the blanket covering her up and I gently pulled her shoes off and lifted her feet up.

I made my way into the kitchen and looked in the

fridge for a drink. I stopped as I saw it was empty except for a few items. I opened up her cupboards to see except a few tins and spices.

Every fibre of my body was telling me to help her, but I wasn't sure how I would be able to do it without offending her and pissing her off. I couldn't help but think about it all night.

*Maybe I should buy her some groceries. No, that would probably piss her off, too.*

Damn me for liking such a stubborn girl. Maybe I could sneak in some groceries and offer to cook for her. I nodded. That was the plan.

I walked out the room heading out the door and got into the car and began to drive to the supermarket. I got out of the car, and Jones stood in front of me. "Alexander, you know you can't go into a supermarket," he said. "You will be recognised."

I looked at him flatly. "I just want to get some groceries."

"That's sweet but impractical, you're a Prince," he said.

"So, I keep being reminded," I grumbled. "Well, will you please go and buy some of the things for me?" I handed him my card. "I promise, I will stay in the car."

"Keys" he held his hand out. I handed it to him. "Get into the car, I'm going to lock you in. Then, I know you won't be going anywhere."

"I'm pretty sure you aren't meant to leave-"

"You're not a child or a dog Alexander," Jones interrupted, making me roll my eyes. "Now get in."

I did as he ordered, getting into the car.

When he shut the door, I pulled my phone out and went onto the App Store. I needed to download TikTok after what the girls were saying. A few seconds later I had my account, and I was scrolling the for you page. I watched as a dog ran from the water with a fish in its mouth and chuckled. I liked the video and got sucked into watching funny dog videos.

A knock on the window jolted my phone from my hand onto the floor in front of me, I turned to see Jones stood by the door.

It unlocked, and I opened the door. "You scared the life out of me," I said, shaking my head. "You're meant to protect me, not kill me."

"Don't be dramatic, Alexander," Jones rolled his eyes. He handed me my card and shoved the bags back into the car. "I brought you things for a few meals and soft drinks, even though you should be able to cook them."

"Okay," I said.

"Follow me to the house and then I want you to make yourself scarce."

I grabbed my keys from his hand, placing them in the keyhole. "Hey, Jones Thanks." He nodded, walking away to his car.

I reversed out the parking bay and drove the short trip to her house. I got out of the car grabbing the bags from the backseat and locked the car heading to her door. I did a quick survey of the area to make sure I wasn't being followed by any paparazzi.

In terms of being with Melinda, I hadn't been caught, but it was only a matter of time before the bubble would be popped. I entered the house heading straight to the kitchen and began to empty the shopping bags and guessed where things went.

I headed back into the living room and looked through the TikTok app and sat with Melinda as she caught up on some sleep.

A few hours later, she twisted and let out a groan as she sat up. "What year is it?"

I let out a little laugh. "It's still the same year you fell asleep in."

She reached for her phone and tapped the screen. "You didn't have to stay, Alex. Thank you."

"You are welcome," I said.

She lifted her arms into the air as she stretched, her top rose showing her skin.

I bit my lip as I couldn't take my eyes off her.

She stood up and headed into the kitchen.

I wondered if she would notice the groceries. Maybe I would get away with it.

"What the fuck? Alex!"

I headed into the kitchen, leaning against the door.

She was staring into her fridge.

I couldn't tell if she was angry or happy. "Yes?"

"Alex, I can't let you buy all this. Let me get some money."

She headed towards me, and I grabbed her arm softly, stopping her in her tracks. "Melinda, I didn't buy this for you to give me money back."

"I'm not a charity case."

I couldn't help but feel slightly offended. How could she think I would assume she was a charity case. "You aren't a charity case. I did this because I wanted to do something nice." I brushed a strand of her hair away from her face. "You carry so much, and you look a little stressed. I wanted to do something that would help you feel less stressed."

She pressed her lips into a thin line as she looked at her feet for a few moments. "Okay.". She looked at me.

I could see apprehension and something else I couldn't quite put my finger on.

"Thank you." She reached up and wiped her cheek, letting out a sniffle. I pulled her into a hug as more tears fell down her cheeks. "I'm not even sure why I'm crying.". "Thank you, Alex. Nobody has ever done something like this for me."

"You're welcome. I'm just glad you didn't fight me too much on this," I said, releasing her.

I heard the car alarm and frowned. I walked towards the front door, opening it to see the lights flashing. I pressed the button, silencing the alarm no doubt a car went past a little too close.

"How many cars do you own?"

I turned to see Melinda stood behind me, and I smiled a little. "Me personally? Two. This one doesn't really get seen. It keeps me under the radar."

"Are you a spy?"

I burst out laughing and shaking my head. "A spy attending university? Not likely."

She grinned. "I didn't say it was a good idea. How about this? If I guess what you are and your secret identity you have to tell me."

I raised an eyebrow as she moved around the kitchen. "Why are you so sure that I have a secret identity?"

She cocked her head to the side and her eyes grew wide. "Really?"

"What?"

"Alex, you have an adult babysitter. You have two very fancy cars, and you have drivers. So, you clearly have some kind of secret."

"Okay. You can guess. You won't get it right."

I was confident. I was sure that she was never going to guess that I was a Prince, so I was safe.

"I'm a good guesser," she teased.

"Not that good. I'd rather you didn't guess. I like you not knowing who I am. I like you a lot. I love that you treat me normally. You have no idea how much that means to me." I hoped showing her a little more of this side of me would be enough. I hoped it would be enough.

"Okay," she said with a little nod. "I won't ask questions. Promise me one thing?"

"Anything."

"I wouldn't promise that so lightly," she said, shaking my head. "Don't hurt me."

"I promise." That was a promise I intended to keep, a very easy one. She shut the front door going back into the kitchen and followed her. "How about we play a game of twenty questions?"

"Favourite colour?"

"Easy," I laughed. "Gold matches my—" I stopped mid-sentence, realising I was about to say crown.

She raised an eyebrow.

"Erm, never mind. It's gold. Yours?"

"Purple," she said, not pressing about what I was going to say.

"Favourite memory?" I asked curiously.

The more I could know about her the better.

"Meeting Megan," she said easily. "That girl is my ride or die. My left leg to my right leg, you know the drill. Do you have any siblings?"

I grinned. "I do." I pulled my phone out, loading up some photos to show her. "I have three younger brothers and one baby sister. Elizabeth is my favourite. She's four. I will have to introduce you both. Let me show you a picture." I turned the phone around to show her.

"Oh my gosh, she's cute! She looks like you. You seem like a good brother."

"I hope so."

If anything I loved Elizabeth and would do anything for her, a fact she did take advantage of so much. "Do you have any siblings?"

"Nope, I'm an only child," she said. "Just me and my mum."

"What about your dad?" I asked curiously.

"He's not my dad. If anything, the man is a sperm donor. Then, I'll have nothing to do with him," she said, frowning.

Clearly, I had hit a sore spot. We stayed in the kitchen asking different questions, and I loved how much I was getting to know her.

"How about we make some food?"

She nodded, pottering around the kitchen and handing me two potatoes. "How about we have jacket potatoes?"

I nodded and placed them on the counter. I reached for the knife and stared at the potato.

How did one make a jacket potato?

The sharp knife was removed from my hand, and I saw Melinda standing there eyes wide. "Have you ever cooked before?"

*Was it that obvious?*

"No," I said, dragging the word out.

She shook her head stabbing the potatoes before wrapping them in tin foil placing them in the oven to cook. My phone started ringing and I frowned, I walked over to the table picking the phone and saw it was mum. I answered the phone, immediately straightening back up. "Alexander."

"Yes, ma'am," I said.

"I'm leaving the country for a little bit, I have a meeting in one of the neighbouring countries," mum said.

"When are you flying?" I asked curiously.

"The jet is going to be taking me in an hour, and I couldn't find you. Now, I know you don't have a lecture, so I am curious where you are," mum said.

"Nowhere," I lied.

"Alexander."

"I'll explain later," I said hoping she would accept that.

"Okay, but you will need to return home. Your father would like to speak with you and Elizabeth is requesting a bedtime story," mum said.

"Yes, ma'am."

"I love you, Alexander."

I ended the call, my mother always ended our phone calls with I love you. "So, what is going with the Jacket potato?"

"Baked beans," Melinda said. "Nothing can beat baked beans and a jacket potato, simple and stunning." She reached into the fridge, pulling out a soft drink and handed it to me.

I opened it, took a small sip, and sat down at the table.

"So tell me, what's your favourite hobby?"

"Horseback riding," I said immediately.

"Wow, really?"

"Yeah, I love horseback riding, we learnt as kids I think we could ride a horse before we could walk properly. I'll have to take you horseback riding someday."

"Are you asking me on a date?" She asked.

"That depends," I mumbled. "Are you going to say yes?"

She nodded a little and I couldn't help but grin. "Yes I'll go on a date with you."

I grinned.

*Hell yes.*

I couldn't wait. Now, I just needed to plan the most amazing first date ever.

I watched her as she walked around the kitchen preparing food.

A few hours later, we had dinner. Melinda and I were currently sitting on the sofa with a blanket resting over us as she was flipping through the channels.

I reached over, taking the remote off her and turning off the TV. "There's only so much flickering between channels one person can take," I said flatly. "You wanted to know more about me?"

"Only if you're comfortable with telling me."

"I don't have a middle name," I said. "My last name is

George. My family is very well known, and we are in the public eye."

She narrowed her eyes, "If you're in the public eye, how come I don't have a clue who you are?"

"You don't pay attention?" I offered. "One day, I will have to take over the responsibility and everything in me wants to escape, but I can't because it's my duty."

"Is this duty a bad thing?"

"Sometimes," I admitted. My phone began to ring, and I groaned looking at the caller ID. "Jones, I'm busy."

"I'm aware of that, sir. I wouldn't call unless it was essential. The paparazzi is at your location."

"I don't care what you have to do, Jones. Just get them away from here."

I ended the call pushing the blanket off me, I noticed a flash at the window, I stood up pulling the blinds a little and saw that some paparazzi was looking at the car.

Dammit, maybe it wasn't as hidden as I thought.

"Alex, what's happening?"

I turned to look at Melinda and gave her a reassuring smile. "It's okay," I said. I had no idea how I would explain this to her. I just hoped she wouldn't ask anymore questions. "How about you show me your favourite reality show?"

She clapped her hands together, sitting back on the sofa. "You have no idea what you are letting yourself in for."

"Can't wait."

"Didn't you have to go home?"

I shrugged. "Eh, it can wait."

# Chapter Nine

## MELINDA

Rolling onto my side, I was met with thin air falling to the floor letting out a groan as I hit the floor.

*How did I fall out of bed?*

I opened my eyes seeing I was in the living room. The memories of last night finally came rushing back to me. We had been binge-watching my favourite reality television show and fell asleep.

Looking behind me, Alex was still fast asleep. He looked so peaceful. With him asleep, I had time to admire him without him knowing it. It had taken a bit for Alex to get comfortable after the incident again. I could tell he was fighting with himself. There must've been a huge part of him that wanted to run and hide, whilst the other part of him wanted to stay.

What scared me the most is that I wanted to know both of those parts of him. The good, the bad, and the ugly. I wanted to know it all. I wanted to know him.

Then, there's the secret.

Could I cope with not knowing what his secret was?

It was obvious he had one, no adult had a grown babysitter without a reason. The security that had suddenly appeared around the campus, it all coincides with when Alex started at university.

I couldn't figure out what the reason was.

Did he have a famous and important family?

Was he secretly a political figure?

Would I end up hurt?

I wanted to google him so bad. I reached for my phone, opening up the browser and stared at it.

*Could I break my promise?*

I told him I wouldn't.

I let out a groan, throwing my phone back on the sofa.

I stood up, made my way to the bathroom, and showered quickly. I wrap the towel around me heading to the bedroom changing into some clean clothes. My body ached so much. Sleeping on a small sofa with someone else was not the best way to sleep.

After finishing getting ready, I made my way downstairs, Alex was still asleep on the sofa, and into the kitchen. I grabbed a can out of the fridge, opening it and taking a small sip.

*Maybe I should prepare some breakfast.*

I know Alex brought breakfast things I couldn't believe he went shopping for me. I don't think anyone would top what he did for me. I walked into the living room and saw he was sitting up looking confused.

"Hey."

"Hi," he said. "I was really confused about where I was then."

"Do you often wake up at random houses not knowing who you're with?" I asked, raising an eyebrow.

"Not happened in a few years," he admitted. "Do you have plans today?"

I shook my head.

"Do you want to go on that date?"

"I'd love to." Butterflies filled my stomach, this was my first real date.

"Great," he smiled. "I'm going to go home and then I'll come pick you up" he looked at his phone "around midday if that's alright with you?"

"Yeah, that sounds good," I said. He stood up, stretching his arms out.

I made my way over to the door and let him out. "I'll see you soon."

"Yes, you will. Just so you know, I had fun last night," he said.

"Me, too."

He got into his car and drove off.

I headed into the living room, grabbing my phone.

Megan answered straight away. "If this isn't life or death, I'm going to fucking kill you, Melinda," she mumbled.

"Does Alex asking me on a date count?"

She squealed, making me pull the phone away from my ear. "Ow. Remember, we're on the phone."

"Holy hell! That was worth waking up for," she said. "When? Where? How? What?"

"Erm, when Midday, where I don't know, and how, he used his voice and asked me," I said answering her questions.

"Are you excited?"

"I am. We've spent the best part of the last day together. I really like him, Megan. Ah, I am terrified," I admitted. "He saw we didn't have a lot of food, so went shopping for me."

"Damn girl, it's like he's getting ready to stake his claim on you," she said. Do you need me to come over and help you get ready?"

"No, I'm just going to go dressed as I am," I said. "I'm not going to bother getting fancy because it's just going to be ruined."

"What are you wearing?"

"Jeans and a T-shirt."

"Melinda, this is your first real date with an actual really nice, amazing man and you're going to wear jeans?!"

"Well, we're horseback riding, so yes," I said flatly.

"Oh, you said you didn't know," she said.

I could just imagine the look on her face.

"I better get the low down on this date. I don't care what time it is you get back. I want all the details, so you better come over."

"I will be there straight away."

"Great. I'm going back to sleep."

Ah, my best friend is not only a pain in *the* ass, but she's *my* pain in the ass.

I pressed my mum's number. I knew she had woken up but I had yet to actually hear from her.

She answered after a few rings.

"Hey, mum."

"Hi, honey," she said.

Relief flooded through me as I heard her voice. I let out a little sniffle.

"I'm okay. I promise."

"You scared me, mum," I admitted.

My eyes began to well up with tears, I didn't want to think about a life without her. Although we argued and didn't see eye to eye all the time, I never wanted to live in a world without her.

"I'm sorry, honey."

"You're okay though?"

"A little bump won't keep me down. You seriously don't need to check up on me. Your dad—"

"Okay, sorry for caring," I cut her off not needing to hear whatever she was going to say about the sperm donor.

I ended the call, throwing the phone on the bed.

Almost immediately, it started ringing again, but I ignored it.

I walked over to my wardrobe, picking up my best looking but not amazing clothes. If we were going horseback riding, I didn't want to wear my best jeans. I pulled out a different pair of jeans with a vest top and got dressed. I let my hair out the bun and ran a brush through it. I winced as it came into contact with a knot. I had really got to start brushing my hair instead of just shoving it up out the way.

I'd like to say I wasn't sitting at the bottom of the stairs waiting for the knock on the door, but the truth is I was sitting at the bottom of the stairs waiting for him. There was only so much watching television that could distract you and I was past that limit. I opened the door and came face to face with Alex.

"Hi," I said.

"Hey, you look beautiful," he said. "Are you ready to go?"

Nodding, I shut the door behind us.

He led us over to an SUV and saw Jones waiting beside the open door.

"Hi."

"Miss Brown." He nodded.

I got into the car putting my belt on as Alex climbed in next to me, I looked at him raising an eyebrow, "is it normal for you to be driven around?"

"Yes," he said instantly. "All a part of my world and my family."

I nodded, not pressing for more information.

He would tell me when he was ready. Well, whenever that may be. Hopefully soon because curiosity would kill this cat that was for sure.

Alex held onto my hand as we began to move. The butterflies in my stomach hadn't slowed down or stopped. It was hard to try and keep my leg from bouncing.

I looked at Alex from the corner of my eye. He was staring out the window biting his lip. It made me want to kiss him so much more.

"How long is it going to take to get to where we are going?" I asked, curiously.

"Jones?"

"Depending on traffic between fifty minutes to an hour Miss Brown," Jones said.

An hour later, we arrived at our destination. It was a little ranch, well when I say little, it was actually big. Dogs were barking, horses were neighing, and cows were mooing.

I imagined waking up to this everyday would be absolutely stunning, although slightly annoying I guess if someone had chickens and other animals that would wake you up.

The smell of manure hit my nose as we walked around the large blue house, "I'll take you for a tour into the ranch soon. It's beautiful there. I didn't decorate though, that is all Marie."

"Marie?" I asked.

"Yeah, she lives here along with Jack. They take care of the ranch and the horses that we rescue," Alex explained.

"Are you here often?" I asked curiously.

"I try to get here as much as possible," he said. "Which sadly isn't often enough, but I love it here."

"I can see why."

The open land, the enclosed horse paddocks, and the different animals seemed like their own slice of heaven.

He reached for my hand as he led me to the stables. "Don't show your fear, stay calm, and they'll be okay."

"Okay."

He pushed open the stable door. There were two horses inside, a white one and a black one. The black horse stood back a little, assessing the both of us. The white one trotted over to us happily.

Alex reached for my hand, lying it out for the horse to sniff. The horse let out a neigh, and Alex nodded. I reached forward, stroking its nose.

"They're gentle creatures," he said softly in my ear.

I bit my lip.

Alex had gotten closer, and I was very aware of it. My arms got goosebumps and I shivered slightly.

"Are you cold?" Alex asked gently.

"No, I'm fine. The horses are beautiful," I said softly. "I don't know how to ride them though."

"It's easy," he said. "I'll help you. You won't be riding him since he's mine. He's more difficult to ride, and he has preferences. You'll be riding Poppy. She's the little Princess' horse—" Alex said, still behind me.

I turned looking at him concerned. "Are you okay?"

He cleared his throat. "Yeah, sorry. Poppy is Elizabeth's horse, but this will be her last ride for a little while."

"Why?"

"She's pregnant. It's why Rocky looks like he's ready to take you down," he chuckled.

I watched in fascination as Alex began to get the horse ready.

The only thing I knew about horse riding is that you sat next to a saddle that was as far as my knowledge went.

Poppy seemed comfortable as Alex put what he needed to on her. He then did the same with Rocky and both horses waited side by side. "So, these are reigns. You use them to guide her and to obviously ensure that you stay up."

I nodded. "How do you get up?"

"These are stirrups. Your feet sit in them, but you also

use them to pull yourself up, so put your left foot on it and then use it to swing your right one over her."

I reached for Poppy and placed my foot on the stirrup and did as Alex ordered putting my foot in and pulling myself up getting on Poppy. I held onto the reins, keeping myself up.

I bit my lip, looking down at what would be a very big drop. I watched as Alex got up onto his horse, and I reached for the reins, holding onto them tightly. They seemed like expensive leather and thankfully felt really nice to hold.

Alex pulled on the reins and trotted off in front of me.

I pursed my lips together. "Help me. My butt..." I mumbled, shaking my head.

"You know what to do Poppy."

She neighed a little, making me laugh a little. I pulled on her reins. She started on trot, quickly catching up with Alex and his horse.

"Told you I'd help." He laughed.

I shook my head. "You left."

"You figured it out though."

I rolled my eyes.

I guess he did have a point.

The horses trotted side by side through the field.

To say we were in autumn was hard to believe. Not all the leaves had fallen yet. They were a pretty orange colour. It smelt like a crisp autumn afternoon, there was a little breeze but thankfully not a cold chill.

The trotting of the horse was an interesting sensation. The jolting up and down and with one hard trot felt like I could fall any second, but that could have been the fact I was not confident.

Alex came to a stop near a lake. I looked out and saw that there were small ripples running throughout the water. A few ducks were swimming around in the lake.

I glanced over at Alex. "If you had to come back as an animal, what would it be?"

"A pigeon, because you'd be able to shit on people that annoy you," he said.

I laughed.

It was a good answer.

"I would be a duck. No, actually, scratch that! A panda. Like pants are so cute and stupid and I have no idea how they survived. I watched a video where pandas just fall over and off everything and it's fantastic, makes me smile whenever I see those videos."

He climbed off his horse, making his way over to me and hold his arms out. I swung my leg around and grabbed onto him as he helped me down.

"It's beautiful, Alex," I whispered.

"I've never shown anyone this before," he admitted. He pulled me over to the blanket and we sat down. He pulled out another blanket covering us. "If it gets too cold, let me know and we can head back inside."

"So have you had Rocky and Poppy since they were babies? Foals, is that what they're called?"

"Yes, they're called foals. Poppy was born here. She's part of a long line of horses we breed. Rocky was a rescue. He was a wild horse. They were getting ready to put him down."

"What? Why? He's a perfectly good horse."

"He is now, but back then, he was in terrible shape. He wouldn't trust anyone. He got abused before he became a rescue. One day, he managed to get out of his stable and Poppy was in the field." He looked over at both of them.

Rocky was next to Poppy as she ate some grass, and I smiled a little.

"The rest was history."

Alex opened up the basket and placed some containers out with two paper plates. "I just packed a little bit of everything."

"Thanks Alex. I love it. This is amazing," I told him. "Thank you for sharing your escape with me."

He smiled, and I couldn't help but smile at him.

Damn. The man that was capturing my attention was slowly worming his way into my life. That much so, I hadn't even called work to explain why I didn't turn up for my shift. I was surprised Cindy hadn't left me a hundred voicemails of her swearing at me.

Anyway, Alex laid out the food on our plates.

I looked at him. "Tell me, what do you think the world has in store for us?"

"I don't believe the world has anything in store for us." He shrugged. "I don't really think the world controls what we do, only we as people can do that."

"You don't believe in fate? That the universe has a plan for us all?" I asked curiously.

"No, I think we make our own decisions when we are born. Fate and the universe don't make those decisions for us. I ran into you that day because I was running away from responsibilities. Then, I was a jerk to you. Fate had nothing to do with this. My mother, on the other hand, is instrumental in a lot of things."

I couldn't help but smile. I think that most mothers liked to meddle or stick their noses in things. I think it was a requirement of being a parent.

So with that thought I took a bite of the sandwich as we spoke about anything and everything random. I loved spending time with him.

He pulled me into his chest and began to play with my hair.

"What was your dream job when you were little?" I asked curiously.

"I wanted to be a firefighter and save people. Although, I don't think I'm actually fit enough for that. What did you want to be?"

"An author."

"Do you write?"

"I have written every now and then, but my drafts mostly stay as drafts. I don't think that my writing is good enough," I admitted with a shrug.

I looked up, and Alex was already looking at me. "What?"

His eyes flickered to my lips and then back to my eyes. "Nothing," he said softly. "You should continue writing."

I shook my head, and a strand of my hair fell in front of my face. Alex reached forward brushing it behind my ear, looking into his eyes he began to come closer as his eyes flickered to my lips once more.

A loud clap of thunder broke us apart.

We both looked up seeing a flash of lightning and like

that the rain began to fall. Alex stood up, pulling me with him and leading me over to Poppy.

I climbed onto her pulling on her reins, and we were off. It didn't take long to arrive back at the stables. I looked to see Alex who wasn't too far behind me. I bit my lip, staring at the floor.

*How did I get off the horse?*

I brought my leg over, so both of them hung on the side and stepped down. I tumbled onto the floor as my foot got caught on the foot-hold.

"Melinda!"

I groaned as I rolled over a moment later Alex stood in front of me holding his hand out.

"Hi," I said with a smile. "That was fun, let's do it again."

"I thought you were seriously hurt with how fast you fell off," he said, helping me up.

I couldn't help but wince as I put weight on my foot. "Okay, I take that back."

He wrapped an arm around me. "Let's get you inside, and we'll take a look at that ankle." He looked behind me. "Are you okay to sort the horses out for me?"

"Yes, sir."

The rain was pouring heavily. I couldn't help but feel I had slightly jinxed it with my thoughts of it being glad it hadn't rained yet. We left the stable making our way to the house.

Just as we reached the stairs, I stopped. "Wait."

"What?"

I placed my hands on his chest, pressing my lips to his. I felt him smile against my lips before he kissed me back, moving his lips in sync with mine. Not even the rain could pull us away from this moment. When I pulled away from him, he rested his forehead against mine.

"We should go inside," I said.

He wrapped an arm around me as he picked me up.

"That wasn't a signal for you to pick me up."

He carried me inside ignoring my comment. "Hush, you would have still been out there hobbling in. It's quicker if I carry you. Stop being stubborn, Ella."

"You are not calling me, Ella, either," I told him.

"Watch me" He winked. "Sit."

"I'm wet."

"I don't care."

I sat down doing as he said.

He sat in front of me, pulling my shoe and sock off. "Looks like it could just be a little sprain, but there's no major damage."

"That's good."

He stood up making his way upstairs and came back a few moments later with clothes in his hand. "The bathroom is through that door," he said pointing to the door.

I stood up, making my way to the bathroom and ignoring the shooting pain in my foot. I stripped out of my wet clothes, putting on his clothes. I grabbed my wet clothes, leaving the bathroom. "Where should I put my clothes?"

"In the basket," he said.

I did as he said, and he pulled me to sit down on the sofa. "Thanks for the loan."

"You're welcome. And of course the rain would ruin our date." He shook his head.

"It was perfect," I told him as I cuddled into him.

In that moment, it truly was perfect. Nothing could ruin our moment. I was falling hard for him. Although, the rain came, the date was perfect. The kisses and spending time together was amazing.

I looked up to the sleeping man on the bed and knew at that moment, I was going to jump in head first. He had broken down my walls, and over time, I was becoming attached to him and falling hard.

# Chapter Ten

# ALEXANDER

I was beginning to fall for her.

Ugh, who was I kidding, I had fallen for her.

In the very short time I had known her, I had fallen for her hard. I didn't understand how it was possible, but it was. For the second time we had fallen asleep together, and I was getting used to sleeping with her. The way she felt in my arms was a perfect fit. In her sleep, she let her guard down.

I couldn't stop replaying our kiss in my head though. I didn't expect her to lean in for a kiss, but a kiss in the rain was the *perfect* first kiss.

I brushed her hair out of her face and studied every bit of her face. I didn't want to forget this moment. I needed to enjoy it, but I didn't know when and where it would turn to shit.

The press had gotten too close for my liking. I didn't

think they would recognise that car, and I hadn't used it enough for it to be recognised as mine, but alas they had.

"Stop staring at me you creeper," she mumbled. "Oh wait, you aren't my creeper, you're my stalker aren't you?"

I let out a little chuckle. "A lot of sass for this early."

She groaned. "I don't want to go back to real life. I need to get mum from the hospital. Plus, I need to see if I still have a job, and I have to catch up with some university work."

"Ella, stop," I said.

She rolled her eyes. "What did I say about calling me Ella?"

"Nothing. You were bitching at me," I said with a small smile.

"Your point?" She raised an eyebrow.

I smiled again. "I'm not going to stop calling you Ella. People call you Mel, El, Melinda, so I need to give you a nickname. I've decided that I'm going with that. You can't change my mind either, so don't even try."

"Most people would go with baby, honey, or sweetheart," she said, rolling her eyes.

I laughed, "I'm not stupid Ella. If I called you one of those names, you would slap me." I leaned forward and pressed a kiss onto her forehead.

"So, do you want to come out for Halloween?" She asked. "You have plenty of time to get a costume."

I tapped the side of my head like I was thinking. "Maybe I should be a Prince."

I was playing with fire but she still had no idea I was a prince. It was too good of an opportunity to not. At least if we were out and people referred to me as Prince, I could pretend it was part of the costume. I was too close, playing with fire.

"Like from Cinderella," she said. "That could work. You could pass for a prince I guess."

"Maybe you should be Cinderella," I suggested.

She laughed. "No, Megan and I usually do a joint costume. This year we are Thing 1 and Thing 2. We were the two guys from the advert last year. You know, the 'I can walk one hundred miles' song, *I'm Gonna Be* (500 *Miles*) by the Proclaimers"

I smiled a little.

A phone started to ring, and we both let out a sigh.

"Do people not know how to leave us alone? It's Thursday."

"Alex, it's a weekday. We should be at university, and I should eventually be at work," she said. "The past few weeks have gone by way too fast. I can't keep up with everything."

"So, I can't tempt you with breakfast?" I asked.

"Not here, but you can tempt me with breakfast back at Daisy's on campus," she said with a smile.

I could accept that.

I let her climb off the sofa and go get her clothes out the dryer.

I quickly went into my room changing into some clean clothes. I was glad I had spread my outfits between here and home. I walked back downstairs hearing her on the phone.

"Mum, I'll pick you up tonight," she said. "I have my lecture first. Mum, I can't keep missing things just because it makes your life easier." She paused. "You know what, if that's the way you're going to speak to me about it, then get him to get you!" She ended the call throwing it on the sofa and she let out a frustrated groan.

I walked over, pulling her into my arms and giving her a hug. "Are you okay?"

She sighed. "My mum wants me to drop everything to go and get her now. She's sick of being in hospital. She wasn't meant to be released until tonight, and I was planning to get her after my lecture and my shift at Daisy's. I mean, presuming I still have a job."

I held onto her a little bit tighter. I didn't know what to say to make it better. Her struggles were different to mine, and I didn't even know how to begin to help her with her struggles. "After your lecture, I will take you to the hospital and we will pick her up together. Then, I will take you both home. I won't hear you tell me no either."

"Wow, it's a serious step meeting the parents," she teased.

I smiled a little.

I loved the fact that I had managed to cheer her up a bit. I wanted to tell her I was in it for the long run but something tells me that might scare her away. I didn't want that yet, the longer I could keep from scaring her the better, even more so keeping the fact I was a Prince from her.

"If you'd like, I will even cook dinner for you."

She gasped. "You don't need to threaten me. I will accept the lift."

I narrowed my eyes slightly. "My cooking isn't that bad, Ella."

"Alex, you didn't even know how to stab a potato. I

don't think I want to let you loose inside of a kitchen," she shook her head.

"I should spank you for that," I teased.

She flashed me a grin as she took the clothes from the sofa and headed up the stairs to change into them.

Damn, the girl had a great ass.

I should really look away, but my eyes were glued on her.

She disappeared from my sight, and I walked out towards the stables, finding Jack feeding the horses. "Hey, man," I said. "Thank you for making yourself and Marie disappear from the house last night."

"You're welcome, Sir. Marie enjoyed her night at the spa." Jack chuckled. "So, who is she? It's got to be pretty serious for you to bring her into your space, but I'm wondering how serious this is considering you made a point to text all staff to not refer to you as Prince if you are around a guest."

This is why I liked Jack. He was a straight talker and didn't hold back from questioning me about things like this.

"No, she has no clue that I am a prince, and I'd prefer to keep it that way for as long as possible."

"Alexander, that is going to bite you in the ass when she does eventually find out," Jack said.

I rolled my eyes. "Right. Anyway, give my love to Marie. I'll see you both soon." I walked back inside trying to get Jack's comment out of my head.

He was right, but I would deal with that when it bit me on the butt.

"I was wondering where you got to."

I looked up to see Melinda sitting on the sofa.

"Just went to go check in with Jack and the horses," I told her.

I reached for the car keys from the side table and made sure I had my phone in my pocket. "Are you ready?"

"Yeah." She looked around the room. "This is a beautiful place. Thanks for sharing it with me."

I pulled her towards me and pressing my lips to her softly. "We can always come here and escape whatever bullshit is bothering us with life."

She smiled at me.

I led her towards the car, opening the door for her. She climbed into the car and shut the door behind her. I got into the car and began the drive to Daisy's. I noticed security following behind us in the other car. I hoped that Ella wouldn't realise it was following us because I didn't know how I would explain that.

An hour later, I parked into the spot at Daisy's.

We headed straight inside and searched for a booth. I couldn't help but smile as I realised it was the same booth in which I did some of my not so covert research from or as Melinda called it stalking. Such an ugly term.

I sat down watching as she looked around the diner.

"Do you know what you're ordering?" She asked, using her server voice.

I raised an eyebrow. "Melinda, you do realise you aren't at work right now. You're a customer."

She grinned sheepishly. "Sorry, bad habit. It's like I just slip into the role."

"Melinda, you're fired!"

Both of our heads whipped around, looking for the voice.

A woman stormed over putting her hands on her hips as she glared at Melinda. She turned her gaze from Mel to me and I saw her eyes widen before she flipped her blonde hair over her shoulder and her demeanour changed from angry to flirty. She knew who I was.

"Well, hello."

Mel coughed and shifted in her seat, clearly uncomfortable, "don't mind me," she muttered. "Carry on flirting."

I ignored her, only paying attention to Mel. I didn't want to give this woman anymore ammunition to flirt with me. I only wanted to flirt with the girl sitting in front of me.

"Ah yes, you're fired." She snapped her attention back to Ella.

"Cindy, please. There was a family emergency," Ella said with a frown.

Cindy the name suited her. What a bitch. Her eyes looked me up and down with a smirk. "Is that what you would call fucking someone well above—"

"Hey," I snapped, cutting her off. "There is no need to be such a bitch."

"Alex, it's fine," Ella waved me off. "This is normal for the devil. Jealousy gets you nowhere, Cindy."

"Jealous? Of you? Puh-lease, you're nothing, you're just a fat ugly-"

"Ugly?" Ella laughed. "The only thing ugly here is your personality. At least I could change my weight and looks."

"There isn't enough surgery in the world to make you look better." Cindy laughed.

It was taking everything in my power to not get involved and defend Ella.

"Either way, you're fired. Get the fuck out—"

"Enough!"

Ella's head spun around to follow the voice, and she broke out into a grin. "Daisy!"

"Melinda, you aren't fired," Daisy said as she approached our table. "Cindy you on the other hand are. Get your things, and please leave the premises. I will send your final pay check in a few days."

Cindy opened her mouth, but Daisy held her hand up. "I don't want to hear it. This is the final straw, Leah, Dave, Lucy, and Sadie all refuse to work with you. I know everything I need to."

Cindy walked away.

"Thank you," Ella said with a small smile.

"You're welcome. Enjoy your meal. Let me know when things have settled down for you, and we will have a meeting," Daisy said.

A small smile appeared on my face.

This was the first I'd seen of Ella's boss, but she seemed lovely. I had a feeling if she had been here when I yelled at Ella, she would have shouted at me and possibly banned me for life.

"This turned into an amazing few days." She grinned. "I think that may be the best thing that's happened."

Of course she would think Cindy getting fired was better than our date. I didn't blame her though. From what I had witnessed, Cindy was not a nice person.

A few hours later, I stood outside of the hospital as Ella had gone in to get her mum.

I was more than happy to stay by the car because it meant less risk of the public spotting me. I saw Ella coming out of the hospital, making her way over to the cars and heading straight to open the door for them both.

"Mum, I'd like you to meet Alex," she said with a smile. "Alex, this is my mum, Elena. Alex was kind enough to offer us a ride home."

"Nice to meet you, ma'am," I nodded, helping her into the car.

We got into the car setting straight off for Ella's home, I had never had a more awkward car ride. That said a lot because I had ended up in a lot of cars with my parents and their disapproving scowls. Ella helped her mum into the house and I followed as she helped her onto the sofa. "Mel, can you go and get my blanket please>"

Ella walked upstairs.

Elena's eyes never left mine. "What are you playing at with my daughter?"

"I like her, ma'am," I said.

"She doesn't need some rich stuck-up Prince sniffing around her," Elena snapped.

So, I guess that cat was out of the bag. The question would be would she tell Ella?

"Ma'am with all due respect, you don't know me. You know what the media portrays me to be," I said. "I'm falling for her. You know your daughter. Trust her judgement. If I was a bad guy, she wouldn't want to be around me."

"You haven't told her you're a Prince, why?"

"She treats me like I'm a normal person. I love that about her. Telling her my title will change everything, and I'm not ready for that."

Elena raised an eyebrow. "I don't know if I can trust you. When you break my little girl's heart, I will break the most precious part of you."

Her eyes drifted down, and I couldn't help but wince as I finally understood what she meant.

My eyes widened slightly.

*Shit, she was scary.*

"Understood. For what it's worth, I have no intention of hurting her."

"I hope not, otherwise my daughter may be visiting me from prison."

## Chapter Eleven

## MELINDA

I'm pretty sure I could cut the tension in the room with a knife right now.

The car ride and the dinner it were all done in strained silence. Every time Alex tried to make small talk to my mother, she gave him one-word answers. I couldn't quite figure out why she was only giving one-word answers. It could be because she was tired from being at the hospital and didn't get a good sleep.

I was surprised Roman hadn't burst his way around. I hadn't seen him since our last bust up whether he was keeping a wide berth or running off. I hoped I would never see him again. I really hope it was the latter of those two options.

"Thanks for dinner, Mel. I'm going to bed. If Ro—"

"No," I cut her off.

I did not want that name or the drama uttered near Alex. I didn't want to have to explain all the backstory and why I was so angry. It would lead to me having to talk about the crippling debt, and the last thing I needed was his pity. That was why I didn't want to tell people.

"You need to go to bed and rest." I shot her a warning look.

She nodded, heading upstairs.

I looked at Alex.

He sloped back into his chair with a sigh, looking a little defeated. "Your mum hates me, Ella."

I didn't really know what to say to that. I had a feeling she did, but I really didn't want to confirm his thoughts. I reached over patting his arm. "She could just be really tired from the hospital."

"Don't fib." Alex chuckled, shaking his head.

He stood up and began to clear the plates from the table and headed towards the sink. "You don't have to wash up."

"You cooked. I can handle some washing up," he said as he began to run the water in the sink.

I walked over to the counter and lifted myself up to sit next to the draining board on the sink. I watched as he began to clean, and I couldn't help but smile. He looked like he had never picked up a sponge before.

"Alex, have you ever washed pots before?"

"That obvious, huh?"

I shook my head in disbelief. "How have you never washed pots before? How is that even possible?"

His cheeks were tinted red.

Was he embarrassed?

"Erm—"

"How rich are you?" I interrupted. "You have a driver and a personal assistant, but something tells me you may also have staff in your house that cook and maids that clean?"

He looked at me sheepishly and stepped in between my legs. "My family is important and as such, we have expectations that we have to follow," he admitted. "The simple things are one of the things that we aren't allowed to do sometimes."

I looked at him confused, "I don't understand. How could your family be raising you to go into a world where you need basic skills to survive?"

Alex stayed quiet. I could see the wheels inside of his head turning, but I couldn't quite figure out what he was thinking.

"We won't be needing basic skills."

What was his job?

What did his family do?

Has he already told me?

"Alex, what does your family do?"

He stepped away from in between my legs going back to attempting to wash the pots.

Had I hit a sore spot and not even know?

Did he still talk to his parents?

Were they toxic?

I had so many questions. I didn't know whether to press him on the issue. What if this pushed him further away? Why didn't I have a better memory?

"Ella, just give me a little bit of time, okay?" Alex asked softly. "I promise I'll tell you, but I need to enjoy this time we have."

I nodded.

My mind was spiralling.

Maybe I should google him.

What did he say his last name was? I felt like it was Dory. I picked up my phone, scrolling through my social media apps. Who was I kidding? I was on one app and that app was TikTok. It must have been made of some kind of chemical because it was very addictive.

"You should send me your username, so I can follow you," Alex said.

I looked at him, puzzled. "I thought you didn't have TikTok."

"Well after you and..." He trailed off, tilting his head up to the ceiling.

"Megan?" I offered.

"Yes. After you and Megan ridiculed me about not having it, I got intrigued and downloaded it. There's a lot of silly animals on that app," he said. "I've also got hooked on watching this woman. She has chicken, and there's this evil chicken, Debora, who keeps stealing Rainbow Cupcake's babies."

My mouth dropped open. I had no words. He got sucked in. I couldn't help but giggle a little.

"What?" He asked with a frown.

I chuckled. "The fact that you said that whole sentence to me is..." I shook my head, not finding the words. "Mind blowing. You've gotten interested in watching short videos of someone who's looking after chickens."

Alex frowned. "Don't give me that look like I'm crazy. Let me get my phone. You'll see." He wiped his hands on the tea towel before putting his hand in his pocket, pulling out his phone.

It took less than a minute before he was shoving his phone into my hand, I looked down watching dumbfounded as this woman shouted at her chicken, Debora.

"So, I guess Debora is off the list for any of your future children," I teased.

"Definitely," he said. "I'm thinking if I ever have a girl she'll be named Rainbow Cupcake."

I laughed. "Because that name won't get your imaginary child bullied at school." I searched for my profile and followed myself, so I could begin to spam him with different TikTok videos. The joy of just sending videos was something else for sure. I handed his phone back to him with a little smile.

He stepped in between my legs and brushed a strand of hair out of my face. I looked at him, and his eyes flickered towards my lips. A second later, he was leaning in. I felt his lips on mine. He deepened the kiss almost immediately, and I wrapped my arms around his neck pushing my body against his.

He broke the kiss, leaning his head against mine. "Fuck."

"Ditto," I whispered.

"I have to go." He sighed.

I nodded, and he stepped back. I slid off the side, walking towards the front door.

He bent down kissing me once more. "I'll see you soon, okay?"

"Remember this weekend is Halloween party weekend," I reminded him. "I'll see you later."

"Bye, Ella."

I watched as he walked out the house and got into the car. I shut the front door, locking it.

I really couldn't figure out this man. He was mysterious and part of that was drawing me further into his aura.

I headed upstairs and pushed open mum's bedroom door. She was propped up, flipping through a book.

"What was your problem?" I asked, folding my arms over my chest leaning against the door. "Alex knew you were rude, and I don't think he believed my bullshit excuse that you're tired from the hospital."

Mum put the book down and stared at me. "I don't trust him."

"You don't know him."

"Neither do you," she snapped. "If you did, you wouldn't be entertaining him right now. It's only going to come back and bite you in the butt. He is not the man for you, Melinda. He will use you and throw you away."

I scoffed, "You mean like the sperm donor did to you? The only difference is you opened your legs as soon as he came back. You didn't care that he destroyed us and left us"

"You don't understand the gravity of the situation. You are a child," she said angrily.

"Yeah, a child who is dealing with thousands of pounds of debt in her name that you wracked up," I shouted angrily.

"Your dad—"

"He is not my dad," I snapped. "He is a sperm donor. He stopped being anything the day he walked out."

"Your dad has offered you the money to pay it all,"

mum said. "We were in a bad place, and mistakes were made."

"Yeah, letting him back was a mistake."

"You don't get to judge me when the man you're speaking to hasn't been honest with you and told you who he really is," she said.

I walked away. I wasn't having this conversation again.

We just ended up going in circles and getting nowhere. The issue was neither of us would accept the other was right and instead of apologising we would just pretend like it never happened.

Was it healthy? No.

Was it ever going to change? Probably not.

---

The bell jingled as I entered the diner, and I headed towards the staff room putting my things into the locker.

I had to admit it filled me with a little joy knowing that Cindy's locker now sat empty. Ding dong, the witch was gone.

I walked out the staff room heading to Daisy's office. Her door was open, and she grinned as she saw me approaching.

"Melinda, how is your mum?"

"She's home now," I said as I entered the office sitting down. "How did you know? I don't remember texting anybody here that I wasn't going to be in for my shift."

Daisy smiled a little. "I was with your mother at the time of her passing out and being rushed into hospital."

I frowned a little. "How do you even know my mother?"

"Your mother and I went to school together," Daisy informed me.

My lips formed into an o. "Oh," I said. "How did I not know this?"

Had my mum mentioned the fact she knew Daisy before? I really felt more and more like Dory these days.

"Thank you for not firing me for missing work."

"I may have not been here physically the past few months, but I still know everything that goes on in my business," Daisy said. "For the last few months, we have been gathering evidence to be able to fire Cindy and not have hit us with an unfair dismissal. I am sorry for all the abuse she has done to you and the girls."

"Builds character right?"

"No. Did I ever tell you the story of how the diner came around?"

I shook my head.

"I used to work in a diner, and I loved it. It was so fun getting to interact with different customers and being able to be creative within the menu," she said. "I had a boss and a manager who were horrible. Our boss would only promote the women who would be willing to sleep with him and the manager was on a power trip. Anyway, to cut a long story short, I always swore that no staff would ever feel like I was made to feel."

I slumped back into the chair feeling slightly overwhelmed.

Daisy had never shared why she opened the diner. Although to be fair I guess I never asked.

"That's a lot."

Daisy smiled. "Anyway, let's forget about the negative. I wanted to talk to you about your work schedule."

I gasped. "Please don't take the hours away from me, I need them," I begged.

"Melinda, I'm not taking them away," Daisy said. "I want to promote you to manager."

I stared at her in surprise.

I was not expecting that. I was stunned into silence.

I opened my mouth and closed it again not really knowing what to say.

"Are you accepting the promotion?" Daisy asked.

"I'm just stunned."

"Obviously with your promotion, there would be a few more hours. Would you be able to cope with the hours and your university schedule? I know your degree is important," Daisy said. "I want to make sure you have your hours here, but also so you can keep on top of your university work."

"I only have three lectures. It would be easier to do my shifts after them and the days I'm off," I said.

"I know you've been working weekends, too. Are you okay with night shifts?" Daisy asked.

"You realise I've worked night shifts before, right?" I asked, raising an eyebrow.

Daisy nodded slowly. "Most definitely. I have hired two new waitresses. One of them has a background in waitressing, and the other is very green." She handed me the CVs, and I flipped through them.

"Would you be willing to train them?"

The only problem with training people up is I had to

remember how I did things properly and not the cheat ways that I had created after working here for years. "Yeah, I can train them. Thank you for the opportunity."

"Melinda, I may have not been here, but I know you are my best staff member," Daisy said. "Obviously with the promotion you'll have increased pay, but if you need anything, my office is always open. I am hoping to be around at least four days of the week just until things at home are settled with the twins."

"How are they?"

"They're both growing beautifully. They came home from the NICU two weeks ago," Daisy said with a little smile. "They're so big now. It's quite trippy considering they were so small. They're healthy, and that's the most important thing."

"Good. I'm glad," I told her with a smile. "Right, I best start work." I headed out of the office into the restaurant.

"Melinda!" I looked up to see Megan in one of the booths.

Did you ever just watch some things happen in slow motion? This was how this moment felt as Megan slipped from the bench, falling to the ground with a bang.

I ran towards her, "Are you okay?"

"Dude, I'm good." She laughed.

"Are you drunk?" I asked. "Megan it's 9:00 a.m."

"It's 5:00 p.m. somewhere. I'm celebrating!. We've broken up. I'm free from him."

I frowned a little that was an odd way to claim a breakup. Free from them. "He can't." She hiccupped.

"He can't, what?"

She yawned and slumped into my leg and almost instantly she was asleep.

"You know the fact she fell and then went to sleep is kind of impressive," Leah said as she appeared above me.

"Isn't it? Do you mind getting my phone from my locker, so I can ring her dad?" I asked.

Leah nodded, walking away. A few seconds later, she returned with my phone, and I hit her dad's contact number.

He answered almost immediately, "Melinda, is she with you? She didn't come home last night."

"Yeah, she just came into Daisy's drunk as a skunk, fell out of the booth and fell asleep," I said.

"She's worrying me, Melinda. She's spiralling, and I don't know how to help her," he said.

I heard his car start and knew he was immediately coming to get her.

"I'll see what I can do," I told him. "Get her home, and I'll come and see her tonight."

"I'll be there soon," he said.

I ended the call and looked down at Megan. "What have you gotten yourself into?" I brushed her hair out of her face and saw her phone light up in her hand. I took it from her looking down at the message from R.

KEEP IT QUIET, OR ELSE. REMEMBER I STILL HAVE THAT VIDEO.

"Oh, Megan, this is so bad" I whispered, putting her phone down. I would have to pin this girl down to try and get it out of her what had happened.

## *Chapter Twelve*

# ALEXANDER

I didn't even know what to say to her. It was still playing in my mind. I couldn't keep the secret for too long, because I knew that eventually someone would spill my secret, and I wasn't sure she'd give me the chance to explain. In one respect, it would be better coming from me, but in another I didn't want to see her face when she told me she didn't want anything to do with me. I didn't know how I'd survive watching her walk away from me never seeing her face again or hearing her laugh.

"Alexander, are you even listening to me?"

"Not really," I said, using a bored tone.

Father slammed the book down on the table in anger, and I rolled my eyes. When would he learn that it didn't scare me when he did that? Or the threat of dungeons, because dungeons seemed mighty fine right now.

"I can't deal with you."

I smiled. "Good, can I go now?"

The door opened. "Alexander, stop antagonising your

father." I turned around to see my mother entering the room shaking her head. She knew me too well. She handed me a piece of paper.

I looked down and frowned. "that's your schedule for the next two weeks. I did have to ask, what were you doing Saturday night?"

"I've been invited to a Halloween party, Mother," I explained. "I have been trying to get friendly with some of the people on my course."

"You don't need friends, Alexander, your path is already set," Father said. "You don't need to waste your time with the people."

I stared at him, shaking my head. Ah, the King, ladies and gentlemen. Although we had to serve the people, we didn't think we should waste our time with the people. "Well, fortunately for the people, I don't think like that."

My father scoffed and laughed. "Was it not you pictured shouting at a waitress?"

I pressed my lips into a thin line.

I didn't need the reminder of the impression I had let Ella have of me that day. I had worked hard to get her to like me and think that I'm a good person. I wanted to be able to have her fall in love with me before she was hit with the reality of what it would mean to be associated with me. There's the pressure, the press, my mother, and my rude father. Mainly, it would be the voices and comments of everyone else that would get to her.

"Silence speaks volumes, Alexander," my father said flatly.

"I apologised to her. If it wasn't for you and your

stupid schedules I wouldn't have been in a bad mood," I snapped.

My father stood up, slamming his hand on his desk. "You have a duty to this country, Alexander. I will not have you flouncing your way through."

"Flouncing? How about I just renounce the throne?" I threatened.

"Stop!" Mother said, putting her hands between us. "You both need to stop before you do or say something you will both regret. Alexander, you may go to your Halloween party."

My father opened his mouth, "I—"

"No," my mother snapped. "Alexander, leave. Now."

I did as my mother requested not wanting to ever be on her bad side, I was brave enough to admit that she scared me still. As I shut the door I could hear them both raising their voices, whenever it came to the children they ended up in a power struggle unless it was Elizabeth, my mother seemed to roll over and accept whatever it was my father said.

I headed away from the office and straight to the bedrooms, finding Elizabeth who's attempting to read a book. I smiled a little watching her struggle with a word leaning against the door. "Ma—" she paused, "age" she frowned. "Mage?" She groaned. "Stupid book."

I walked over sitting down next to her on the bed, I pointed at the word. "Sound it out, Little Princess."

"I tried." She groaned. "I'm done, Ander."

I shook my head. "Nonsense," I said. "How about we do it together?" I pointed at the m. "M-a-."

"M-a-g-i-c," she finished. She turned to me with a smile. "Biff picked up the magic key. I did it, Ander."

I smiled. "Of course you did, Little Princess. You're really smart. You just need to persist when things begin to get challenging for you." I pressed a kiss to her head. "I love you, Elizabeth Paige George. Never forget that."

"I love you, too, Ander."

I laid against her headboard. "Read it to me, Little El," I told her.

She nodded eagerly and continued reading the book. It was moments like that I loved so much. I never wanted her to grow up. I wish I could keep her at this age where she was small, cute, and innocent. I also knew that was a silly thing to hope for. One day, she was going to change the world, I didn't know if it was for better or worse yet.

El finished reading her book and placed it onto the side, curling up on to my chest.

"I miss you, Ander," she said, clinging onto my top not wanting to let go.

"I'm sorry, El. University has been kicking my arse," I told her softly.

"Mummy and daddy were arguing about you being with a girl. Who is she?"

I looked down at her. "Have you been eavesdropping, Little Princess?"

"It's not ea—" She paused. "Dropping, especially if they're shouting."

I laughed, and that is why I didn't know if her talent would be used for good or evil. "Her name is Melinda," I said. "I call her Ella."

"What is she like?" El asked. "Is she mean like Victoria?"

I bit my lip to hide the smile, I don't know what El had against Victoria but whatever it was it made a mental note to keep them apart. "Ella is stunning, and she is so kind. I don't think she has a bad bone in her body. She told me off the first time I met her."

"Really? She told you off?" El crinkled her nose in confusion.

"You know the best part, Little Princess," I said softly. "She has no idea I'm a prince. She treats me like our titles don't matter. One day, you'll grow up to realise how much you need that. You will need that one person in your life that will centre you and give you a reality check whenever you may need it."

"I don't want to grow up, it sounds hard." El said, letting out a yawn.

"It is," I told her. "Go to sleep. I love you." I pressed a kiss to her head, climbing out of her bed pulling the cover over her.

I headed into my room, flopping down on the bed with a sigh.

I reached for my phone noticing that I had a few notifications from TikTok. I opened the app and saw Ella had spammed me with a few videos. I clicked on the inbox, seeing the tiny red box with the number thirty staring at me.

I didn't know whether to be impressed or scared that she had sent me thirty of them. For the next fifteen minutes, I watched them all and couldn't help but smile. She had sent me various ones of kids, people and animals doing stupid things, and with each one I couldn't help but chuckle at each and every one of them. I laid back scrolling constantly and as I saw videos I sent them to Ella.

A knock on the door brought my attention away. "Come in," I called out, sitting up.

My mother entered the room holding a cup. I narrowed my eyes at it slightly.

She sat on my bed. "How are you feeling?"

She handed me the cup, and I looked down to see it was her famous hot chocolate with marshmallows. "What's the bad news?" I asked instantly.

She looked at me confused.

"Mother, I don't know if you realise this, but anytime you come to give me bad news..." I lifted the cup. "You bring this beautiful thing to help soften the blow. So, what is the bad news?"

She looked down at the floor before looking back at me. "I guess you haven't looked at your new schedule that your father just sent?"

I opened my phone looking at the email immediately. I read through it seeing almost every second of my day was filled with meetings and even worse, sightings with Charles and Arthur. He had blocked up every possible second.

"Mum, this isn't fair," I said, crossing my arms across my chest. "How am I meant to keep on top of my university work if he is making me be royal during all my free time?"

"Alexander, you did just threaten him with renouncing the throne," Mother said softly.

I took a sip of her hot chocolate, placing it on the side

of the table and walking over to the window. "How is something so beautiful a prison?" I pushed open the balcony doors, and the cold air hit me immediately.

I wanted to run away. The more he pushed me, the more I wanted to be free.

"Can't you do something about the schedule?"

"Alexander—"

"Mum, please," I whispered. I turned to look at her, "I can't do this anymore." I shook my head letting out a breath.

I don't know why I bothered. They wouldn't do anything about it. They would both go on about the birthright, and that we owed our life to service the people of the crown. "I want to be alone."

"Alexander—"

"Mother, please leave," I said, not looking at her.

I heard her sigh and she left the room. I looked down at my phone and dialled Ella's number. After a few rings, it went straight to voicemail. She was either asleep or at work, I wasn't sure which. I hit Jeremy's number, and he answered immediately. "Next race?"

"What happened to hello—"

"Jeremy," I cut him off.

"In thirty minutes, can you be here?" He asked.

"Leaving now."

I walked out the bedroom and headed to the garage, grabbing the keys to my black BMW XM and unlocked it.

Getting into the car, I sped off and out of the grounds, knowing that the guards would still be able to find me. I wondered if there was a place I could disappear, Antarctica maybe.

I hated the cold, that wasn't a good idea.

*Turn your brain off, Alex.*

I put my foot down driving to the race tracks, I arrived just five minutes before the race began. I drove over to where Jeremy was standing, and I rolled down the window.

"I thought you weren't racing anymore," Jeremy teased.

I let out a sigh. "Dad's being a dickhead. I need to blow off some steam."

"Where's your girl?"

"She's not my girl yet," I said. "She's asleep or working."

"I got you, dude." He tapped his hand on the car and I rolled the window back up.

*I needed this.*

I revved the engine and smiled a little. I missed this.

## Chapter Thirteen

# MELINDA

I was missing him.

The only thing we had currently been able to do was swap TikToks, but that alone wasn't cutting it anymore. Anytime I was free, he seemed to be busy. And when he was free, I was busy. We were like passing ships, and annoyingly, I had begun to miss his presence. It was weird how used to seeing somebody you got. At least tonight I would see him, tomorrow was the Halloween party, and I couldn't wait. I couldn't wait to blow off all my problems and just get drunk. I couldn't wait to forget about the university work, the debt, and the struggling relationships with my mother and sperm donor.

I could forget it all.

Tonight was for *us*.

I wanted to give Alex that part of me, and I wanted to have that part of him.

"Ella, are you going to come out of the bathroom yet?" Alex asked.

I looked in the mirror and let out a breath.

*I could do this.*

I opened the door walking into my room, Alex was laid on the bed in just his blue jeans and he looked incredibly hot.

"Fuck," he muttered under his breath.

His eyes looked me up and down, and I couldn't help but smile a little. I loved his reaction.

I was in a black babydoll lingerie outfit with a little advice from Megan.

I was very thankful for it right now.

I walked over to the bed, and he pulled me to sit on top of him. I bent down pressing my lips to his and kissing him softly. I pressed little kisses from his lips down to his neck before sucking on his neck and leaving my mark on him. Alex's hands were running up and down my body but settled on lifting the black babydoll away from my body.

"I don't know whether I want to ravish you in this or whether it would look better on your floor," Alex said before capturing my lips once more. I smiled against his lips as I felt him slowly take the babydoll off. He broke the kiss, pulling it over my head as my arms lifted. He tossed it on the floor and kissed me softly. "It definitely looks better on your bedroom floor."

He wrapped his arms around me as he rolled us over, so I was now lying on the bed with Alex hovering above me. He pressed little kisses down my neck and towards my chest. His mouth quickly wrapped around my nipple, sucking on it gently. He scraped his teeth across them gently, and I moaned. He switched over sucking on my other boob as he played with my nipple. I could feel how wet I was getting and he had barely touched me.

"So responsive," he murmured against my skin.

Ugh, he looked so good.

I ran my hand across his chest before running my fingers through his hair. His mouth left my boobs, and he trailed a finger across my thigh before he slipped a finger between my pussy making me moan. "Oh, you're so wet already," he whispered.

"Alex," I whispered.

He pressed a finger inside me, making me jump slightly. "You're so tight," he whispered. I pressed my lips to his, deepening the kiss, "Oh, you feel so good."

I broke the kiss and let out a moan. "Why am I fully naked and you aren't?" I sat up.

He took his fingers out of me, putting them to his mouth and sucking on the juices.

"You taste so good," Alex whispered, pressing his lips to mine.

I kneeled on the bed, pulling his trousers down. He lifted up his knees making it easier.

His dick was rock-hard.

I gulped slightly as I stared at it. "Are they all that big? How big are you?"

He shrugged.

"Will it fit?"

I saw him smile.

"Don't laugh at me."

He bent down kissing me softly. "Never, baby," he shook his head as he sat back on the bed. "Climb on."

I did as he said, climbing onto his lap. I shivered as I felt his dick pressing in-between the folds of my pussy.

"I'm nervous," I admitted, biting my lip.

"That's okay." He brushed my hair out of my face. "You look beautiful."

"Is it going to hurt?"

"It might at first, but you're wet enough," he said.

I nodded.

I could feel how wet I was. I wanted this, but I was also nervous.

"We can stop if you want? We don't have to have sex, Ella."

"I want to," I whispered. "I just can't stop thinking."

He pressed his lips to mine, and I felt him begin to lift me onto his dick.

I gasped as he started to enter me. My eyes widened.

He pressed kisses down my neck until he reached my breast and began to suck. As he did, I felt myself sinking lower on his dick. I bit down on his shoulder as I felt him break my hymen. I could feel his fingers playing with my clit. Pretty soon, the small amount of pain became pleasure, and I let out a breath.

"Fuck," I whispered.

"Baby, you're so tight." He pressed his lips to mine and I deepened the kiss wrapping my arms around his neck.

I moved my hips grinding on him. "I want you to fuck me, Alex."

"With pleasure," he said. He held onto me as he kneeled and pressed me down onto the bed. He pulled his cock out slowly, and I moaned. As he reached the opening he pushed all the way back into me making me moan loudly. "You feel so good." He pressed his lips to mine and kissed me again, "I'm going to fuck you, Ella, so hold onto me."

I wrapped my arms around his neck. He began to move his dick inside me going hard and fast. I clutched onto him, moaning. There was nothing like this. Alex was groaning in my ear, and it made me even hornier. I was beginning to thrust with him meeting him halfway. I crashed my lips onto his. I raked my hands through his hair, pulling it. I could feel my orgasm building as Alex fucked me. "Fuck, Alex."

"Ella." He groaned.

He pressed small kisses on my lips, and I smiled against his.

I threw my head back as I felt a rush, and my toes began to curl as I felt myself coming. I held onto Alex tightly as I came apart around him. I could feel him moving inside me, I held onto him, lying there and breathing heavily. as I came down from my orgasm. If that was how good sex felt, I don't understand how people got out of bed some days.

Waking up the next morning, leaving Alex was harder than I thought. The only good thing is I would get to see him in a few hours, but first I had a best friend to sort and grill.

I knocked on the door and pushed it open. Oliver was sitting on the sofa with Lily. "Hey Mel, can you...?" He asked quietly, nodding into the room.

I stood by the door. "What's up?"

"Has she said anything to you? I'm really worried about her," Oliver said softly.

I couldn't help but feel slightly bad for them as they spoiled and doted their only daughter as much as possible.

"She's going for a breakup," I said, only telling them half the truth.

There wasn't much more I could tell them, especially when I still had to grill her about the texts. She had been avoiding me or grounded for the last few days since coming into the diner.

"She'll be okay."

"Thanks, Melinda. You're a good friend."

I nodded and headed up the stairs pushing open her bedroom door.

Megan was lying in bed with her laptop, watching something. I peered over seeing that it was *Julie and the Phantoms*. I pushed her over slightly and climbed into bed with her. "Comfort show, not answering my calls, now I know there's something wrong," I told her.

"Can't a girl just mourn her break up?"

I laughed, "Maybe, if you hadn't told me you were celebrating. Come on, Megan. We've never kept secrets from each other before." I hit pause on her laptop, closing the lid and looking at her. "Ride or die, remember? When we're together, there's no judgement. You can get that from anyone else."

Megan sighed, reaching for her friend, and she handed it to me. "Read it," she whispered.

I looked through the message thread, and it went from him telling her how he loved her, and then to threatening, to blackmail to loving. I was getting whiplash just reading her messages. I could only imagine what she was going through. "I saw the message when you came into the diner. You should report him."

"It's not that easy," she whispered. "Let's just say I got myself into a situation where I need to figure out how to get out. I need to do it on my own. He'll go away."

I looked at her, tilting my head.

I could tell that she was shutting down, And I couldn't understand why.

"Please, Mel, you can't interfere."

"I'm worried about you, Megan," I said softly.

"I'm fine." Her voice cracked. She shook her head and looked up at the ceiling as if she was trying to stop from crying.

"If you need me, day or night, ring me, and I will be here, okay?" I told her. She nodded.

"No, Megan. I need to hear you say it."

"I promise. If I need you, I will call you," she said. She reached up, wiping a stray tear that had fallen. "I'm okay. I'll be okay."

At that moment, I knew she was trying to convince herself rather than me. "You got this, you're a strong independent..." I paused. "Woman."

"Exactly. Just one that still lives at home and relies on mummy and daddy for everything."

I let out a laugh.

She was the epitome of a bratty only child. "Anyway, we can't be sad."

She gasped, pushing the covers off her, "No, we can't! It's Halloween!" She let out a squeal and I smiled. She did love Halloween.

"We're going to get fucked tonight," I said. "It's been too long since we last got drunk."

Megan laughed. "Well, no. I got drunk the other day, and it's been too long since you have. Are you excited for your Prince to come?"

I furrowed my eyebrows in confusion. "You know Alex's costume?"

She bit her lip and nodded slowly, "Yes. So, are you coming?"

"Yeah, I've not been able to see him for a few days and other than TikToks exchanged. We haven't really communicated," I admitted. "If he didn't warn me before, I would've said it was because of the kiss."

Megan reached over to slap my leg. "Excuse me?!"

I frowned slightly. "Did I not tell you?"

She slapped my arm this time.

I held my hands up. "Girl, stop with the abuse or you aren't going to find out."

"No, you didn't tell me you and the..." She paused. "Alex kissed?! When? Where? How? Was it good? Was there tongue? Did he get handsy at all?"

I laughed a little. "Erm—"

"Actually, rewind," she said. "You never told me about the date. What kind of a best friend are you?" She folded her arms over her chest and pouted. "You know what, maybe I just need a new best friend. I'm sure I could find someone."

I rolled my eyes. "You should have taken a drama class, clearly," I muttered.

She grinned.

"We went to a ranch, where he had some horses. We

went on a horseback ride and had a picnic. Then, as usual with England weather, it rained. I fell off a horse, and we kissed in the rain under the stars."

"Aw, it's like something out of a romance film," Megan said. "That's so romantic, like honestly I bet that was a perfect first kiss."

"You know what, it was stunning. Ah, it was perfect," I admitted. "Then, he got mum from the hospital and we had dinner. Man, she hated him. She was so rude. Thankfully, I just lied and said it was due to the fact that she had been in hospital and was probably tired."

"Did your mum say what her problem with him was?" Megan asked curiously.

"No, she just kept making claims that I didn't know him, and he wasn't who I thought he was," I said. "It ended in an argument." I wasn't going to bring up the good, old argument of my sperm donor. "He joined TikTok, by the way. I have been spamming him with random videos, and he's been watching something about an evil chicken stealing babies. Anyway we kissed and he said goodbye."

"So, where do the two of you stand?" Megan asked curiously.

I let out a breath. "I have no idea where we stand," I admitted. "I don't want to think about any of that tonight. Did you get the thing one and two costumes?"

"Yeah," she drew out the last letter. "About that..."

"You forgot to order it, didn't you?" I asked.

"I'm just a girl!"

I shook my head and pulled a costume out of my bag. "Luckily for you. I had a feeling you would forget."

"Oh, thank God," she said with relief.

"I will be a sexy fairy, get drunk, and not worry about all these other problems we currently have."

"Amen, sister!" She laughed. Megan jumped off the bed and ran to her wardrobe pulling out an outfit. "I'm a sexy bunny."

I laughed. "Are we getting ready then?"

Megan grinned and nodded. She put her phone onto her dock and music began blasting out.

The one thing I loved about our music taste was that it wasn't what you think it would be. There was some what people would call old music but we loved it, you couldn't beat a little bit of Steps, S Club 7, or even One Direction. There is something about that music that slaps. They had some catchy tunes, and also some banger party hits like the *Cha Cha Slide*. Has there ever been any better party song? Or the ketchup song where everyone thinks they can speak Spanish but really someone is just babbling.

"You got pre-party drinks?" I asked grinning.

"Always," Megan said.

She ran out of the room, and I let out a little chuckle.

I looked at my phone and saw there was a TikTok notification. I clicked on it straight away, and Alex's username popped up. I couldn't help but let out a laugh because he sent me another video of Debora, the evil chicken. Maybe I should see if he can adopt a chicken and name it Debora. I needed to find out Alex's birthday or wait until Christmas if we were still talking at that point. I watched the video with a smile and sent back a little emoji.

Megan waved the can of vodka in front of me, and I took a sip.

"Let's get ready!" She said with a grin.

For the next few hours, we spent doing our make-up, putting false lashes on and then doing our hair. Megan was a genius when it came to hair and makeup, which is a good thing because I couldn't make myself look nice if I tried. Megan had curled my hair and straightened her own. We both got changed into our costumes.

My best friend did the slutty bunny well. I looked in the mirror and smiled as I looked at the green fairy outfit I was wearing.

"So, your Prince is going to have a fairy. Now the question is, are you a good fairy or a bad fairy?" Megan asked, grinning.

I let out a little laugh. "I'm a good fairy when sober and then a mess when I'm drunk."

She reached for her phone, and we took a few selfies. She uploaded them immediately to Instagram.

I grinned and made her send them to my phone. I reached for my little green bag, shoving my phone and my cards in there.

"Let's go." She clapped happily. "I also invited an extra person with us, you know just in case you go off into a love bubble."

"Love bubble?" I laughed.

"Love bubble." She confirmed. She hooked her arm in mine and we headed towards the front door and it didn't take too long to get into town. "So, we're going to start with pre-party drinks and Revs, and then drinks at Walkabout before we head on our ghost walk through town. Then, we will go clubbing and maybe hit pop world or route one or even the be one I think it's called. Maybe we should just bar hop."

"Is this going to be like the time you tried to convince me to do a Spoons Pub Crawl?" I asked, raising an eyebrow.

"That's still a good idea, Mel. I think we should do it one day. Like could you imagine what an achievement it would be to hit every Spoons in the country? How many people can say they have been to every Spoons?" Megan said, shaking her head. "Like that is an achievement."

I shook my head, "It really isn't."

She scoffed, whipping out her phone. She turned it to me as she whipped out the Spoons app and I couldn't help but laugh when she showed the check in. Low and behold, someone could check off every spoons place possible.

We entered Revs and went straight to the bar. I looked at my phone, seeing if there was a message from Alex, but there wasn't. I hoped he would actually come and not let me down.

I missed him this week.

# Chapter Fourteen

# ALEXANDER

I couldn't keep my eyes off her.

She was stunning.

The way she danced and moved was making me want her more and more. It wasn't like she was even dancing to lure men to her, she was letting loose and having fun.

The green fairy outfit showed every inch of her curves. Her boobs looked even more suckable. Her outfit was small enough that it just covered her ass, and I wanted to bite it.

I wanted to permanently mark her as mine.

"Dude, I can't believe you dressed as a Prince, and used your actual fucking crown." Jeremy laughed, shaking his head.

I looked at him. "At least if anyone catches sight of me, I can say they are addressing me as a prince because of the costume."

Jeremy raised an eyebrow. "You got a plan for the paparazzi, genius?"

"University photographer?" I offered.

Jeremy scoffed. "Mate, nobody is going to believe that."

I rolled my eyes.

I didn't need his negativity. I hoped the fact that it was Halloween would help hide my identity.

I walked away from Jeremy towards Ella. I wrapped my arms around her waist.

"Get your hands off me." She spun around with anger flashed on her face. Ella's face softened. "You came."

I brushed her hair out of her face and grinned, "Of course I came, Ella."

I pressed my lips to hers, kissing her softly. I deepened the kiss, immediately pulling her closer to me.

I loved having her pressed to me because there was nothing better.

She was like a drug, one I always wanted. She pulled away resting her forehead against my chest. "I missed you."

She held onto me tighter, and I leaned down to kiss her head.

"I missed you more. You look so handsome, Mr. Prince."

I bowed my head. "Why thank you, my Little Green Fairy," I said, skimming my hand down her outfit. "You look sexy." She looked around and frowned as her eyes landed on something, I turned to see what she was looking at and saw Jeremy talking to Megan.

"Who is that?"

"Jeremy," I said. I pulled her with me towards the bar as the songs finally started playing music. Having to shout to be heard was the one bit I didn't like about clubs and bars. "What do you want to drink?"

She mumbled.

I looked at her confused, and she leaned up on her tippy toes, pulling my head down.

"Coke Zero and cherry sours!" She yelled.

I nodded and typed it on my phone along with coke and vodka. I hated shouting it when there were easier things to get your order across to them.

"What can I get you?" A man yelled.

I flipped my phone around, showing him what it was written, and he nodded.

A minute later, the drinks were placed in front of me. I pressed my phone against the card machine, paying and handing the drink to Ella.

She pulled us onto the dance floor and pressed herself against my body.

"How drunk are you?" I shouted in her ear.

"Where are we?" She shouted back.

I raised an eyebrow.

I guess that answered my question of how drunk she is.

Her hands rested on my waist as she grinded herself against mine, taking small sips of her drink.

I guess I was going to spend the rest of the night being hard. It didn't take long for me to get Ella drinking some water and me having a few more drinks to catch up to her. I pulled her out into the smoking area where it was a little quieter.

"So, how were you planning to get home tonight, Ella?" I asked, holding her against me.

She let out a laugh, and damn it was one of the best things I have heard. "That was a problem for 5:00 a.m. Melinda and Megan."

"That's not safe, baby," I told her disapprovingly.

"What are you going to do? Spank me?" She teased.

I lowered my hand to her lower back and leaned down to whisper into her ear. "Don't tempt me. I will spank you."

She shivered against me, and I laughed. "Does my Little Fairy like the idea of that?"

She bit her lip, not answering me.

I pulled her lip away from her teeth and held her chin in my hand. "Are you a secret brat, Ella?"

"I think it's time for our ghost walk!" She exclaimed happily. She grabbed my hand, pulling me through the crowds and back into the loud bar.

We pushed through people as she walked towards Megan. She grabbed onto Megan's arm and yelled in her ear. It only took a few minutes until we left the bar.

"Ghost walk, ghost walk," Ella and Megan chanted excitedly.

I looked at Jeremy, raising an eyebrow.

His eyes hadn't left Megan, or his hand that was currently placed on her waist. "Ghost walk!"

"Alright, I think you woke up the dead," Jeremy chuckled.

"Good! I want them to be awake," Megan said, moving from Jeremy's grip to link arms with Ella.

They both stumbled ahead in front of us and I followed.

*I needed to make this girl my girlfriend already.*

They were both yelling as they stumbled the streets towards wherever this ghost walk was starting.

"Has anyone actually approached you as a Prince yet?" Jeremy asked.

"Not yet," I admitted. "They know it's me though. They have that wide-eyed look, stumbling over words. It's only going to be a matter of time before either someone blows the secret or paparazzi realise where I am."

"What are you going to do if someone blows up about who you really are?" Jeremy asked.

I let out a breath.

I had no idea.

"Could I use the fact she's drunk, and maybe it was her imagination?"

"No, bro, that's something that shocks someone sober," Jeremy said, shaking his head. "Honestly you're so smart, but you can be a fucking idiot sometimes."

"Fair." I reached for Ella's hand, holding it and giving her a light squeeze.

*I missed her so much.*

She clutched into me just as tight and I couldn't help but smile. "So, where is this ghost walk going?"

"Everywhere!" Megan exclaimed. "They take us everywhere." She stopped in her tracks turning to Ella. "OMG! I just had the best idea ever!"

"OMG? Girl, we aren't in texts," Ella laughed. "Anyway, best idea ever? Is this like the time you thought it would be awesome to make a slide down the stairs?"

"Number one, that was a good idea. The execution was bad. Skinny dripping!" Megan exclaimed.

"Dripping?" I asked, raising an eyebrow.

"Dipping," she corrected.

"That's a no from me," Ella said matter of factly. "I am not drunk enough for that."

I was glad she had the sense for that.

I didn't want to have to convince her that it was a bad idea, especially if I did manage to attract the paparazzi. I didn't want her body splashed all over the papers. That was something only I wanted to see, and I didn't want anyone else to see her that way.

"There's a solution for that, Mel," Megan said.

"Nope try and convince, Jeremy," Ella said flatly as she pushed her best friend towards my best friend. She linked her arm through me and rushed ahead putting a good distance between us and them. "How's your week?"

I felt her shiver against my arms, I pulled off my suit jacket placing it around her shoulders, and she slipped her arms into it pulling it tighter around her. "My week just turned a million times better," I told her softly. "I missed you Ella. Sending tiktoks just doesn't do it for me."

"Not even your rainbow cupcake?" She asked teasingly. "My buzz is going away. Why did you give me water?"

I looked at her sheepishly.

"Alex, why?"

I stopped walking to turn around and look at Ella. I bent down, placing my lips on hers and kissing her softly. "I like to kiss you when you at least have some awareness, Ella," I told her.

"You can kiss me anytime," she said quietly, putting her hand in mine as we continued the walk to wherever this ghost walk was starting.

"I like to have your consent, Ella. When you're drunk, you can't give consent," I told her. She rolled her eyes slightly, and I frowned, "I'm serious. I will never do anything whilst you are drinking and may be drunk."

"I hope you know we are going to drink and from that we will be kissing," she said matter of factly.

She ran ahead to Megan and Jeremy, and I couldn't help but smile as she hooked arms with Megan. They both ran ahead to the church. I followed her to the church and wrapped my arms around her chest, pulling her back to me.

I loved holding her close to me.

I was highly aware people were looking at me. I prayed that no one would leak the location.

"Alex, are you okay?" I looked down at Ella who was looking at me with concern.

I shot her a smile, "I'm perfect. I have you in my arms. How could I not be?"

"Smooth," she giggled. "I'll ignore the fact you have tensed up."

I was the luckiest man in the world because this girl was truly the best I have ever known.

Having her body pressed against me did nothing for the hard-on I was currently trying to hide. Although she was only slightly drunk, she was doing a great job at rubbing against me.

The wind had begun to pick up, slightly making Ella's hair whip backwards into my face. She was concentrating hard on the tour guide in front of us who was just chatting to a few people. It helped set the mood for Halloween night that was for sure.

A man clapped bringing our attention to him. "Right. Tonight is a special night. It's the night where two worlds can cross and intertwine. This night is known as All Hallows Eve, the one night where the beyond can come forth."

"Beyond?" Ella snorted as she looked at Megan. "You couldn't have thought of a better word."

"Tonight, we will encounter the ghosts and spirits as we tour some of the most haunted places in the city. Starting with the church, rumours say that in the dead of night, you can hear a scream of a woman crying in pain for the baby that was ripped out of her arms."

"Not original," Ella muttered.

I bit my lip to keep myself from laughing.

We began to walk to different places in the city. Ella and Megan kept passing the bottle of vodka between the four of us and taking swigs. Either the tour was getting better or we were getting drunker, but something told me it was the latter. It was hard to let loose completely because it seemed like wherever we went someone was with their phone out, or they would look like a reporter. The tingling in my chest wouldn't stop or the sour taste in the back of my mouth.

Part of me wanted to hide but the other part of me wanted to spend as much time as possible with Ella.

The tour finished, and we pulled straight into the next bar and ordered a round of shots and some beer. The girls immediately started to dance while Jeremy and I waited for more shots at the bar.

The girls were getting attention from everyone

surrounding them, "I want to punch any man that is looking at her," I grumbled slightly.

"I mean your jacket is doing a good job of covering her," Jeremy said, shaking his head. "Unlike her best friend who is one slut drop away from being naked."

"Jer, I know you want her, but you can't make her naked in the club," I laughed.

"She's pushing back on all my advances, and I can't work her out," he admitted.

The man handed us the shots and I walked back over to Ella turning her to face me, "I want to try something!" She yelled.

I looked at her curiously.

She took the shot drinking it before pulling my head down to her level. She moved forward, pressing her lips to mine. As we both deepened the kiss, the alcohol flowed between us. She moaned into my mouth, and it was the hottest sound I had heard.

*I needed her.*

I broke this kiss, licking the side of her mouth. The remaining alcohol that had poured out. I drank my shot, holding it in my mouth and kissing her again. We pulled away, taking down the last bit of alcohol. She reached up, licking round my mouth. I took her tongue into my mouth, biting on it gently.

"Fuck," she mumbled. "This might be my new favourite way to drink. When I get you alone, I want to do some body shots."

I laughed. "As long as I get to drink off your stunning body," I told her.

She grabbed my hand, pulling me through the crowd and out of the bar into the street. The wind hit us immediately, but I didn't care. I pushed her against the wall, crashing my lips onto hers. She deepened the kiss, and I pressed my body against hers. She began to grind against me.

*Fuck, she was hot.*

"I want you," she moaned. "Alex."

"I love when you moan my name," I told her, biting her lip. I rested my hand on her waist as my other hand grazed her thigh.

Fuck. I wanted to feel all of her body. I wanted to taste and lick every inch of her.

A flashing light pulled us apart. "Does someone have strobe lights?" She asked.

"Prince Alexander! Prince Alexander!" Multiple people shouted.

I turned to see us surrounded by paparazzi.

"Shit!" I snapped.

I looked at Ella's face. She looked stunned more than anything, and I felt horrible. This isn't how I wanted her to find out.

"Alex, what's going on?" Ella asked.

"Prince Alexander, who is the new girl? Is she your girlfriend? Prince Alexander." I looked around us, and the crowd was getting bigger.

I needed Jones.

"Alex, why are they calling you a Prince?" Ella asked, trying to put distance between us.

I pulled my phone out of my pocket and hit Jones' number. "I need you." I ended the call, pulling Ella into my chest to try and protect her from the paparazzi.

She was trying her hardest to move away from me, but the truth was, she was safer here than she was away from me. Not only was the paparazzi surrounding us but the public crowd was getting bigger. And just like all the others, they were getting their phone out and recording and taking photos.

"Prince Alexander. Who is the girl?"

Just like that my night was ruined, and my whole world had come crashing down. Ella had the truth exposed to her in the worst way possible. I was unable to hide in the little bubble we had created with each other.

# Chapter Fifteen

## MELINDA

*Prince Alexander?*

My mind was spiralling. So much about him was finally making sense to me. It was hitting me all at once.

The cameras were flashing crazily as Alex tried his hardest to bury me into his chest.

I wanted to run and hide. It was too much. Just like that, all the alcohol I had consumed disappeared. I was sober.

"It's okay, Ella," Alex whispered.

I looked up at him, and his face was eerily calm.

I suppose for him this was nothing new.

I heard cars screeching to a stop and looked around Alex to see two black cars, and two police cars pushing the paparazzi away. It was the crowd we had drawn to the side.

"Jones, give me your jacket," Alex ordered.

Jones did what Alex said and looked at me. "I'm going to put this over your head, ok?"

I nodded.

A second later, it was dark. I held the jacket a few inches away, so I could breathe. I felt an arm hold onto my back as they directed me towards what I was assuming was the car.

"Duck," Jones said softly.

I did as he said, climbing into the car, but I kept the jacket over my head until I heard the car door shut. I pulled it off, throwing it to the side next to me.

I frowned.

*Where was Alex?*

The front car door opened, and Jones stepped in. "Where is he?" I asked automatically.

"He's just telling Jeremy that we're leaving, ma'am," Jones said. "He'll be in the car momentarily. How are you feeling?"

"Well, I'm not drunk anymore," I grumbled.

The car door opened once more, and Alex got into the car, strapping his seatbelt on. He slammed his hand on the door making me jump. I reached for the door handle to get out of the car. I didn't want to be around him right now.

"If you open that door, I will spank you Ella," Alex said sternly.

I raised an eyebrow, really the spanking threat again. As much as the idea seemed appealing right now all I wanted to do was kill him.

*Oh shit, I was mad at him.*

I glared at him. "Are you serious?"

"It is a circus out there, and you will be trampled," he

said. "I'm sorry, okay? I'm really fucking sorry this happened." He reached for my hand, and I pulled it away from him. "Ella, please."

I could feel the tears welling up in my eyes.

I had no idea why I had the urge to cry. It wasn't a sad situation. I was angry though.

*How could he lie to me?*

A cop car pulled out in front with flashing blue lights on and Jones followed.

"To the ranch please, Jones," Alex said.

"I want to go home," I told him.

"Ella, I know you're angry and confused. I know you probably want to be anywhere that isn't near me, but right now, you are safest with me," Alex said.

"Does this fancy car have a stash of alcohol?" I asked curiously ignoring his statement.

"Do you think getting drunk is the best idea right now?" He asked.

"Do you think me being sober and angry is the best idea right now?" I counted.

He reached between the seats and pulled out a bottle of vodka, "Fair point. It already has lemonade mixed in with the full bottle," he said.

I pulled open the cap taking a swig of the bottle, and the vodka burned my throat, but holy fuck it felt so good. I took another swig, leaning back in the car. As I drank the vodka, all I could think about was the promise of sucking it off each other that we had suggested earlier.

I had shared some experiences with a man who hadn't been truly honest with me. He lied about who he was.

*How could I be so fucking stupid?*

I took more swigs from the bottle. The signs were all there.

Megan's reaction.

The people in the diner.

The shock of people we encountered.

I must have had a giant sign above my head that read 'gullible idiot.' I took another swig of the vodka bottle. I wondered how long it would take me to feel blackout drunk. Maybe I could just pretend it had all been a dream.

I yawned, lying my head back and closing my eyes. I felt my head falling to rest on Alex's shoulder. The vodka bottle was removed from my hand, and I felt a blanket being pulled over me.

"Sleep sweetly, Ella. I'm so sorry."

---

I groaned, flinching from the bright light. "Holy fuck."

I blinked a few times and looked around.

*Where was I?*

The pounding in my head intensified as the whole world began to spin.

I sat up and gagged, standing up and running to the door. I hoped there was a bathroom behind it.

I pushed it open and relief flooded through me as I dived onto the floor as I threw up into the toilet. I retched as more sickness came up, and I let out a groan.

Was the alcohol worth it? Hell yes, it was.

I leaned my head against the toilet bowl as tears

streamed down my face. I know nobody liked being sick, but I fucking hated it. That was for sure.

My stomach stopped churning, so I stood up to reach for a glass from the sink and rinsed my mouth out.

In the mirror, I caught sight of the way I looked and grimaced. Mascara and eyeliner had turned my eyes into panda eyes, and my foundation had turned patchy. I looked around for a flannel and rinsed it under the water, cleaning my face.

After a few minutes, I felt a little fresher and not as rough. I walked out of the bathroom, looking around the room now to figure out where I was. I headed towards the window looking out and smiled.

I was at the ranch.

*Was that always the plan to come to the ranch?*

I looked around the room for evidence that Alex had been in bed with me, but it was empty. His side of the bed was cold.

I opened the bedroom door and headed down the stairs

*Where was he?*

I frowned slightly.

*Did I embarrass myself in front of him last night?*

I tried to rack my brain around what happened last night.

I walked through the house, not finding him. I exited out of the kitchen and went onto the back patio.

As my eyes landed on him riding his horse, it all came flooding back to me.

The paparazzi.

The prince.

The lie.

The deceit.

I stumbled back like I had been punched in the stomach. I had trusted him, and he had lied to me. I blinked seeing him in front of me off the horse. He looked at me hesitantly.

I shook my head, not finding the right words. "How could you?" I whispered.

"I'm sorry, Ella—"

"No!" I snapped. "You don't get to...no."

I needed to escape, but I was trapped.

"You've put me in a place I can't even run home. I don't know what to say to you!" I began to wave my hands in front of me. "I don't know how to act around you. Alex? Prince Alexander? Prince Alex? What do I call you? You're a Prince, and you lied about it!" He grabbed my waving hands. "This isn't—"

His lips touched mine, kissing me and silencing me.

I froze.

He pulled away hesitantly to see if I was going to punch him for kissing me.

I shook my head out of my trance and slapped him. "Don't kiss me!" I yelled. "You don't have the right to do that. You don't get to drop a bombshell..." I shook my head. "No, you didn't even drop that bombshell because you weren't being honest with me. The paparazzi dropped that bombshell for you! You're a fucking Prince." He stepped closer, and I shot him a dirty look. "Don't even think about kissing me again."

Alex stepped back like I had physically hit him again. I ran past him, heading for the lake where he had our picnic and ignoring the fact I was only in his T-shirt and wearing no shoes. I sat down in front of the lake as I felt a tear slide down my cheek.

*How did everything get so messed up? How had I been so dumb to miss all the signs?*

I looked out at the water as my thoughts raced around my head.

*Where did that leave us? Was there even an us?*

If I could slap past me, I would.

*How many times did I ignore people trying to tell me?*

I would be a millionaire probably with the amount of time I had ignored all the signs.

"Melinda."

I flinched from the use of my full name. It sounded weird coming from him now, especially as I had come to love the nickname Ella. Although, I suppose I told him he didn't get to do anything anymore.

"If I sit next to you will you hit me again?"

"If you deserve it." I sniffled.

He sat down to the side of me but so I could see his face. "Melinda, I am sorry you found out the way you did," he said.

"You're not sorry you lied?" I asked, raising an eyebrow.

He shook his head, "Would you have given me the time of day if you knew I was a Prince?"

I looked at the floor. I suppose he had a point there.

"Would you have shouted at me the way you did?" He asked.

My eyes widened. "I shouted at a Prince!"

"You just also slapped him now." Alex added helpfully.

I looked at him deadpanned.

"Melinda—"

"I don't like it when you call me that," I whispered.

Alex smiled a little, and a look of hope shined in his eyes. "Ella, at first I was surprised you would even talk to me that way. I wanted to know more and I wanted to know you. I started hanging around Daisy's, the library, and sitting near you in lecturers and seminars, hoping you'd give me a chance. Hoping that I could wear you down to at least go on a date with me. I figured if I could make you like me the rest wouldn't matter."

"The fact you're a Prince wouldn't matter, Alex?" I questioned. "You can't be that delusional."

"Delusional? No." He shook his head. "Hopeful? Yes."

I looked back out at the lake. I had no idea what to do.

The shock of finding out the way I did and then it all came flooding back today. I was confused.

"Why me? Was I just some game? Play the girl that had no idea you were a Prince?"

"Never," Alex said. "Everything I said to you and about you and my feelings for you was the truth. I may have lied about my title and lineage, but I never lied when you asked me a question."

I thought back to all of our conversations when he was saying that his story was already written. He was right. he technically hadn't lied when I asked him questions. "Where do we go from here?"

"Ella, be my girlfriend," he said.

My eyes widened. "Alex I..." I trailed off. I had no idea

what I was going to say. I liked him. A lot. Could I deal with all the extra parts of him?

He sighed. "It's okay. I get it." He stood up. "I'll order a car to take you home."

I reached for his hand. "Alex."

He stopped, looking down at me.

"I can't give you an answer right now. I need time."

"Everything I said is the truth, Melinda. I care about you. I don't want this to destroy us before we even have a chance to start," Alex said. "I'll order you a car to take you home."

"Can I stay here?" I asked. "I'm not ready to face life just yet."

"Of course, Ella," Alex said. "I'll be with the horses if you need me."

"Thank you," I whispered. I turned my head and stared back at the lake.

I could ignore all of the problems I was facing right now.

I liked him. A lot.

Could I deal with all the extra parts of him? It wouldn't just be him as a person. It was all the extra.

The breeze felt so good and it helped settle my stomach a little. Dealing with all this whilst suffering from drinking so much was making it worse.

God, he had wormed his way into my life and heart. I had no clue what life with Alex would look like. I didn't know anything about his world or the expectations that came with his world.

I wondered if I could just stare into the lake and stay here forever.

# Chapter Sixteen

## ALEXANDER

I didn't want to leave her. I also knew she needed space from me.

What was that saying? Let someone go, and if they come back, it was meant to be.

She stared back at the lake, and I made my way back to the stables where Jack was brushing Poppy.

"How is she?" Jack asked curiously.

"Angry and confused," I said, leaning against the door and making sure I could still see her. "I don't know how to help her."

"Darling, this isn't something you can help her with," I turned to see Marie coming out with two cups. She handed one to me and patted my arm walking away.

I watched as she headed towards Ella and put a hand on her shoulder before handing her the cup. Marie stayed with her, and I just stood there watching.

"Alexander, watching her isn't going to help. You need

to distract yourself," Jack said. "Rocky needs washing and you know he only really likes you doing it."

I nodded.

I headed into the shed grabbing my waterproofs out and slipped them on before heading into Rocky's stable. I stroked his nose, and he leaned his head against mine.

A smile appeared on my face.

This is why I was glad I saved him. Behind all the fear inside of him, he was a lovely, caring, and stunning horse.

I reached for the halter and lead rope placing it on him leading him out of the stables into the field where I could wash him. I tied him to the post and stroked his nose once more. "What do you think Rocky? Will she forgive me?"

He let out a neigh.

I reached for the sponge in the bucket that Jack had left for me and began to wash his coat.

Half an hour later, Rocky was trotting around the field happily. As much as he enjoyed our riding time, he still needed his free time to roam. I hated keeping him cooped up, so when it was possible, I'd let him out.

"What's his story?"

As much as I wanted to turn around to see where Ella was, I kept my gaze on Rocky.

"You said you rescued him? Something about him being a wild horse?"

"Rocky was used for breeding stock by his old owners," I told her. "They would keep him trapped in the stables. His only purpose was to breed mares. The moment he was rescued, they couldn't even get him into the trailer. He sprinted and didn't stop. He was free."

Something that I wasn't. Defined by the crown, to live my life in service to it.

"I was at the vet with Poppy because it was time for her vaccinations. Rocky was being pulled by like five other men to where the vet was waiting with a needle. Rocky managed to escape from them, and he trotted over to me and Poppy."

"He knew," Ella said.

I finally turned to face her where she was sitting on the fence. "Knew what?" I asked.

"He knew you were a person he could trust. He knew that you wouldn't hurt him," Ella said, nodding towards Rocky who had stayed within distance of us.

"The workers were shocked when he bowed his head to me and let me stroke him. He hadn't let anyone near him since the attempted rescue. He was scared of humans and a horse with no owner can be..." I trailed off. "Wild and unpredictable. The rest is history. I brought him here to the ranch. It took a year for him to step back into a stable and then another six months before I could shut the door. He gets nervous around new people so he stays here living in retirement, he'll never breed again, or race anything like that. He's just a horse living his best life."

Jack opened the gate letting Poppy in. Rocky trotted right over to her and began nuzzling her. "That will never get old," Jack sighed, leaning on the gate.

"Agreed."

I looked at Ella who was watching them with a small smile on her face. "Oh to be a horse." She hopped down off the fence, walking inside.

I grabbed onto it, keeping myself from following her.

"Progress. She spoke to you," Jack said softly. "It'll get better, Alexander."

"I'm not so sure. She struggled to let me in, and she's right. I betrayed her trust by not telling her who I was," I said. I heard a car door shut and frowned. "Are we expecting anyone?"

"Not that I know of."

I jumped the fence heading through the backdoor. I heard voices almost immediately, one in particular that I couldn't help but grin. I rushed through the kitchen into the living room and my little sister was standing there in a bright yellow sundress, "Ander!" She squealed excitedly, running into my arms.

I caught her picking her up squeezing her tightly. "Hi, El," I let out a little laugh. "Who let you out?"

"I let myself out," she said, rolling her eyes.

"Sir, your mother thought if the Princess came she would be able to bring you home faster," Jones explained.

"I'm not due home until tomorrow," I said.

"Ander, is that her?" El asked, trying to whisper but failing.

"Yes, El. That's her," I whispered back.

I looked at Ella who was biting her lip to keep herself from smiling. "That's why I'm Ella and not El," she mumbled.

"She's pretty," El said.

I put her back on the floor, and she walked over to Ella who was bent down to her level.

"Hi Elizabeth, my name is Melinda," she introduced.

"We're both El!" She squealed excitedly, making Ella flinch slightly from the loudness.

"Sir, a word," Jones said, nodding away from them. I followed him into the dining room, keeping my eyes on Ella and El.

"Ander really likes you," El said again, trying to whisper.

I really had to teach my sister to talk quietly. Something tells me that she would be no good with state secrets that was for sure.

"Sir, there has been an emergency meeting called regarding you and Miss Brown. The King and Queen require your and her to be in attendance," Jones explained.

I let out a sigh.

Would nothing go my way?

I knew taking Ella to the Palace would push her further and further away. I looked over at seeing the way she was interacting with my sister and right then I knew I couldn't lose her. "I can't," I whispered.

"Sir, you don't have a choice," Jones said.

I stared at them, not taking my eyes off either of them. I didn't care what my mother or father wanted. I couldn't throw her into the deep end like that. I'd lose her for good.

"Oh," Jones said.

I looked at him confused. "Oh, what?"

"You love her," he said.

I shook my head. "No, that's silly, I don't—"

I looked back at Ella.

What did love feel like? I had never been in love before.

"I..." I didn't even know what to say.

I walked out the room leaving them together sitting on

the porch, "Recalled back, huh?" Jack asked, sitting next to me.

I looked at Jack. "What does love feel like? I don't mean love for your family either. How did you know Marie was the one?"

"You just know in your heart," Jack said.

I rolled my eyes.

*Ugh, people and their crypticness.*

I pulled my phone out of my pocket and saw at least a dozen messages from mother and father recalling me back as well as a message from Jeremy checking in. I let out a sigh and opened up google before entering my name. Almost immediately, coverage of last night spread across my screen. Us kissing, grinding against each other, and me touching her. It was everywhere, but fuck, it looked hot.

*Would it be wrong to ask for originals of some of those photos?*

As much as it turned to shit, I wanted those memories.

My eyes widened. "I love her," I whispered.

I heard someone let out a small chuckle. I turned to see Marie with a cup of tea in her hand. "About time, Alexander."

My eyes stayed on my phone, looking through reports and comments. There was some name calling and insults. I hated the way they were speaking about her, calling her ugly or a slut and other names. I clenched my fist. I wanted to hit them all. I had to protect her from seeing this, but I had no idea how. I couldn't put a gag order on the press or the public but keeping her in the dark wouldn't be protecting her either.

"What am I going to do?"

"Being in love isn't a bad thing, Alexander," Marie said softly. "It's life-changing."

I looked at her. "Have you ever thought about writing fortune cookies?" I raised an eyebrow at her.

"It's my pastime," she teased. "Look, you can sit out here panicking that you love a girl or you can go inside and tell the girl you love that no matter what happens you will protect her. Show her the raw honesty of your world. If you love her, you will tell her everything to protect her from your world."

I stood up, heading inside.

El was chatting Ella's ears off who was nodding along and looking so invested at the story she was telling.

"El, could you give Ella and I a minute please?" I asked her. "Marie and Jack are on the porch if you want to go and see Poppy."

El jumped off the sofa and ran out the door. I couldn't help but let out a little laugh.

"She's amazing."

"She's something," I rolled my eyes. "Can I sit?"

Ella shrugged. "You're a Prince. You can do anything."

I let out a sigh, sitting down. "Please don't do that. I don't want you to see me like a Prince. I'm still the same person I was twenty-four hours ago. Now you know my title and heritage. I don't want to give up on us, and I hope you don't want to either."

"This is a lot for me, Alex. This isn't normal in my world," she said. "I don't know how to act, I don't know what to do, And I don't know how to deal with this."

"I'll help you, Ella," I said. "I'll protect you. And as much as I don't want to show or tell you any of this, keeping it in the dark will take you by surprise and will hurt you in the long run. My mother and father have organised an emergency meeting in regard to last night. They would like you to attend."

Her eyes widened. "You want me to meet the King and Queen?!" She shouted, jumping up off the sofa. "Dude, did you see what happened when you told me you were a Prince. I slapped you."

I took a step closer to her knowing she was going to be spiralling.

Would I kiss her again? Yes. Even knowing she'll probably slap me again? Absolutely.

"I can't meet them I don't know how to—"

I pressed my lips to hers kissing her. She kissed me back almost immediately. I nibbled at her bottom lip and deepened the kiss. I felt her hands in my hair pulling and I groaned into her mouth. She pulled away breathless, narrowing her eyes.

"You can slap me, it'll be worth it," I teased.

She laughed. "I don't know if I can go and meet them yet."

"Ella, you need to know what you're going to be faced with in the outside world," I told her. "I can't let you leave unprepared."

"Who says I have to leave?" Ella asked. "Look, I'm not ready to face it out there, and right now, I need a clear head to decide on this." She waved her hands between us. "Can we not just stay here for a week? I won't meet them until I'm sure of this."

I nodded. I could understand that. It was a big and not normal thing. "Okay, I can get mother and father to hold off for a week, but by next Sunday, we will have to be there, especially if you decide this is worth it."

"Thank you," she whispered.

"I have to go and speak with them. Is there anything you need before I leave?" I asked her.

"More clothes, and Megan," she said.

"I'll have it organised," I told her. "Thank you for staying."

"I need time. Also, do you think you can pull strings at university for us to have our work done at home?" She asked.

One of the things I loved about her was that she was not willing to stop working. I nodded, bending down to her forehead, "'Of course." I stood up. Before I could walk away, she grabbed my hand, "What?"

"Alcohol," she said.

"Yes, ma'am."

# Chapter Seventeen

## MELINDA

It felt like a dream.

I didn't know how to explain what I was feeling.

*How was he a prince?*

I began to fall for a prince.

I was glad Alex left when he did because I was way too confused. A huge part of me wanted to hide in this bubble we had, but I knew that was silly. We had to face the outside world eventually. Well I definitely had to, I guess. Alex could technically hide as much as he wanted. I had to go back to work and university soon.

"Well, that was not the Halloween night I had in mind." I turned around to see Megan walking in with a bag in her hand.

I snorted. "You're telling me."

Megan flopped down next to me.

I reached over, slapping her leg. "How could you not tell me?"

"Hey, I tried," she protested. "Multiple times. You didn't want to listen. Do you not remember that whole rant when he knocked you over?"

I rolled my eyes. "Megan, what am I going to do?"

"It's simple, Mel. Do you like him?"

I sighed. "You know I do."

"Well then..." Megan trails off. "You stay with him and by his side."

"What about everything else? The paparazzi, his title, his legacy, his family. His parents are the King and Queen of the country and how am I meant to fit into that? I'm just Melinda. How am I meant to fit into that world?"

Megan headed into my bag and pulled out a bottle of cherry sours, "We are way too sober for this shit."

I took the bottle from her and took a swig of it before handing it back to Megan.

My best friend was right on that front.

We were way too sober.

Was getting drunk the answer to all my problems? No.

Was being drunk right now a good thing? Yes.

I grabbed the bottle from her and took another swig. I loved this.

"Anyway, the other stuff is just stuff, Melinda," Megan said. "If you like the man, then stay with him. Explore this world that he is going to open your eyes to."

I reached for the bottle taking another swig of it. "There's so much I don't know."

"Mel, nobody is expecting you to marry the man. You're just dating," Megan said. "He's not proposing."

I mean she had me there.

"Go with the flow, Mel," she shrugged.

"I just can't believe I didn't fucking know," I groaned throwing my head back. "Like how dumb am I?"

Megan stayed silent.

I reached for the bottle off her and took another swig of the drink. "Beating yourself up isn't going to help the situation you know," Megan said, stealing the bottle back. "You know what will help?"

"What?"

"More alcohol," Megan said, handing the bottle back to me.

I took another swig and smiled.

She was right about that. Who was I to judge all of my life problems without a little bit of alcohol?

"The alcohol has arrived!" Alex shouted as he walked through the door. "Let's ignore all of life's problems and get drunk."

Megan pulled me into a hug. "Amen!"

I laughed, reaching for the bottle and taking another drink.

The alcohol was finally beginning to hit and just like last night I wanted to make some questionable choices regarding a certain prince. A do-over so to speak. I could pretend today was Halloween.

I walked into the kitchen, grabbing some glasses. I headed back into the living room where Alex and Megan were staring each other out. I wondered if she had said something whilst I was grabbing glasses.

He poured us some vodka in a glass and handed it to me.

"Cheers," he said, tapping the glass.

We both downed the shot before pouring some more

and that's how the next few shots went. We sat in silence, drinking away.

I thought back to all our previous conversations.

How well did I actually know him? Was he right that it was just the title he didn't tell me about?

"Your favourite colour," I said. "You said it was gold and began to say it matches and then you stopped. Were you going to say crown?"

Alex smiled sheepishly. "Yep."

Megan scoffed. "Unoriginal Prince, unoriginal."

Alex stared at her, not saying a word.

I pressed my lips into a thin line to keep myself from laughing. I didn't want to get into whatever they were disagreeing about.

"If you could travel anywhere in the world, where would you go?" I asked curiously, taking a sip of the cherry sours and coke.

"I'd really like to travel to the Maldives. It would be like my own little island. It's stunning. Where would you go?"

"I'd really like to go to places like Rome, Barcelona, and Greece. You know. They're places with history, and *The Lizzie McGuire Movie* got to achieve those dreams." I laughed.

"*Lizzie McGuire?*"

Megan gasped.

I sat up shaking my head. "Right, the streaming service that has the movie." I reached for the remote and loaded onto the service and pressed play on the film. "This film is like a comfort film for me. Although, most of those films tend to be."

"I think that might be my cue to leave, so you can watch the movie and chill." Megan pulled a face. "Doesn't have the same ring to it."

I laughed, agreeing with her. "Thank you, Megan."

"Welcome bestie, see you later." She took one more shot before standing up.

"How are you getting home?"

"The Prince here got me a car to send me home," she said.

"Text me when you're home."

She nodded, walking out the ranch.

I reached for the blanket covering us, "Thanks for organising her to go home."

"Anything for you and your friends," Alex said softly.

We held up our drinks and watched the film. Something so simple healed a little part of me that was unsure about us.

"So, when you first watched this, did you have a crush on Pablo?" Alex asked curiously.

I laughed. "That's not his name. No actually, Gordo all the way. He was literally trying to save Lizzie's arse. Like if that isn't a man waiting for a girl to notice him, I don't know what is."

"Yeah, but he didn't win the girl? He got a little tiny kiss at the end of the film," Alex rolled his eyes. "So, was it worth it?"

I grinned. "Let me know after you're finished chasing me."

He pressed a hand onto my chin, turning me to look his way. He pressed his lips to mine, kissing me softly. He pulled away resting his forehead against mine. "Ella, you will always be worth it to me. I'd travel to the ends of the earth if it meant I could spend time with you."

I took another sip of my drink.

I didn't really know what to say to him. In my heart, I knew he was right about his feelings, but I didn't know if I could deal with his world and everything else that came with him.

I reached for the bottle of vodka and took a swig. "I think it might be time for more drinking."

Alex gently pushed me back and lifted up my top, pouring some alcohol into my belly button. He bent down, sucking it up. I giggled, squirming as he sucked. "Would you be comfortable taking the top off?"

I smiled a little and pulled my top off. "If you wanted me naked, you just had to ask."

"Are you attached to this bra?"

"No," I whispered.

He poured the alcohol on my chest and let it drip down. As it did, he began to lick it up again. "This is definitely my new favourite way to enjoy alcohol."

I sat up, pushing him back and pointing at his shirt.

He didn't have to be told twice. He took it off, throwing it onto the floor. I poured the alcohol onto his chest and watched it drip down before I started to lick him.

"Is this a case of you licking me so I'm yours?" I asked with a laugh.

"Definitely, Ella." He laughed and stood up, reaching for the TV remote. "We're doing karaoke. I need to know your karaoke song."

I laughed a little. "My karaoke song?"

"Yes, Ella. Everyone has a song that they sing for karaoke, and I need to know yours." He reached for his shirt and pulled it over my head pulling me up off the sofa. He began pressing buttons on the remote as he was searching.

I raised an eyebrow as my eyes landed on *Barbie Girl*. "Don't judge." Alex stood up and put one hundred and ten percent into his performance of the song.

I clapped as he finished.

"Woohoo!" I cheered.

"Now it's your turn," he said. "Karaoke song."

I looked up at the ceiling pursing my lips together thinking, what would I say my karaoke song was. I had favourites but I wasn't sure which one I would say would be my go to.

Alex sat back on the sofa and stared, "I'll wait." I couldn't help but chuckle. "What?"

"You just reminded me of secondary school when people don't shut up, so the teacher stands there and says: 'I'll wait."

He furrowed his eyebrows in confusion.

"Ah, of course not a pretty boy like you though. I bet you went to some fancy private school where they wouldn't say boo to a goose." I rolled my eyes.

Alex batted his eyelashes. "You think I'm pretty?"

I ignored him and decided on *I Will Survive*. For the next three minutes or so, I put my all into singing the song. Terribly, might I add. By the end of it, Alex was on the floor, crying with laughter and tears streaming down his face.

"And that my friend is why I don't do karaoke," I told

him matter of factly. I reached for the alcohol, taking another drink. I let out a yawn. "I think I need a nap."

Alex reached over, picking me up and carrying me princess-style through the house. He entered his room laying me on the bed. He climbed in next to me covering us both with the blanket. "I wish our first sleepover happened in better circumstances," he said, pulling me into his arms.

"Technically, our first sleepover has already happened." I closed my eyes, enjoying the feel of being in his arms. Tonight, I could forget. I found myself falling asleep easily.

"Night, Ella," he whispered.

I felt him brush my hair away from my face, but I didn't have the energy to move or even open my eyes. "Ella? I love you. No matter what happens, I will always protect you."

If I had the energy, my eyes would have widened.

A moment later, I heard a soft snore, so I cracked open an eye to see Alex fast asleep. Maybe I had heard him wrong. It had to be the alcohol. I was drunk. Yep, that seemed to be a good idea. I was drunk. My ears didn't work.

I sat up, and his arms loosened straight away. "Alex," I said.

He let out another soft snore. Clearly the man was a sleep talker or a drunk talker. I slipped out of bed and reached for my phone on the desk, sitting down on the floor and staring at the bed.

*He loved me.*

I unlocked the phone and pulled Google up.

I guess it was time to see the stories about him. I knew the good and the sweet parts of him, but I wanted to know the bad.

If I was to go all in, I didn't want to be taken by surprise with anything.

I typed in his name, pressing the search button. Almost immediately, the results appeared. My eyes widened as I saw pictures of us. I clicked on the images spread across the first four rows. There were pictures of Alex and I not just from last night, but pictures from the diner and the university.

*How did I not notice any of these other ones being taken?*

I smiled a little as one from Halloween caught my attention, and the pictures looked as hot as it felt when Alex pushed me against the wall and devoured me.

*Would it be wrong to save them?*

I shrugged.

Eh, what the hell. I was saving them. We did look cute. I went back to my search and started to read some news articles.

He had a reputation. That was for sure.

The more I scrolled, the more I realised the press loved painting him out as a bad boy. And that was what was wrong with the media. They loved to build people up just to tear them down.

# *Chapter Eighteen*

# ALEXANDER

I groaned, rolling over burying my face in the pillow.

*Could I suffocate my hangover out of myself?*

I spread my hands out and reached for Ella, but my hand was met with coldness.

I frowned, opening my eyes slightly.

She was gone.

If I felt like this, how the fuck did she managed to get out of bed without feeling like she wanted to die?

My head was pounding.

I sat up and fell back down as the room started spinning.

*Holy fuck.*

Right now, I wish I was back at the Palace where I could have a maid or butler bring me water and drugs.

Jesus, the girl could drink.

It was hard keeping up with her.

I flipped the covers off and stumbled down the stairs. I

could hear banging around in the kitchen. "Marie, you're being too loud," I grumbled, entering the kitchen. I stopped in my tracks as I saw Ella in the kitchen, "oh hello. Am I still asleep?"

She jumped, turning around as she pulled out her earphones, "holy shit you scared me."

"How on earth do you feel okay right now? I feel like the whole world is spinning. The light is too bright, and the noise is too loud." I groaned sitting at the table.

"Quite simply, dear Prince. I haven't really slept," she laughed. "I sobered up. I've eaten a shit ton of toast and done some university work. I've been busy whilst you've been snoring."

I stared at her. "I hate you right now."

"Stop being a baby. Nobody forced the alcohol down your throat."

"Let me whine and moan. Was I being dramatic? Yes. Did I care? No.

"Aww, poor baby, I'll take care of you," she mocked. "I was actually planning to bring you breakfast in bed."

"Perfect girl," I said smiling.

She really was the girl of my dreams.

I wanted to ask what all of this meant. Was she staying? I also didn't want to ruin the bubble we had. "How about I just sit here and watch a beautiful girl cook?"

She nodded, pottering around the kitchen. I had no idea what she was making, but I was here for it.

I needed it to appear in front of me like magic.

She hummed as she began to cook the bacon in the frying pan.

"I'd offer to help but—"

"No thank you, Alex. You'd get in the way," she said flatly.

I should have been offended, but it was the truth. I would just get in her way. I'd wrap my arms around her and never let her go. Boy, I really did sound like a lovesick fool.

Ten minutes later, she placed a plate in front of me, "A full English breakfast Well it's as full English as you can get. I don't cook black pudding or French toast."

"Ella, I don't care what it is. As long as it's in front of me, and I can eat it, then the room can stop spinning."

I dived into breakfast and let out a moan of appreciation.

Damn, it tasted good.

"Where's your paracetamol?"

"In the junk drawer," I said. "Why?"

"I was going to be nice and get you some drugs to help with that hangover, you poor baby," she mocked.

I glared at her. I did not need her mocking me whilst I felt like I was going to pass out.

She walked over, pulling open a drawer. I watched in amusement as she opened random drawers, trying to find the junk drawer. The next drawer she opened was the junk drawer and things fell to the floor. "I think you found the junk draw, Ella."

"Dick," she muttered, rolling her eyes.

A second later, she came over and handed me the packet.

I popped two tablets out, taking them.

Ella sat down with her plate and started eating, too.

*I loved this girl.*

She was everything I could imagine wanting in a wife. Although that was jumping ahead. First I had to get her to agree to be my girlfriend. Then, it would be the case of getting her to love the life I saw as a prison, a life that I wanted to escape.

"Alex."

I looked up to look at Ella who was biting her lip and playing with the food on her plate. "I..." she trailed off.

*Is this where she ended it?*

"I don't."

I slumped back in the chair. This is where she ended it.

"It's okay, Ella. I understand."

She raised an eyebrow. "You understand that I'm saying I will give it a shot?"

My mouth dropped open in surprise. "What?"

She let out a little giggle.

"Ella. You better not be playing with me right now. Are you serious?" I stood up, walking over to her chair and bending down to her level. "You're giving us a shot?"

"I'm giving us a shot," she said.

I pulled her into my arms, crashing my lips onto hers and kissing her deeply. I put every ounce into the kiss. I couldn't tell her I love her yet, but I could certainly show her. "I won't let you down, Ella. I promise."

She smiled, "Eat your breakfast, you hungover potato."

"Potato?" I questioned.

"I'm trying out some new pet names, my little tomato," she teased.

I shook my head going back round to my breakfast and

finishing what she made me. "Thanks, Ella." I took her plate and began washing the pots and cleaning up.

"Look at you, what a domesticated potato," she teased.

"You are not calling me a potato as a pet name," I said flatly.

"Okay, potato."

I rolled my eyes and finished washing up. Ella was doom scrolling on her phone, and I could hear various TikToks playing. I wondered if we would ever see videos and pictures of us on that app. Maybe I should search my name and see what comes up. Although, on the other hand, ignorance is bliss. I wiped my hands dry on the tea towel and sat down with her.

"We need to have a serious conversation," I told her.

She nodded.

"We will have to have a meeting at the Palace regarding us and the images that have been circulating. Reporters are at least held to some standards of not being able to post cruel comments, but the same can't be said for the public."

"Yeah, I'm already an ugly slut," she looked away. "Gold digger."

"You looked at the pictures, didn't you?"

"Yeah," she whispered.

"Ella, I really wish you hadn't." I sighed. "Comments from the public are simply from jealous people. You aren't an ugly slut or a gold digger. Nothing good can come from looking at that stuff. I know it's easier said than done, but you will get hurt from reading that toxic shit."

"Would you have told me about the comments?" She asked, folding her arms over her chest.

"Yes," I said. "Do you think I'd send you into a situation blind?"

She raised an eyebrow. "Are you serious? You wouldn't send me into a situation blind? Oh, how about finding out you're a prince from the fucking paparazzi, whilst we were basically dry humping outside of a club? I'd say that was pretty blind."

I winced. She was right about that. "I deserved that."

"You think?"

"I'm sorry. If we can't get past this that I didn't tell you I was a prince, I don't know if this will work. I want this to work," I told her.

"I can get past it, but I might just throw it at you every now and then," she admitted. "Let me throw my petty shots every once in a while. I want honesty from now on though, Alex. I can't be left in the dark, even if you think it's the right thing."

"I can try, but there may be some things that I may not be able to divulge," I said. "When it comes to me and your honesty, always."

"Thank you."

"There's so much that I'm going to need you to accept and it's not going to be easy," I admitted. "Some of it will feel like no big deal, but it will be important and it will be about safety."

"I am not having someone follow me around," she said immediately.

"You wouldn't," I shrugged. "There would be no need. You're just a person of interest to them. I don't think you'd be in any real danger, but if that changed, we would reassess the situation."

She nodded.

"If we are together, my security will now be seen by you and not hidden like they have been," I told her. "My parents will have the last say and what occasions you come to. You will be required to attend some functions as my girlfriend. Also, I'd like for you to come to my polo game."

"Polo?" She asked in confusion. "Isn't that like you know that game Marco? Polo? You hide and they try to find you?"

"Ella, that's played in water," I told her.

"Shut the front door," she gasped. "It's not."

I nodded slowly.

She pulled up her phone, and I could see her googling it. I shook my head slightly.

She definitely was a different kind of person.

"Huh, what do you know it's true," she mumbled. "Polo?"

"It's a game that's played on horseback," I told her. "I'll take you to a game when I play."

"Rich people sport," she said.

"When we are together in public, you will have to follow the rules of my security. It can't be a case of just running off and not assessing the area," I said. "I understand you will want to get out of a car, and that's a natural instinct, but you will need to wait for my security team."

She nodded.

"Last thing, are you going to be ready to come to the meeting at the Palace? It won't be easy, but we need to do it. If anything, I'm lucky Mother allowed me to push it back and not force me to come back immediately."

"Sounds like I don't have a choice, Alex. If we're going

to do this, I need to accept that this needs to happen," she said.

I leaned over, pressing my lips onto her forehead. "Thank you, Ella. I will arrange the meeting." I left the room, heading into the office and sitting in the chair.

I couldn't believe she had agreed to give us a chance. I felt like the luckiest man on earth right now. The girl I loved was willing to give it all a chance.

I picked up the phone, pressing my mother's number. She answered the call almost immediately. "Hello, Alexander. I didn't know if my son was alive."

"That's very dramatic, Mother." I snorted. "You sent Jones and El here. I also popped back to see you."

"My baby boy, when will you learn that a mother's worry never disappears?"

It wasn't often my mother referred to us as her babies, but when she did, it meant she was feeling maternal and ready to fight for us. If that was the case, I was going to be using this to my advantage. I knew father already hated the idea of Ella and alas will probably hate her, but Mother was still to be decided.

"Sorry," I said. "Ella has finally come around and agreed to give us a shot, given that she knows the truth."

"I'm happy for you son," she said. "You realise you will be bringing her for this meeting?"

"Yes, mother. That's what I'm ringing you for. We're ready, so if you could set up the meeting, that would be appreciated," I said.

"Yes, son. I'll get it organised and put on the calendar," mum said. "Just enjoy the next few days with her before all of this becomes real."

"I will. Thanks, mum," I said.

"I love you."

"Love you more," I told her, ending the call. I put the phone down, slumping back in the chair.

We could do this.

We could get through it.

## Chapter Nineteen

# MELINDA

I didn't want to leave our bubble.

The last few days had been perfect.

Alex and I had been going horseback riding daily, watching tv shows, and cooking together.

We were both going to be behind on university work, but I couldn't help but feel like it was worth it. I had gotten to know so much about him, what his favourite royal jobs were, and stories about Elizabeth. I knew so much more about him now. I also realised how much he carried on his shoulders.

We were currently on our way to London for our meeting with his parents. I was nervous as hell, and it didn't help that Alex looked cool as a cucumber. He looked so fucking hot, too.

I looked at my phone to see Megan had texted me back. I shook my head as I saw that she texted me a row of GIFs.

My best friend was so helpful.

Not.

I felt a hand on my knee looking at Alex with a frown. "What?" I asked.

"You're tapping your feet. You don't need to be nervous," Alex said softly.

"Easy for you to say," I muttered, shaking my head. "It's just your family."

He rolled his eyes. "They're normal people, Ella."

I snorted. "Only you would think that, Alex."

I looked out the window as the streets of London passed by. The city looked beautiful.

One day, I would have enough money to explore. I heard sirens and then one passed by us, but it didn't speed ahead like I thought it would. Instead, it remained in front of us. I looked behind us to see we were also being followed by police. "Why are we being followed by the police?" My eyes widened looking back and forth.

"Oh, it's an escort. I forget that it's not normal for you," he said, shaking his head amused.

"An escort?" I asked.

"Yeah, Ella. The closer we get to the Palace, the more we need an escort. Although, my travel plans haven't been leaked yet. We have to be ready in case anybody is watching the Palace and attempts to kill me," he said.

"I have a question, and I promise I'm not a killer or terrorist," I told him with a little laugh.

"You're really selling this, Ella."

I laughed. "So the police...Are they here to make sure nobody is going to ram the car or kidnap you? Who says that someone can't throw a bomb at your car or hit you with a missile?"

Alex pursed his lips. and I couldn't help but chuckle a little.

Clearly, this is something he had never thought about before.

"Well, usually, we have dummy cars, too, so it's not actually clear which one we are in. Maybe I should worry about you."

I laughed. "Or watch a crime show and that would tell you that these are completely normal questions, potato."

Alex grimaced at the nickname, and I couldn't help but smile.

Who knew the man could be set off by being called a potato?

"I should put you on some kind of watchlist," Alex said, looking at me suspiciously.

I scoffed. "You better put everyone who watches *Criminal Minds*, *Swat*, *FBI*, *NCIS*, and *Law and Order* on your watchlist then."

"Maybe we need to limit your screen time," Alex said, shaking his head.

"I'm not a toddler." I scowled. "It's good background noise and these shows help me escape."

"I wish I could relate to finding a good TV show," Alex mumbled.

"Oh, potato. I can open your eyes to many good television shows," I said with a smile. "Maybe that's what we should do one date night. A little television binge-watching."

"Hide away from the real world forever. I like it," Alex smiled.

I smiled. "I wish."

Pretty soon I would have to go back to the real world. I'd have to go back to working, studying, dealing with my mother and sperm donor, and the debt. This week had been a good distraction from all of that, but I wasn't going to be able to be distracted forever.

I watched as the gates to the Palace opened, and we drove in with the police cars splitting away from us. We pulled to a stop, and I put my hand on the car door. "No," Alex shook his head.

"What?"

"You won't be able to do things like this. You have to wait for the car door to be opened," Alex explained. "Just in case."

I nodded.

Is this what his world was like? Always wondering when danger was going to hit. Was I going to be in danger?

The car door opened. He stepped out before offering his hand to help me out. I stepped out of the car, seeing two people stand there in suits.

I looked down at my leggings and baggy t-shirt and back at Alex. "The staff here are dressed better than me."

Alex shook his head, "Don't be silly. You're beautiful."

I rolled my eyes. "I don't need your corny compliments."

He grabbed my hand, leading me inside my eyes widened as I took everything in.

The palace was stunning. It was everything the history books said it would be.

The one thing that the history books didn't take into account was the little girl running down the corridor covered in flour. She ran straight to Alex, wrapping her arms around his legs. "Ander! You're home!"

He laughed, letting go of my hand and picking her up. He didn't care that she was covered in flour. She hugged him and cocked her head as she saw me.

"Hi," I said softly.

"She's talking to me, Ander," she whispered, making me laugh a little. "Can I say hi?"

"Of course, little El," he said.

"Hi," she said. "I'm El. You're El. We're El."

I laughed. "Yeah we're El."

"Can we keep her?" El asked, turning back to Alex.

I smiled, it was amazing how much she was like Alex. I could find myself getting attached to her that was for sure. I had to wonder how often Elizabeth came to him covered in things because Alex didn't bat an eyelid to it.

"So, Little Princess," Alex said, tickling her. "What trouble have you been up to today?"

She gasped in fake shock, and I couldn't help but giggle slightly.

"Nothing, Ander. Absolutely nothing."

"Hmm, I don't believe you," he said flatly.

"Nope. Innocent until proven guilty!" I declared defending whatever the little princess had been up to.

"I like her," El said, matter of factly. "Down."

Alex did as she said.

She ran ahead, and he let out a sigh. "I don't know what chaos I am going to be walking into."

"Does she do this a lot?"

"Way too often to count."

He reached for my hand, pulling me through the house. As we got closer and closer to the loudness, I looked at Alex in concern.

"I'm going to kill you!" I heard someone yell.

My eyes widened.

He smiled. "Welcome to chaos, baby." He pushed open a door and chaos was right.

There was a trail of flour all over the floor and two teenage boys covered in flour and Elizabeth stood with another child looking very proud of herself.

"How did a four-year-old cause this much chaos?" I asked with shock in my voice.

Alex chuckled. "This is nothing."

"I hate you!" A boy screamed.

"That's enough, Charles," Alex said, his voice cold. "She is a baby."

"I'm not a baby!" El stamped her feet in anger.

I pressed my lips into a thin line to keep from laughing.

I loved her. She was great.

"Charles and Arthur, go and clean yourselves off. Henry, stop helping Elizabeth with her pranks."

Henry's mouth dropped open. "I didn't."

Alex scoffed. "Are you telling me the four-year-old climbed up to put flour on top of doors and was smart enough to put all of this together?"

"Yes," Henry offered with a smile. "She's a really smart four-year-old."

"Henry."

"What? I'm getting tired of them picking on me," he

snapped. "So, what if Elizabeth wants to pull some stupid harmless pranks?!" He stormed off, slamming what I could only assume was his bedroom door.

Alex sighed and rubbed his forehead. He turned to the two teens shaking their heads. "Are you two for real? Leave him alone."

"We'll just call it character building," one of them shrugged.

"I call it being a dickhead to your brother," Alex snapped.

"You shouldn't swear. Anyway, who is this thing?"

My mouth dropped open in surprise.

"Talk about her like that again, and we will have a problem," Alex threatened. He grabbed my hand, pulling me away. "Don't kill your brothers," he whispered to himself.

I squeezed his hand, reassuring him. "I love El. She is my second best friend," I told him, trying to cheer him up.

Alex laughed and pushed me against the wall, pressing two hands either side of my head.

I bit my lip as I looked up at him.

"Do I have competition?"

I laughed. "Are you jealous?" I raised an eyebrow. "Are you jealous of your baby sister? My poor potato."

He rested his forehead against mine. "I don't know what pisses me off more Ella, that you're amused by this or that you keep calling me a potato."

I smiled, batting my eyelashes.

Was it wrong that I loved seeing him like this? Something about it was incredibly hot.

He pressed his lips to mine and deepened the kiss,

almost immediately pressing my body to his. He pulled away, and I smiled. "Alright. Let's go to the lion's den before I change my mind and decide to throw you away."

He grabbed my hand as we walked through more of the palace until we reached an office.

Alex knocked and walked in, pulling me in with him. He sat down, pulling me to sit on his lap. I tried to get up, but Alex held me in place. "Stop moving," he whispered.

"I am not going to sit in your lap," I hissed.

"Ella—"

I glared at him, "Do you need another lesson again?"

I heard a chuckle and turned to see the Queen sitting next to the desk.

My eyes widened.

"I love hearing someone put my baby boy in his place," she mused.

I stared at her not knowing what to say. Alex released his grip on me and moved up on the seat allowing me to sit next to him.

"Alexander, I think I broke your girlfriend," the Queen said amused.

"I'm not his girlfriend," I mumbled.

Alex looked at me. "You said you were giving me a chance?"

I grinned. "I am, but you haven't asked me to be your girlfriend yet."

"I think I like you already, Melinda," she said. "I need to hear this story of slapping my son though."

"Mother," Alex frowned.

She groaned, throwing her hands up dramatically. "Nobody lets me have any fun anymore."

I couldn't fathom how this woman ran the country, especially when she was standing there acting so normal.

"Mother," Alex said. "Can we get on with the meeting?"

She sighed. "Alex will fill you in with the nitty gritty in regard to the reporters. It won't be easy, but I hope you like my son enough to stay by his side. It won't be nice—"

"Yeah, I already read some of the lovely comments," I said, pressing my lips into a thin line.

"Yes, so there will be that. I'd like for you to attend some formal events with Alexander," she said. "In fact, we have a royal ball happening next weekend. I'd like for you to attend. We will have you dressed and get your makeup done here."

"The balls are boring, but we will make it fun," Alex grinned.

I nodded.

"I hope you understand the importance of keeping things that happen in the palace and with Alexander. We do not need our business splashed all over the papers—"

"Mother, she isn't like that," Alex defended.

"Alex, it's okay. She's protecting your family," I defended his mother.

I could understand why she felt the need to say it. I couldn't help but wonder how many times they had been burned by allowing people into their life.

"I still think she should sign an NDA," a new voice said. I turned to see the King walking into the office and standing by his wife. "Alexander can be too trusting. For all we know, this girl could be a spy or a gold digger."

I looked to see Alex's fist clenching in his hand, "We aren't going through this again."

"Alex, if it would make your family happy I'll sign—"

"No," he snapped. "I am not tainting my relationship with a NDA or a background check. I trust her." I bit my lip not knowing where to look. I could feel the tension between them both.

"She is not—"

"We aren't having this discussion again," Alex snapped, standing up. "Do not test me father."

I bit my lip as I had never seen Alex this angry and annoyed before. He wasn't kidding when he said that his relationship with his father was strained.

"Look, if it will make everyone happy to do a background check..." I trailed off.

"Melinda," Alex said sharply.

I couldn't help but flinch slightly at my full name.

"A word," he said.

I followed him obediently out of the office.

"You don't need to offer bullshit like that."

"Alex, if it gets your dad off your back, do it. I have nothing to hide."

"It feels like I'm slapping you in the face by making you do this, Ella." He sighed.

"You aren't making me do anything. I'm the one who's offering to do it. I'd rather do a background check than an NDA. Like, could you imagine if I couldn't tell Megan things? Um, no thank you," I said. "Let me make things a little easier for you."

"What did I do to deserve you?" Alex asked, wrapping an arm around my waist. He pressed a small kiss onto my forehead as he reached for my hand and peered his head back into the office.

"Do the background check."

I didn't really care about the background check if it made the King feel better about me and Alex being together. I was more than willing to do it. There wasn't anything they'd find that would put major red flags. So, I didn't worry.

# Chapter Twenty

## ALEXANDER

I still couldn't believe Ella had entertained my father by allowing him to do a background check on her.

I suppose she was right it did get him off my back for a little bit.

The week passed fast. Thankfully. Ella had gone back to university and I was doing online courses because I had so many duties this week.

Ella had gone back to work which was taking up most of her time, too. Other than texting throughout the day, we hadn't spoken to each other much.

I was currently parked outside of Daisy's, waiting for Ella to finish. I looked in the mirror behind me, seeing security still waiting behind us.

I hated that the press was still trying to catch glimpses of me and Ella. They seemed to be respectful when she was on her own because they didn't have any information about her yet. So, their only solution was to follow me and hoped that I would lead them to her.

I stepped out of the car seeing her through the window walk towards the door. She came out with her hair in a messy bun and wearing leggings and one of my shirts. As she got closer, I pulled her into my arms and kissed her softly. "I missed you."

"Hmm, I really couldn't tell," she teased.

"Are you ready to see my world?" I asked her.

"Yep. Although, I need a detour to my house to grab my bag because I was running late this morning, so I forgot," she said.

"Now I have a question for you, Miss Ella," I said, raising an eyebrow.

"Yes, sir?" She asked, batting her eyelashes.

I narrowed my eyes. "Where are you getting all my shirts from?"

"Well, my little potato, you dress me in them, so that makes them mine," she said, matter of factly.

"Get in the car," I said, slapping her ass gently.

She got into the car, and I sat down in the driver's seat, driving to her house.

"Don't bother getting out. It's by my door," she said.

She opened the door and ran towards the house. She came out a few moments later getting back in the car. "So, tell me about your world. What should I expect?"

"Spoiled, rich, pretty much anything someone could want. Well, almost anything. It's missing you," I said, honestly.

For the first time ever, I was looking forward to one of the functions and that was because I had her.

"You promise you won't let me embarrass myself?" She asked, biting her lip.

"I promise."

I think I'd die before I let anything happen to her.

I needed to find a way to tell her that I loved her without chasing her away. She reminded me in some ways of Rocky when I first got him and needed to give him a chance to get used to everything.

I started the car and began to drive to London with guards in front and behind. "So, tell me about your week. I missed you."

For the majority of the drive, I listened to Ella talk about her week and how much she was enjoying work now that Cindy wasn't there. She had also started our university assignment, which meant she got further than me because I hadn't even opened the module handbook that said what our first assignment was. That would be a night before problem, which I would then hate myself for leaving it the night before.

The sirens finally joined us as we approached the Palace.

I couldn't help but smile as I remembered Ella's face from the week before. She was so unsure and nervous about everything I wanted to ease her into the world, but there was no easing her when it came to my world.

We pulled into the Palace and the car doors were opened, I stepped out walking around to Ella's side of the door. She reached back in for her beg and I pulled her hand in mine and headed straight to my bedroom, I didn't want to risk bumping into my parents or Elizabeth mainly because then I would be stuck with my little sister and after not seeing Ella all week I just wanted to chill with the girl I loved in my arms.

Once we were in the safety of my bedroom, I sat down on the bed and pulled her in between my legs. I grabbed her chin, gently pulling her down and kissing her.

She deepened the kiss, pulling away when she needed to breathe. She climbed onto my lap, and I held onto her tightly. I kissed her again, putting all my feelings into it. I laid back on the bed pulling her to lay down with me. She was directly on my cock. If there were no clothes between us I would have sunk straight into her sweet pussy.

She pulled away, breathing heavily and biting her lip.

Damn, I wanted her.

"Ella, you look fucking amazing. I want you so badly." I ran my hands down her body, resting on her hips.

"I think we need to have a chat," she said, sliding off my lap.

"Uh-oh, that can't be good," I said with a sigh.

She raised an eyebrow, "Alex I'm not stupid enough to have a dumping conversation while I'm stuck in a palace in London. I'm not that much of an idiot."

"Fair enough." I moved to sit up on the bed. "What do we need to talk about then?"

"Us," she said. "You're the only person I slept with. I'm not experienced or amazing. Megan said I should be honest about the fact I haven't slept with anyone else."

"I'm glad she spoke some sense into you," I admitted.

I would hate to think how it would have happened if I didn't know she had only slept with me. "That's the kind of thing that you share with a partner."

"It's embarrassing," she mumbled, turning away.

"Why?" I frowned.

"I'm an eighteen-year old girl who has only slept with one person," she said. "Most girls my age have slept with plenty of guys. Before you, all I had done was kiss a boy and it wasn't even a good kiss."

I grinned. "All that means to me is I get to be all of your firsts."

"It doesn't make you view me differently?" She asked.

I pulled her to me kissing her once more, "Ella, it makes me even more horny and want to make you mine. The fact I get to ruin you for life, and you'll remember my cock as your first is better than I could've imagined."

"Alright there, caveman." She giggled.

It wasn't far from the truth. Something about claiming her for the first time.

A knock at the door pulled my attention from Ella. "Enter," I called.

The door opened, and Slate entered. "Sir, Lady Annie has requested to see you," he said. "She's in the lounge waiting for you."

"Thank you," I said.

I completely forgot that I was meant to have a meeting with her. I pressed a small kiss to her lips. "I'll be back soon, baby."

She nodded.

I climbed off the bed heading away from my room and towards the lounge.

Annie was pacing the floor.

"Are you okay?" I asked softly.

She shook her head. "They're trying to force me into

marriage, Alex. I can't do it. I'd rather lose the lady title than bend to their will," she said.

I felt bad for Annie.

She did everything possible to be the perfect daughter, and it still wasn't enough for her parents. She had fallen hard for a man, and the news of her impending engagement had broken them up.

I wasn't sure what she saw in Charles, but one thing was for sure. She was good for him.

"Annie, have you spoken to him?"

"He won't see me, Alex. I don't know how to get him to talk to me. I don't want this engagement, but he just won't listen to reason," she said.

I could see her wanting to cry, and I reached over hugging her.

"God, I'm pathetic."

"The joys of being in love," I told her softly. "Are you coming to the ball?"

"I have to," she mumbled. "I don't want to."

"Well dress to impress. You are beautiful enough, Annie. You will get the attention of the men in the ball, and hopefully, Charles will begin to see reason," I told her.

She rolled her eyes, "Ha, a man seeing reason? Don't be silly."

"I'll pretend to not be offended," I said, rolling my eyes. "Annie, I've told you since you first started coming around here. You will always have a safe space here, regardless if you are with Charles or not. Elizabeth loves having you around. Plus, I think you keep her from going too crazy with her pranks."

"Thank you," she said.

I sat down.

She sighed, slumping into the arm chair. "Do you think I could just hide out here with you?"

I smiled. "Unfortunately, no. I have my—" I paused.

I didn't quite know what to call Ella since she hadn't specifically said she was my girlfriend, and she denied me when I asked. "Something here."

She grinned. "Is this girl you were splashed all over the internet with your tongue down her mouth looking like you were about to fuck her against the wall?"

*Jesus.*

I looked at her sheepishly. "We got lost in the moment, and I forgot about the cameras."

"That's like saying you forgot that you were a Prince," she snorted.

"With her, I do," I admitted. "She didn't know I was a Prince. She found out that night. It was kind of a shit-show. I'm surprised she's here right now. I need to introduce her to this world without scaring her away."

"Alex, I'm going to give you some advice," she said. "The fact the girl is even in this Palace speaks volumes. A girl wouldn't be willing to even try if she didn't have any kind of feelings for you."

"Thanks, Annie," I said softly. "Keep me updated ok?"

"I will. Thanks for listening."

"Anytime." I smiled at her.

I headed back to the bedroom.

As I opened the door, I saw Ella was lying on her bed typing away on her laptop. I reached over, tapping her ass gently.

She squealed, turning around. "You're back."

"What are you working on?" I asked curiously.

"Our assignment," she said. "You know the thing you should have started by now."

"Eh, I have time," I shrugged. "What? Another three weeks?"

"Alex, it's due next week," she said.

My eyes widened slightly, "Oops, I better get started."

"Who is Lady Annie?" Ella asked, frowning.

I smiled a little. "Ella, are you jealous?"

"Shut up, potato," she grumbled.

I couldn't help but smile at her nickname for me as much it annoyed me when she started calling me it. I had gotten used to it.

"Come with me," I held my hand out to her.

She took it, begrudgingly.

Jealous Ella might be my favourite type of Ella.

I walked towards the balcony and pulled back the curtain, opening up the door. I pulled her out onto the balcony, and she leaned against the edge.

"This is what I see every day."

"It's beautiful," she whispered.

I had to agree with her.

London was stunning at night with the way the lights shined. Watching the girl I love staring at the city made it even more beautiful..

"Yeah you are," I whispered.

She spun around. "Wait. Is this the balcony?"

"The balcony?" I asked.

"Yeah, the one where you all gather, watch events and weddings, and the first kiss?"

"Yes."

"Holy shit," she muttered.

I pulled her into my arms, kissing her softly. "I love the way you react to all of this. It makes my little prison seem that much more special."

"Thanks for inviting me to prison then." She chuckled.

I looked at the girl I loved, and I smiled. "Ella, I love you."

She stared at me wide eyed as her mouth dropped open in shock.

"You don't have to say it back, but I needed to tell you because I've nearly said it a few times," I admitted sheepishly.

I hoped she would say it back. Oh, I wanted her to feel the same way.

She stared, blinking her eyes and looking at her hands.

I had to admit it hurt that she might not feel the same way.

"So, the ball is tomorrow night," she said. "What are we doing on Sunday?"

I guess she didn't love me yet.

"Sleeping," I said, trying to keep emotions out of my voice.

I guess I would have to work harder at getting her to fall in love with me.

"Well, how would you feel about us exploring London instead?" She asked. "I haven't explored London before."

"In that case, yes." I laughed. "Let me show you where the ball and everything will be happening. Hopefully seeing what will happen might make you less nervous." I led her away from the balcony and into the ballroom. "This is where the ball is going to be held. We will enter through the stairs, as well as all the royal family and important people."

"So, I will wait for you at the bottom?"

I couldn't help but laugh at her hopeful expression.

"Nope, you'll be by my side." I grinned.

"Shit," she mumbled. "I'm suddenly even more nervous."

"You would be stupid not to be nervous Ella," I told her. "I get it okay? This world is scary. There are different rules and it's overall a different world than what you are used to. But believe me they're still the same asshole people that you can encounter. I will be by your side. I promise."

I pressed my lips to hers, kissing her softly, "So where's the kitchen?" She asked curiously. "I'm getting kind of hungry. We should watch a film."

# Chapter Twenty-One

## MELINDA

I woke up to people in Alex's room whose main mission was to get me somewhere.

I turned away, hiding under the covers and snuggling closer to Alex. I didn't have to get up for work, and they were waking me up.

"Idiots, leave me alone."

"Wow, you really aren't a morning person," I heard a new voice say.

I pulled my head from under the cover to see the Queen.

I quickly pulled the cover over me. I was okay with hiding from the world. When the curtains opened, I felt Alex flinch against me as the covers were pulled away from our heads.

"Up now, Melinda. We have a full day of getting ready for the ball, and breakfast is the most important meal of the day," she said.

"Later, babe," Alex mumbled, pushing me away from him.

"Nice try, Alexander, you are getting up. Your father wants to see you in his office after breakfast," she said.

"Ha, sucker" I poked him.

"Mother, take her and let me sleep," he complained as I got off the bed.

"No, go and see your father," she said.

"Do I get breakfast?" He asked.

"Alexander."

He followed us out of the room as we began to walk towards the dining room.

"Does this make you feel like a naughty child?" I whispered.

He nodded.

"What's the crime?" I asked curiously.

"Sleeping," he pouted. "Mother has that effect on all of us. She can make you feel guilty without actually doing it. I hope when we have kids I can do it."

We? He was planning a future with me?

I can't stop thinking about how he told me that he loves me. Part of me was waiting for him to look at me and say, 'no, just kidding.'

He was worming his way into my heart. It scared me because I didn't want to be able to give him power to hurt me. Day by day, I was falling hard for him. We arrived in the dining room and sat down at the table I followed sitting next to him. "So, how does this work? Breakfast I mean."

"You put it in your mouth," he said teasingly.

I chuckled, shaking my head. He really thought he was

a comedian, that was for sure. A few of the butlers came in, placing trays of food in the middle of the table and walked off again. "Does anybody say thank you?" I asked.

"No, they're paid to work."

"That's a really shitty attitude, Alex," I said. "No wonder you said what you did when we met. You would be lost if all your staff went home."

"You finished with your lecture now?" He asked, rolling his eyes.

I glared at him as I reached for two pieces of toast placing them on the small plate in front of me. "Come on, don't be mad." I crossed my arms over my chest.

"Your boobs pop out when you do that."

"That's really helping your case right now." I frowned.

I stopped looking at him as I began to eat the two toast. After I finished, I sat back, trying my hardest to not glare at Alex.

"Melinda, girls, come on," the Queen called walking into the room.

"Ella, you can't stay mad at me," Alex complained.

I stood up and winked. "Actually, I can," I said. "I'm not one of your staff you can control." I walked over to the Queen as Elizabeth latched onto my hand.

I heard Alex groan behind me, and I couldn't help but smile. We walked into another room, one that I hadn't seen before. I made a note to ask Alex how many rooms the palace had. Well, when I was talking to him again I would.

"Girls, you know the drill," the Queen said as they both rushed into the chairs with the two women standing behind them. "I better introduce you to all the craziness."

"Thank you, your majesty," I said.

"Melinda, something tells me you're going to be a part of this family, call me Victoria," she said. "So, this is Taylor. She'll be doing your hair. Pablo is going to dress you, and the lovely Lady Annie here will be doing your nails."

"You came to see Alex yesterday," I said before I could stop myself.

Lady Annie grinned. "My hunch was right it seems," she said. "Actually, it's just Annie now. I renounced my title."

"Oh—"

"No, and I'd rather not discuss it right now," she mumbled.

"Very well," Victoria nodded. "You'll be in very safe hands here, even if you are in a disagreement with my son."

"You heard that?" I asked slightly embarrassed.

"Word travels fast. Melinda. One thing is for sure you have gained favour with our staff." She chuckled.

I sat down in the chair with Taylor as she began to wash my hair and blow-dry it, "So, do you have any ideas about what to do with your hair?" Taylor asked.

"Erm, no. I haven't been to anything like this before," I said. "I don't know what to expect."

I looked over at Elizabeth who was having her hair brushed. She was watching a video on her iPad.

"Do whatever you want to my hair. I honestly have no clue what hairstyle to suggest."

For the next hour and half, my hair was pulled in

every direction possible as she began to curl my hair and pin it up and back.

After she finished, I went to sit with Annie as she looked at Elizabeth. "She's not usually this perky," Annie said. "Are you okay with acrylic nails?"

"Sure," I said. "I've never had them, but it would be cool to actually have nails for a change."

"Learning curve, but once you are used to them, it's easy," Annie said.

"What do you mean she's not usually like this?" I asked curiously.

"The Prince. His list of women is long, and they don't last long either. Elizabeth looks up to Alexander, and these women always ignore her. If you ever argue with him, which believe me, you will, don't hurt her. That was my mistake with Charles."

"Charles?" I said as my eyes widened in surprise.

"Yeah, we dated for about a year, but we got into a fight and broke up. I didn't come around for a few months. I ended up hurting her, so please don't make the same mistake as me. Forget the boys, it's about her."

"I won't," I said softly.

Annie spent the next ten minutes finding the right size acrylic for my nails. "Ella, can I talk to you?" I looked up seeing Alex at the door. "Hey, Annie."

"Dog house already, hmm??" She teased.

I stood up, following Alex out the room.

"I'm sorry for being a dick," he said.

"Do you understand why I'm mad about how your attitude was in there?" I asked.

I needed him to realise what it was about his

behaviour that upset me. I couldn't be with someone who treated people like they did before.

"Yes, but Ella you have to understand this is how we were raised. I can't change that. I can try and do better but—"

"No. You will do better, Alex, it's a matter of respect." I interrupted him. "You have a little girl in there who adores you and you could make that change by showing her that your staff are not here to do everything for you."

"I mean we pay them to do that, but I get your point," he said.

"Also, I'm sorry about being jealous yesterday with Annie," I admitted.

He smiled, pressing his lips to mine and kissing me softly. "You look beautiful," he said. "I can't wait to see how you look later."

"Ander!" I watched as Elizabeth came running out the room and gave him a hug.

"There's my beautiful Princess," he said. "I have a present for the both of you." He reached into his pocket as he crouched on the floor, and pulled out a necklace and placed it in Elizabeth's hand. "Rules, remember?"

"Lena has to put it on," she said. "I'll find you tonight to take it off so I don't lose it."

"Good girl. Go inside while I talk to Ella for a minute," he said.

"You truly are a good brother," I said with a grin.

He stood up as he pulled out a box from his pocket. He placed it in my hand. "I got you this."

I opened it and gasped. It was a heart necklace with a green gem stone with his name underneath. "Alex, this is beautiful," I whispered. "You didn't have to get me anything though."

"I want every stuck up asshole to know that you are my girl," he said. He placed his lips onto mine. I couldn't help the butterflies in my stomach at him calling me his. Slightly possessive but also hot.

"Let me put it on you."

I turned around and held the box up for him as he took the necklace out of the box. He placed it around my neck, clicking the clasp into place. "Beautiful." He kissed my neck.

I spun in his arms. "Thank you. I'll see you tonight, Alex."

I walked back in, sitting with Annie.

From that moment it was go, go, go. Time was slipping away fast as Annie did my nails and Pablo showed me dresses to which I said no to some.

Before I knew it, the ball was starting. I stood in front of the mirror as I looked at what I was wearing. I didn't even look like me.

I was wearing a one shoulder red dress that flowed down nicely and had a little drag on the floor with black heels with red bows on.

"Are you okay?" I turned to see Victoria standing at the door. "Annie said you looked a little panicked."

"Not panicked, just scared," I admitted.

"You don't need to be. My son will be right by your side as you walk down those stairs. You have nothing to be scared of. In all honesty, it's when you're on the floor," she said, letting out a chuckle.

My eyes widened. I wasn't sure how that conversation helped calm my nerves.

Talking to Victoria, I saw how much Alex was like his mother and where he got some of his personality from.

We left the room, and I followed her down the familiar path of the corridor near the stairs where we made our entrance.

Alex stood at the balcony, looking down at the party. "I found the runaway girlfriend." I watched as she headed down the stairs looking as graceful as ever.

He turned around.

My breath caught in my throat as I took in the sight of him. He looked handsome. The man knew how to wear a suit, that was for sure. It fit him perfectly, showed off his muscles. His brown hair had been neatly combed back.

I walked over to him, taking his hand.

"You look stunning, Ella." His eyes looked up and down taking in the one shoulder red dress that I wore.

I leaned up, I pulled away as I looked at him. "You look handsome, stunning, and I think I have quite possibly run out of adjectives."

"Are you ready?" He asked.

"As ready as I'll ever be," I said.

I held onto his hand tightly as we walked down the steps into the ball where there were a few reporters at the bottom waiting.

Once we reached the bottom, Alex stood with his arm wrapped around me as a few photos were taken. As the photos were being taken, I looked around the room, a giant chandelier hanging in the middle of the room. A band stood on the stage paying some soft music. The room was packed with people; some I recognised from television others not so much. It was such a different world than to what I was used to.

"There's going to be some questions. I figured you wouldn't want to know that in advance," he whispered.

"Who is your date, Prince Alexander?" A reporter asked.

"This is my girlfriend, Melinda Brown. We met through university. She is in one of my lectures," he said.

I made a mental note about the girlfriend thing being that I never agreed to being his girlfriend.

"Two," I told him. "Monday and Thursday, you know the one you forgot about."

"Oh yeah," he said sheepishly.

"How are the courses going, Prince Alexander?"

"They are going alright. I'm glad to finally be doing something I wanted to," he said.

"Is your relationship going to be just another fling?"

"This relationship is not a fling," Alex looked at me. "Ella is special, and I'm crazy about her."

I didn't get a chance to hear another question before I felt a tug at my hand. I looked to see Elizabeth pulling me away from Alex and the reporters. "Can you dance with me?"

"Of course I can," I grinned.

I picked her up, and we began to sway to the music as she chatted my ear off. I had no idea what I was going to do if we ever didn't work out. I was growing more and more attached to Elizabeth.

"Hey, my beautiful girl." I looked to see Alex coming

over. He took her off me, placing her on the floor and whispering something into her ear.

She nodded, running off.

Alex pulled me into his arms and I wrapped my arms around his neck.

The song changed, and I smiled. "The greatest story ever told," I said.

I laid my head on his chest as we swayed together to the song.

I wanted this moment to last forever.

It was perfect.

"Ella, thank you," Alex said.

"For what?" I asked as I looked at him.

"For trying," he said. "I realise how hard this must be for you and I appreciate it. So, next date you can do whatever you want."

"So, this is a date?" I asked teasingly.

"Royal engagement," he said with a shrug. "Dates and royal engagements are all the same to me."

I smiled a little, "So tell me, Mr. Alexander George, I don't remember agreeing to be your girlfriend."

He shrugged with a little smile. "You didn't say yes or no. The way I see it, it's a win-win."

I smiled and shook my head.

At that moment, I knew I was falling in love with him and that thought terrified me. I never wanted to be in a position where I could be hurt by someone yet he had entered my heart.

# Chapter Twenty-Two

## ALEXANDER

Ella had headed off to my room once the ball had finished.

I had no idea what my father would want at this time of night, but if it was anything like normal, it would end with me storming off because he was insulting her or me.

I walked into the office sitting down in the chair straight away. "What do you want?"

"I'm giving you one last chance, Alexander. End this with her before she gets hurt," he said. "Once I start this background check, I will dive so far in I will know if she got a scolding at nursery."

If things were on better terms with my father, I may have believed he was doing this out of concern, but I knew better.

He was only bothered about the heir. Charles, Arthur, Henry, and Elizabeth could pretty much do anything and he wouldn't bat an eye, but where the throne was concerned, I was the one that matters. I was the heir, and they were the spares.

"I'm trying to protect you, Alexander. I know you don't see it that way and that I'm ruining your life, but I am looking out for your best interest as well as the country. You are the heir."

I looked at my father. I had no idea whether to talk to him as the King or as my dad, the one who used to tuck me into bed at night who let me pretend I was a knight in battle.

"I love her dad."

His eyes softened a little as he sunk into his chair.

I couldn't tell what he was thinking or what he was going to say. I was honestly in uncharted territory.

I had never told my parents I loved a girl, never mind bringing her into my life.

"I just want to protect you from ruining your life. You are going to be King one day. This little fling isn't going to go down well with the public."

"Dad she isn't a fling. She's it for me. I don't ever see myself being with anyone else. I would marry her in a heartbeat if I could."

Dad let out a sigh. "You may leave for the evening."

I stood up, leaving the office.

I walked through the palace, heading to my room.

I opened the door and saw a breeze blowing through the curtain. I watched Ella wrapped in a blanket still dressed soaking up London. God, I really hoped this background search wouldn't pull anything up. She may have been confident, but I was less so.

"It's cold. You should come inside," I said softly, approaching her.

"It's peaceful out here," she whispered.

I walked over, wrapping my arms around her and resting my chin on her shoulder. "Yeah it is, especially at night."

"More and more, I can understand why you didn't tell me you were a Prince. That little bit of freedom must have felt like heaven to you."

"Spending time with you is heaven to me. It was so much easier to block out all the other shit. There were so many times when I thought I had blown it all up with reporters getting closer or appearing at your house that time. I panicked because I thought I'd lose you. I've never met a girl who made me want to be around you all the time, you were on my mind. I didn't want to make a mistake with you. I don't know when I fell in love with you but I did and now I never want to let you go."

She turned around in my arms. She had a small twinkle in her eyes. It was something that always drew me to her.

"Tonight wasn't as bad as I thought it was going to be. You may be able to convince me in the future to attend some more by your side."

"Good," I kissed her softly. Breaking the kiss, I placed a small kiss onto her forehead. "You make the events a little less boring." She shivered against me, and I shook my head. "Come on, we don't need you getting a cold."

"I won't. I don't get sick," she protested.

"You know when people say that they usually always get sick," I told her slightly amused.

She shook her head. "Not me."

I shut the balcony doors as she came in. She reached for her pyjamas, walking into the bathroom,

I stripped off my suit, quickly leaving only the boxers on and climbing under the covers. Ella came out of the bathroom dressed in one of my shirts which did a good job of hiding her body and reached mid-thigh on her.

"I love seeing you in my clothes," I said.

She grinned jumping on the bed.

I wrapped my arms around her, pulling her to my body.

"I fear I'm going to get far to attached to you," she whispered.

"Good." She climbed under the covers before getting back into my arms and I smiled. "I want to sleep with you every night and wake up to you in the morning."

"Hmm, that would be a nice break from reality," she said, yawning.

She snuggled into me closing her eyes and pretty soon the sound of soft snores lulled me into sleep, too.

---

Waking up with her in my arms felt amazing. It would have been even better if I wasn't woken up by Elizabeth jumping on the bed.

I groaned, trying to grab her but she kept moving around the bed.

"It's time to wake up," she squealed. "The sky's awake."

I looked over at the alarm clock and saw it was only 5:00 a.m..

"Elizabeth, lay down," I grumbled.

"Alex?" Ella mumbled.

"It's okay, Ella. Go back to sleep, it's just El," I told her softly.

She let out a small groan, snuggling back into the pillow. I grabbed Elizabeth's hand, pulling her down to lay with us. "It's sleep time, Little Princess."

"I'm not tired," she whispered.

"Well Ella and I are," I said. "So, you either lie down and enjoy snuggle time or you go back to your own room."

"Fine," she mumbled, snuggling into my arms.

I looked over as she settled in between Ella and I. She had rested her arms around Ella's stomach snuggling into her, too.

God, I did love my baby sister. but I'll admit not at 5:00 a.m.. I guess it wasn't too bad though.

I closed my eyes trying to get back off to sleep once more. It was no use though, so I watched both of the girls sleep as I scrolled on my phone, watching TikToks of Princess Cupcake and Deborah. I had become attached to the chickens. They amused me to no end.

I detached myself from both of them and put some joggers on, leaving the bedroom and made my way towards the kitchens, as I entered the kitchen went silent. "Erm, are you lost?" The chef asked with a raised eyebrow.

I let out a snort. "No, I'm in the right place," I said. "You think you can help me make breakfast for Ella?"

"Of course," Chef said with a nod. "Has she been criticising your lack of cooking knowledge?"

I smiled sheepishly. "Yes, she was also offended that I didn't know how to cut or grate whatever vegetable it was she handed me. So, I figured I'd try and surprise her. You might want to kill me after that."

"Oh, lordy," Chef said, shaking his head. "I'm going to need all the patience God can give me." He looked at the ceiling, and I couldn't help but chuckle. "Alright, come on then."

For the next two hours, Chef spent the time walking me through how to make breakfast for Ella. And during that time, there were a few near misses of me chopping my finger off, which even the Chef was confused about how I had managed it.

I looked down at the plate of food and smiled to myself. Maybe Ella was right. It did feel different when you did things yourself.

I carried the two plates from the kitchen heading towards the bedroom. I pushed open the door. She was awake in bed watching TikToks with Elizabeth snuggled into her watching, too.

"Good morning, girls," I said smiling.

"I was wondering where you went off to," Ella said, sitting up and leaning against the headboard.

"I couldn't get back to sleep when El decided to gate-crash our sleepover so I went to the kitchen," I said.

Her eyes finally landed on the plate and her eyes widened. "Do we need to get an ambulance on standby? Is the Palace on fire?"

I pouted, "Ella, I'm not that bad."

"You didn't know how to cut or grate a potato or carrot, yes I would be worried," she teased.

I rolled my eyes. This girl was lucky I loved her.

I sat on the bed handing her a plate with the cutlery and watched her.

She frowned, "Stop staring, it's creepy."

I grinned, "I need to know if you like it."

She took a bite and her eyes shot up in surprise, "Damn, that's pretty good. We may have to change your nickname, potato."

I started eating my plate and giving bits to El as she turned her attention from the phone. She really wasn't a big eater so she did a lot of snacking throughout the day. El jumped off the bed, running out the room. It meant that Ella and I were alone. I finished eating and placing the plate on the floor. I laid next to her in bed. "Thank you. Alex. That was amazing."

"You're welcome, Ella," I said.

I reached for my phone, scrolling on TikTok. It didn't take long before Ella had finished breakfast and laid her head on my chest as we both doom-scrolled.

"I wish we could stay like this forever."

"Wouldn't that be nice," she mumbled. "I have to go back to work and university eventually."

A knock at the door stopped me from replying, "Enter."

I looked over my phone, seeing Mother enter the room. "Alexander, you are required in meetings all week next week."

I groaned. "I don't want to deal with parliament. They're annoying, and they argue over random shit like the entitled pricks they are."

Ella let out a snort, and I narrowed my eyes.

"I said nothing," she giggled.

"Alexander," Mother said sharply.

"Fine," I grumbled. "We're going around London. I'm going to take her home afterward. I will be home for my duties later on."

Mother nodded leaving the room.

I turned to Ella, digging my hands into her sides and tickling her.

She let out a squeal, moving away from me as she slipped off the bed. She tried to crawl away from me, but I reached over and pulled her back onto the bed.

"Stop!" She squealed. "I'm sorry I'll take it back. You're not entitled at all. I was talking nonsense!" I hovered over her, and she smiled.

God, she was beautiful. I was so lucky. I wanted to spend the rest of my life with her.

I bent down, pressing my lips to hers.

She pulled me closer, deepening the kiss. She let out a small moan as her body pressed against mine. I broke the kiss before pressing a small kiss to her forehead.

"Right, we need to get out of bed before I don't let you leave," I told her.

"Hmm, I do love our bubble," she mumbled.

I rolled off her getting out of bed and stretched. "We better get ready."

I walked away from her leaving her to get ready and walked into the bathroom and got to brushing my teeth and getting ready. I walked out the bathroom and she was dressed brushing her hair. "You look beautiful, baby."

We left the Palace, and I led her to the car. We were having a driving tour of London. It would be the only way to show her everything before she decided which part of London to physically explore.

"Wait!" I turned to see El running over to us and pushing past me to get to Ella. "Hold your hand out."

Ella did as she instructed.

"Close your eyes."

Again, Ella listened to her orders, my eyes narrowed as she placed a friendship bracelet in her hand. "Open."

She opened her eyes and smiled, "aww Elizabeth I love it!" She pulled my sister into a hug and I smiled a little. I loved how much Ella seemed to be letting El in a part of me filled with nerves because I hoped I would never have to break either of their hearts.

Ella got into the car. I climbed in after her, crossing my arms over my chest and pouting. "I'm jealous. I usually get her jewellery."

"Do you wear it?" She asked, raising an eyebrow as she pointed to her wrist.

"Not always."

"Which is why I'm clearly her favourite now," Ella teased.

I loved how much Elizabeth liked Ella. Even if she was stealing my best friend and all of her jewellery.

## Chapter Twenty-Three

# MELINDA

Driving around London wasn't quite what I had in mind, but it kept us away from the crowds and for that I was thankful. I did want to explore London like a tourist one day but I guess I would have to bring Megan for that.

A few hours later, we arrived at the diner. I got out of the car going to the boot and grabbed my bag out of it. Alex wrapped his arms around me pulling me closer to him. "I don't want you to go." He groaned. "Not seeing you for the whole week is going to suck."

"It will go fast," I don't know who I was trying to convince.

I pressed my lips to his, kissing him before he deepened the kiss.

"I'll see you soon, Ella," he whispered.

I watched as he got into the car and waved as it drove away. I walked into work, and I saw Daisy behind the counter. "Hey," she said.

"Hi." I grinned.

I walked into the back dropping my bag on the floor and reaching for my apron. For the next few hours, I concentrated on the work and not on the fact that I was not going to be seeing Alex. It was weird how much he had invaded my life.

Work finally finished, and I headed straight to Megan's house.

I walked into her house and saw Oliver sitting on the sofa. "Hey, my other daughter. I was wondering when you would be coming," he said.

"I've been in London," I said.

"Tell her to bathe," he said.

I laughed walking up the stairs into her bedroom, she was laid in bed scrolling through one of the various apps on her iPad. "Why did your dad tell me you need to bathe? What's going on? Is it him?"

"Not here, can we go to your house?" Megan asked.

"Yeah, pack a bag," I said with a shrug.

It didn't take too long for Megan to get her stuff together. We left her house and walked to mine. As we turned the corner onto my street, I saw paparazzi waiting.

"Ugh, stupid paps. I don't think they're going to move now, so I guess it's official." I unlocked the front door.

As we reached it and walked inside, I locked the door behind us and ran upstairs, changing into my pjs.

Megan sat on my bed, staring at her phone.

I sat next to her. "Talk to me then."

"The man I was seeing, he's married," Megan said quietly. "I let myself get sucked in by all his promises and bullshit. I thought I was in love. I didn't want to disappoint my dad."

"Your dad?" I asked. "Megan, what was his name?"

She looked at the ground, and my heart sunk. "Robert. It gets worse."

"Worse how?" I asked.

"I'm late," she said. "I think I could be pregnant. I took three tests. One was positive and two were negative. I don't want a baby like this, Melinda. I don't know what I'm going to do."

"We don't know anything for sure. Tomorrow, we will go get another pregnancy test, the clear blue ones. They are crazy accurate apparently, and we will call the doctor. If you are pregnant, it'll be okay. I will be by your side, supporting you with whatever you decide to do. If you aren't pregnant, we'll have a celebration."

"Thank you," she whispered.

"You know what, let's forget about everything. The rest of today, we are going to spend ignoring the world."

We ignored the world until 5:30 in the morning when Megan woke me up, squealing excitedly. She had started her period, the one time someone was actually excited about their period. After she had woken me up, it was hard to get back to sleep. In the end, I had finally given up trying to get back to sleep. We made our way downstairs, and I began to make us breakfast.

"Good job, you can cook," Megan chuckled. "If not, we'd be ordering breakfast in bed because I burned the rice."

I laughed as I remembered that fiasco. "Yeah, we're keeping you out of the kitchen unless you're eating."

I pottered around the kitchen, making us bacon sandwiches.

I handed her the plate as I sat down at the table, taking a bite out of my sandwich. I hoped with her finally having answers that she would finally be able to be free. I wanted to do everything for my best friend, but I also knew she wouldn't accept any help. I was worried that hopefully she could begin to be on the mend.

"Thanks. Okay, tell me about the ball. The pictures looked amazing." Megan took a bite out of her sandwich as she stared at me.

"It was amazing, but I finally understood something though," I said, taking another bite of my sandwich.

"Which was?" Megan asked with a mouthful of food.

"I get why he didn't tell me who he was, the time he spent with me where he was normal it was heaven compared to what that ball felt like. It was amazing but the eyes, everyone was watching," I said. "In the end it was worth it."

"You really like him don't you?" Megan asked softly.

I bit my lip, "I think I love him Megan."

"Woah the L word already, must be serious," she said.

"He already said it, I heard it once when we were going to sleep and then he just came out and said it," I admitted.

She let out a squeal, and I flinched from the noise.

"He told you he loved you and you didn't think to tell me?!"

"Can you shout any louder? I don't think the reporters outside heard you," I said sarcastically.

She looked at me sheepishly. "Sorry."

I rolled my eyes. "I don't know if I'm ready to fall head over heels in love."

"Oh sweetie, you're already there," she said.

"I don't know when I'm going to get to see him again. He's at parliament all week other than this polo game he wants me to go to."

"Polo?" Megan asked, scrunching her face up in confusion. "I'm assuming it's not like Marco Polo?"

"I didn't realise that was played in water," I said with a grin. "Alex told me that."

"You have your very own fairytale, every girls' dream."

"Not a fairytale, and it might not even last," I said with a little shrug.

Megan scoffed. "Puh-lease. I have read my fair share of romances and let me tell you girl, a man doesn't bring a girl around his family that he's going to break up with, especially if he's a royal in line for the throne."

A knock on the door stopped me from answering Megan.

I stood up, eating the last part of my sandwich as I opened the door. As per usual, I saw the garden filled with paparazzi. I was surprised to see Victoria standing there..

Hi," I said. "Erm, come in." I let her in, shutting the door behind me. I made my way into the kitchen with her following behind me.

"Your majesty," Megan bowed in the process, slipping onto the floor.

I burst into a fit of giggles, grabbing my sides as I struggled to breathe "Oh my God." I laughed. "I wish I had a camera in this house."

"Not funny." She grumbled, sitting back at the table.

"Sorta was." I shook my head. I looked at Victoria. "Sorry I'm not very presentable."

"I should think not." She chuckled. "I looked worse at your age. As you are aware, Alexander is in parliament for most of the week except for Wednesday for the polo game. I hope you can attend. You may also bring your funny friend."

"Hey, she thinks I'm funny," Megan said, looking pleased with herself.

"I have made some arrangements because of your relationship with my son now being fully in the public eye. You will have a guard to escort you places safely because the press can be brutal, and we wouldn't want bad things to happen. You may not like it, but it is for your safety and that will be the end of that discussion," Victoria said.

"I don't even get a say?" I asked.

"Afraid not. Alexander doesn't want your life to come to a standstill because of your relationship. At the end of the day, your safety is what matters to him," she said.

"Does he know about this?"

She grinned, "No. I figured the best time to slip your security when he is in parliament and is too preoccupied to argue with my interfering ways," she said. "I shall see you Wednesday. I'll see myself out. A guard will be posted outside your house in a car similar to Jones. Goodbye, Melinda."

I watched as she walked out the kitchen and stared until I heard my front door open and close. "Is she for real?" I asked.

"The Queen was just in your house! The motherfucking Queen!" Megan squealed. "How did she know where you live?"

I stared at her. "She's the Queen."

"Did I just hear the Queen was in the house?" A voice shouted from upstairs.

"Your mum is home?" Megan asked.

I shrugged and turned to look up the stairs, low and behold my mother was sitting at the top of the stairs. "When did you get home?" I asked curiously.

"Late last night," mum said, letting out a yawn. "I'm going to go back to bed, so girls try to be quiet."

I watched as she went back into her room, something told me she wasn't alone and she probably had the sperm donor there. "How is she after the hospital stint?"

"She's started to relax more and doesn't work as much, so I think she probably realised how much she was draining herself," I said, making my way into the living room sitting on the sofa Megan followed, sitting next to me.

"One episode of *Ex on the Beach* before we have to be at university?"

"You read my mind, babe."

Two hours later, we watched an episode and left for university. As Clarissa said the moment, I opened my front door and saw that a guard was waiting. It seemed they were ready to take me anywhere.

This was going to take a while to get used to, and I truly was not keen on the idea at all. Somehow I knew I would be losing this battle. We arrived at university.

I got out of the car and looked back at the guard. "I'm sorry I never got your name."

"Jimmy," he said.

"Erm, you're not following me around university right?" I asked, raising an eyebrow.

"No ma'am, just to and from places. The university shouldn't have any paparazzi in as it is off limits due to the Prince," he said.

"Cool, bye," I said.

We walked into the building, and I couldn't help but feel like everyone was watching me. "Hey Megan, call me paranoid but people are staring."

Megan looked around the university and nodded, "Yes, but get used to it girl," she said bluntly.

I suppose she had a point, if I was going to stay with Alex I would have to get used to it. "I guess so," I whispered.

"Are you working tonight?"

"Yeah, five until eight, pretty easy shift. I need to ask if I can switch my shift on a Wednesday. I may have to suck it up and work Sunday. I hate Sunday shifts."

I laughed. "Subway?"

"I'm not going to turn food down," she said.

We queued for Subway, getting our order. The line was thankfully short, so after a few minutes, we managed to find a table near the corner and sit down. We both started eating, and I tried to not let the staring bother me. I had to get used to it.

"His sister gave me a friendship bracelet. She's my new best friend," I told Megan.

"What? You can't replace me."

"Sure I can. She gave me a bracelet. When have you ever given me a bracelet?" I raised an eyebrow.

"I give you endless entertainment duh."

I laughed. She had me there. Megan certainly did give me endless entertainment.

We finished eating our Subway.

Before we knew it, it was time for our lecture.

I could get through it. I just needed to tell myself that everything was good.

People weren't staring.

I could pretend to be invisible, even if I wasn't.

# Chapter Twenty-Four

## ALEXANDER

Mind-numbing.

That was what the week was like.

I still had two full days left of it. At least tomorrow was the polo game, so I had a bit of a reprieve from it.

Ugh, I missed Ella.

My phone had been confiscated by my mother and father during all meetings so I would focus. I knew a punishment would come, but I didn't realise the punishment would be taking my phone away, so I have to pay attention.

I tapped my hand on my leg, hoping this meeting would soon be over.

I had to wonder if the people around the table found these conversations stimulating or boring like me.

As I looked around the table, I noticed them all staring at me.

*Shit.*

What were they talking about?

"Erm, could you repeat that?" I asked with a small smile.

"We were just talking about being finished for the day, your Highness," John, one of the members of the board, said. "We were going to ask if you were okay with that?"

I smiled. "Yes."

"Oh, thank God," I heard someone mumble. I turned to see Tessa who had slapped a hand over her mouth. "I am so sorry. I did not mean to say that out loud. I apologise, your Highness. I meant no disrespect."

"Disrespect?" I asked, raising an eyebrow. I looked around the table, leaning my elbows on it.

They were all shifting uncomfortably.

"Do your meetings usually last this long?" They all looked down, and I groaned. "Why?" No one answered and I narrowed my eyes. "Tessa. Why have these meetings lasted so long if they usually don't?"

"Well, your Highness, we figured the reason you came to the meetings this week was because you wanted to know everything."

I bit my lip to try and keep myself from insulting my father in this circumstance. I let out a small laugh. "No. I'm going to be blunt when I say this. I could think of much better ways to spend my time. You guys have this all wrapped up usually much earlier than this?"

"Usually within two hours, three at the most," John admitted. "Your father did request that you were to be here all day."

I rolled my eyes.

*Of course he did.*

"How about we do normal meetings for Thursday and

Friday? We can just pretend that we've been here all day." I offered.

They all nodded with relief.

"Great." I grinned. "Thanks. I need to go and see my girl." I stood up and walked out of the room.

I walked out the building and saw Jones' car ready and waiting. I got into the car as he opened the door.

"To Ella's please, Jones."

He nodded, shutting the door.

A few moments later, he began driving.

I couldn't wait to finally see Ella. I had missed her so badly. God, I was attached and obsessed.

After a couple of hours of driving, we arrived outside her house. I got out of the car, knocking on the door.

A few seconds later, the door opened.

Ella's mum stood there.

"Hi, Ms. Brown."

Although I knew her name, I wasn't about to call her by it. Not when I knew she hated me.

"I warned you about hurting my girl." She glared at me.

"With all due respect ma'am, I wouldn't say I hurt her. I'd call it a blip in the road," I defended myself. "Ella and I are on good terms."

Elena scoffed and opened the door, letting me in. I followed her and as I did I heard Ella talking to herself. "Stupid idiot. Can't even text. Stupid parliament making him work."

"Melinda," her mum said, shaking her head. "I know you're annoyed, but don't take it out on the ice cream."

"He hasn't even texted me, mum. I'm like one of those annoying girls you want to slap." She groaned.

I couldn't help but smile. Ella definitely did hate showing her emotions, but it made me smile when she did.

"Anyway, who was at the door?"

"If you actually turned around, then you would know," she said.

Ella groaned. "I can't believe you're making me move." I heard the bowl be put onto the table.

I appeared next to Elena.

"Alex!" She climbed up over the sofa.

I rushed forward as she began to fall and grabbed her before she could hit the floor.

"I missed you!" She hugged me tightly.

I noticed Elena walking away and rolling her eyes. She really did hate me and my relationship with her daughter. I just hoped she would come around because Ella was forever.

"My girl missed me," I said, holding onto her tightly before sitting us both down on the sofa.

She moved her legs, so she was straddling me. She reached back for her ice cream, and I couldn't help but laugh a little.

"Did you go to class today?"

She shook her head. "I lost all free will," she said, taking a spoonful of ice cream.

"Sorry I couldn't text. I still don't have my phone. My father has been interfering to keep me away," I admitted.

"It's fine, baby," she said.

I smiled a little at the pet name. Anything was better than potato, that was for sure.

"You warned me. I just didn't realise how much I would miss you." She reached for another spoonful of ice cream and offered it to me.

I took the spoon and inserted it into my mouth, eating the ice cream. "Ice cream has been comforting."

I laughed. She placed the tub on the floor resting her head on my chest, I kissed her head holding her tight. "Ella, can I stay the night? We can travel back to London tomorrow."

She nodded, reaching for the blanket and wrapping it around us.

I could stay here forever.

She let out a yawn, and I smiled a little. "You want me to take you to bed?"

"I'm not tired, I'm comfortable," she said.

I couldn't tell if she was lying or whether she was actually tired.

"So, what happens at the game tomorrow?"

"You will sit by the track and watch us play. It's one of the nicer events you get to attend," I told her softly. "Mother said Megan is coming?"

Ella let out a small laugh. "She made a complete and utter fool of herself with your mother, she curtsied and fell down. It was interesting," she said. I couldn't help but chuckle. I could just imagine how amused that made my mother. I kind of wish I could have seen all of their faces.

"It was one of those moments I wish we had cameras in this house," she said.

"I bet. Dress appropriately though, please."

Her mouth dropped open. "When have I not?"

"I'm talking about Megan, Ella," I told her, shaking my head.

"Oh." She sat up removing her head from my chest and looked at me with a little smile, "Can I tell you a secret?"

"I'm listening."

"I think I love you."

My heart stopped.

"Actually, I don't *think* I love you. I *know* I love you."

I crashed my lips onto hers and deepened the kiss immediately. I had wanted to hear those words from her ever since I said them to her.

*She loved me.*

She pulled away resting her forehead against mine. "I love you, and I'm all in."

"I love you, too."

"Thank you for being so patient with me since I discovered who you were. I know it hasn't been easy, being in a little bit of a limbo but thank you."

"Ella, I love you and our bubble. I'd wait forever if it meant I'd be able to hold onto these moments," I told her honestly.

"Do you want to watch a film upstairs? In a bed, where it will definitely be more comfortable."

I nodded.

She went to climb off my lap, and I held her tighter. "Let me carry you."

She wrapped her arms around my neck, and I lifted her princess-style. I headed up the stairs, and Ella directed me into her bedroom. I shut the door behind us and laid her down softly on the bed.

I looked around her room and grinned. "This is exactly how I imagined your bedroom."

She leaned up on her elbows, raising an eyebrow. "You imagined my bedroom?"

I nodded, not elaborating anymore. Her space was filled with photos of her best friend, and her work spread all over a desk.

One of the things I loved about her was her work ethic.

"So, since you're avoiding that question...do you want to explain to me why you have the guards? I thought you said I wouldn't have them," she said.

I smiled sheepishly. "I thought I had escaped the lecture."

My mother said she took it well when she suggested it, but clearly she was waiting to try and argue it out with me. It wasn't my mother's order either. It was mine, but I didn't think I wanted to admit that to Ella. "Ella, you could argue until you are blue in the face, but believe me it does nothing. They will be staying. That is the end of that discussion."

She stayed silent for a moment, and I had to wonder if she was gearing up ready for an argument or if she was going to accept it. She was keeping me on my toes that was for sure. "Okay."

My mouth dropped open in surprise. "Didn't think it would go that way."

"Well, I thought about arguing with you but at the end of the day I'm wasting my breath," she said, rolling her eyes.

I kicked off my shoes and stripped my suit off, leaving me in just boxers. I got into bed with her.

She laid on my chest as she began to flicker through Netflix, looking for something to watch.

As she clicked on a film, I rested my head against hers and found myself falling to sleep easily with the girl I loved in my arms.

---

I rolled over and coldness hit my chest.

I cracked an eye open.

*Ella wasn't here.*

Is this how she felt when I left her in my bed?

I looked around for my phone and let out a groan when I remembered it was still in London.

I really must remember to get my phone back.

I looked around Ella's room and couldn't see anything with the time on it. I flipped the covers off and looked on the floor to see a pair of my joggers. I narrowed my eyes.

*Was Ella stealing my clothes?*

I slipped them on and headed downstairs. As I started coming down the stairs, I saw Ella and Megan in the living room. I could hear them talking about something to do with men.

I stood at the living room door and saw that they were watching ex on the beach. "You actually watch this crap?"

Ella's head spun around, and her eyes stayed on my chest.

I couldn't help but smile from my own amusement.

My girl really didn't hide her lust well, but I loved it. "You finished staring, Ella? You can take a picture if you want."

"Shut up," she mumbled, blushing.

I noticed Megan was eyeing me up, too.

I looked at Ella as she grabbed my hand, pulling me to sit on the sofa and placing herself in front of me.

"Roar," Megan teased doing a clawing motion with her hand. "Don't worry, he's all yours, but it doesn't mean I can't stare."

"Actually it does," she said flatly.

"Shh." She waved her hand turning back to the television.

"I love you, Ella," I whispered in her ear. She turned slightly in my arms and kissed me softly. "I suppose I can watch this shit if it means I get to stare at my beautiful girl."

"Swoon," Megan said, waving her hand in front of her face.

I let out a laugh.

I really liked Megan. She reminded me so much of Jeremy. It was hilarious.

By the end of it, I was glued. She was right. This shit was addictive. "Not bad for shit huh?" She teased.

A few hours later, a knock on the door made us all jump. "What's the time?"

Ella reached for her phone, and I looked at the time. "Shit. We're going to be late. I bet that's Jones."

I climbed off the sofa, heading towards the door and seeing Jones standing there.

He looked at me disapprovingly as he handed me clothes and my phone. "Thank you, Jones."

"Please hurry, sir. We don't need to be late."

I nodded, shutting the door. I looked in the living

room, seeing Ella and Megan had gone. I quickly changed into the jeans and shirt that Jones had provided leaving Ella with the joggers she had stolen. I ran a hand through my hair and made my way upstairs and I could hear them talking. "Come on girls, we're going to be late."

"What does one wear to a polo game?"

I rounded the door, seeing Ella standing in her underwear and I grinned. "Not that baby girl, you look sexy." I pressed a kiss to her neck and started to suck on her neck, leaving her a love bite. I pulled away and grinned.

I was impressed with my little mark on her.

"Anything, Ella. Whatever you're comfortable in."

She reached for leggings and a black top that said something about adulting. She got dressed, and I smiled. "You look beautiful."

I tapped my phone screen, looking at the time.

We were definitely going to be late.

"Where did you get that picture?" I looked to see Ella concentrating on my screensaver which was a picture of us from the ball.

"Mother got a few, and I also asked the photographers for copies."

"Send them to me. I want those photos," she said.

I nodded. "I'll send them to you in the car. Go find Megan. We're already late." I bent down, kissing her.

I headed out the house to the car where Jones was looking disapprovingly. "Yes, we're late. I know."

He chuckled as I got into the car tapping my foot as I waited for Ella and Megan to come out.

# Chapter Twenty-Five

## MELINDA

I couldn't stop staring at the photos from the ball. It was amazing how much you could tell from the look on our faces how in love we were.

They were my new favourite photos.

"You're so in love it's gross." Megan said, sitting next to me under the heater.

I don't know why they decided to have an outdoor polo match in November. It was freezing. No amount of wrapping up in the coat and being stuck under this heater would make us warmer.

"I'm regretting that love right now," I admitted. "I'm freezing."

"All these people look like snotty rich people that have a stick up their ass," she muttered.

I chuckled. "They are rich and probably stuck up," I said quietly.

"El!" I turned looking around knowing there was only

one person that called me that. I looked to see Elizabeth, running through the crowd and jumping into my lap.

I hugged her tightly. “I missed you!”

“I missed you, too,” I said. “Elizabeth, this is my friend Megan.”

“Hi,” she said.

I watched as Megan sat there dumbfounded while Elizabeth spoke to her about everything and anything.

Megan looked at me and let out a sigh. “I just had a brilliant idea!”

“What?” I asked wearily.

“We should have been his cheerleaders.” She laughed.

“That would have been hilarious. One of your better ideas, I’ll give you that. Next time, I’m pretty sure I can convince the little one to help, too.”

“You could at least watch.” I turned to see Alex on a horse with a stick of some sort in his hand. “You know, be a supportive girlfriend.”

“Is someone jealous that their baby sister is getting my attention?” I teased. I stood up, kissing him. “Go win, baby. Then, you can have my attention.”

He laughed as he trotted off on the horse.

I sat and watched the game. I had no idea how it went or what the purpose of it was.

Elizabeth was telling me stories, and I couldn’t help but laugh at some of them.

The game ended, and I believed Alex won, but I still wasn’t sure.

Megan had left me to go and get a drink.

I stood up as Alex walked over, and he wrapped an arm around me. “What did you think?” He asked.

"Did you win?" I asked curiously.

He laughed, pressing his lips to mine.

I smiled against his lips, deepening the kiss. "We did. I'm going to have to teach you the game. Where did Megan go?"

I looked over to the bar where I saw Megan being chatted up by somebody. "Who is that?" I asked curiously.

"He's a good guy if that's what you're asking me. He won't do anything to hurt her," he said.

"That wasn't my—" I paused. "Never mind."

Alex chuckled.

The conversation ended as some people came over.

I stood next to him as he spoke.

I couldn't stop watching Megan and the other bloke though. I couldn't help but be a little protective over her. After the shit she had been through the past few weeks, she didn't need to be hurt again.

She came over a second later, handing me a drink. "Who was that?" I asked curiously.

"Some guy. He tried to hit on me. He was funny. I'll give him that. He's hot, too," she said. She turned around, and as quickly as she did, she looked at me. "He's coming over right now."

I looked just in time to see him pull Alex in for what I could only describe as a bro hug.

I looked at them both.

"Jeremy, I would like you to meet my girlfriend, Melinda, and her best friend, who you already hit on, Megan. Ella and Megan, I'd like for you to officially meet one of my oldest and best friends, Jeremy."

"Jerk," Megan muttered, making me laugh.

"Nice to meet you. Please stop hitting on my friend," I said.

"Megan, what a beautiful name. How about you give me your number?" Jeremy asked, looking straight passed me.

I rolled my eyes, burying my head in Alex's chest.

I'd give the man ten out of ten for trying. He was really aiming to get shot down every time.

"Any plans for the rest of the day, Ella?" Alex asked curiously.

I looked at Megan who was already looking at me. "No," we said in unison.

"I was asking my girlfriend," Alex frowned.

"How about a double date?" Jeremy suggested.

"I don't know if you can handle me bruising your ego for the rest of the day," Megan teased.

"That seems like a challenge," he said.

"Bring it." She grinned.

"Daisy's?" I offered.

Megan and Alex nodded. Jeremy shrugged; it sounded like he really didn't care where we ended up, as long as he could carry on talking to Megan.

It took a few hours to get to Daisy's, I pushed open the door seeing Daisy and Daphne working at the front of house and noticed Chef at the back in the kitchen.

We sat in the booth and I grabbed the menu laying it out in front of Alex and I. "Hello, welcome to Daisy's," Daphne said.

I couldn't help but chuckle.

"I know it's weird."

We reeled our orders off, including drinks and food and Daphne went off putting the order into the kitchen.

I leaned my head on Alex's shoulder as I watched Jeremy and Megan interact. Alex took his hand in mine and began to trace small circles on the top of my hand.

I reached up with my spare hand, playing with his necklace. "This is nice," I mumbled.

"It is. Although, I miss our bubble," Alex complained. "I really hope people aren't posting pictures."

I turned his arm to face him and pressed my lips to his. "I don't care if everyone can see me kiss you or be with you. That means everyone knows that you are mine, Prince Alexander," I said resting my head against his.

He pulled a face, and I laughed.

"I hate hearing you call me Prince Alexander. It's so formal, and you are anything but formal to me," he said.

"I love you, Alex," I whispered.

"Get a room," I heard Megan tease.

I looked at them both and buried my head in Alex's chest. I couldn't help but blush.

"It's amazing how she thinks it's going to protect her," Megan chuckled.

I turned to face her, sticking my middle finger up at her.

"Tut tut, future whatever you are going to be," Megan said tutting.

"Queen," Jeremy said. "She'll be the Queen."

"What?" I asked, shocked.

I spun around to stare at Alex who looked amused.

"You mean if we...?" I trailed off.

Alex looked at me hesitantly and then shot a glare at

Jeremy. "You don't need to think about that just yet," he said.

"But it's a possibility?" I asked.

"Possibly." He sighed. He looked at Jeremy and pointed at him. "I should really give you a list of topics that you aren't allowed to mention."

"How was I meant to know that you haven't even mentioned Queen to the girl?"

If not for the shocking statements, I could have found this funny instead of terrifying. None of that even entered my mind as a possibility. I mean, I was dating a Prince. I was in love with a Prince. Of course if we went all the way, I'd end up with a title, too.

Food was served and there was no talking as we ate in a comfortable silence. We finished, and Megan grinned. "Chef!" She shouted.

A second later, Chef popped his head out.

"Can we have two more bowls of chips?" She asked, batting her eyelashes.

"Of course." He chuckled.

Megan grinned to show she was proud of herself.

I fist-bumped her, making her chuckle.

She looked at Jeremy and raised an eyebrow. "What? Have you never seen a girl eat so much? Well, let's face it, you probably haven't. I bet you only date sticks."

I couldn't help but laugh. She was really teasing him, and he didn't seem the least bit phased by it.

"I like girls with curves, too," he said, looking her up and down.

She scoffed. "Please these aren't curves, it's pure fat.

This is how I'm going to live my life, so you may as well give up now because I'm going to become fat and lazy."

I laughed and high fived her. "Amen to us being fat." I grinned.

"You're not fat, Ella," Alex said, rolling his eyes.

"Here you are, girls." I looked up, seeing Chef bringing the plates down in front of Megan and I.

Chef looked from us to the boys sitting next to us. "And who might you be?"

"Alex," he said, holding his hand out.

Chef shook his hand. "Nice to meet you."

"You too," he said. He looked at Jeremy, "And you?"

"Jeremy, his best friend," Jeremy said. "Currently trying my luck with this one." He nodded his head towards Megan.

"And failing miserably," Megan chuckled.

"Those are my girls." Chef chuckled.

"You are so good to us." Megan grinned.

Chef nodded, walking away and back into the kitchen.

We carried on eating.

As soon as we finished eating, I pushed the plate to the side. "I'm kind of glad I have an employee discount because I cannot afford to keep eating out," I muttered, shaking my head.

Megan scoffed. "Girl you aren't eating that much, you're dropping weight."

I frowned slightly, I didn't think I'd drop that much weight. I knew I hadn't eaten much or regularly but weight wise I had stabled I think. I didn't make any choices to know my weight it wasn't something I wanted to fixate on.

"Where does your money even go?"

"Where most money goes for bills." I sighed.

I noticed Jeremy looking at Alex with a little frown. "You don't have money?"

"I mean I have it, but then, it goes away," I said, pursing my lips. "I don't like talking about money. It makes people sound superficial."

"No wonder Alex likes you," Jeremy said.

"If we get to that point, I know she'll be a fantastic Queen. Honestly, it's one of the things I look for in someone I want to date. They don't have to be right for me. They have to be right for my world for what they could become."

I looked at him. "What are you passionate about?" I pulled my knees to my chest, lying my head on my knees and looking at him.

"Other than horses?" He asked. "I want to show you something. What are your plans after this?"

I looked at Megan and she shrugged, "I'm going to sleep."

"Erm, nothing," I said. "I guess I'm all yours, boyfriend."

We finished eating and paying the bill.

Alex led me to the car, and I waved goodbye to Megan as she headed home.

"To the farm please, Jones."

I looked at Alex. "I am not dressed for a farm. I need wellies."

"You can borrow some," he said, rolling his eyes.

"What are we doing there?" I asked curiously.

"You'll see," he said vaguely.

A couple of hours later, we arrived at our destination. He helped me out of the car, wrapping an arm around me.

"This is my thing," he said. "I save wild animals and the centre here helps rehabilitate animals. I got Rocky from here, so on my rare free days, I like to come here and help them. This is a huge part of my world."

I smiled, leaning up to kiss him. "Show me."

He grabbed my hand and pulled me gently towards the farm.

It was a lot different than the ranch. The ranch was calmer and more peaceful where the farm was active and busy, there were many people doing different jobs. Some were mucking out stalls, milking cows and lambs, it was interesting to see a working farm.

He walked us through the horses, and he handed me a pair of wellies. I kicked off my Ugg boots and slipped the wellies on.

"Do you mind getting messy?" He asked.

I shook my head.

He pulled me outside the barn. "I wonder where everyone is." He pulled me into another barn and this barn was busier than the other one.

"Hello, your Highness," the woman said.

"Hi, this is my girlfriend, Melinda. Ella, this is Courtney. She's one of the vets that work here," Alex explained.

"You may want to move back," she said, waving her hand. "The mare is about to give birth."

I stepped back, listening to her. I did not need to be getting horse baby goo on me.

Although, I was curious to see a horse being born. It

definitely wasn't every day that someone got to see something that special.

We watched as the horse gave birth, and I couldn't help but be disturbed. "That is absolutely disgustingly gross."

Alex laughed. "That's life. The circle of life, one day you will have to give birth, I mean probably not as gross and in a hospital, but it's life. Life is precious."

"Pro-life for you I see," I said. "Do you agree with abortions?"

"Melinda, I'm not stupid enough to answer that question." He laughed.

"So, that's a no?"

He raised an eyebrow and pulled me away from the others, so they couldn't hear us. "You aren't going to let this go are you?"

"Nope. I feel like we need to have this conversation just in case something ever pops up in the future. I need to know your views," I told him.

"I don't have a uterus, so no opinion," he said.

I couldn't help but be surprised by his view.

"Not the answer you were expecting?" He asked, raising an eyebrow. "Ella, how can I, a man, tell a woman that she has to keep a baby that she may not want? There are enough unwanted children in this world. What is the point of bringing an unwanted child into the world?"

"So, now the horse giving birth has scarred me for life, what's next?"

"Drama queen," he rolled his eyes.

We walked around the farm.

I loved how passionate Alex was about it all, and the

way his eyes lit up when he was doing even the simplest of jobs.

We stayed at the farm for the majority of the night before he took us back home.

I kissed him good night and entered the house. My head was pounding and all I could put it down to was lack of sleep.

I walked into the kitchen, seeing a letter for myself and opening it.

I scanned it, reading a statement from the credit card company.

Only another eight grand left to pay.

I could do this.

I could clear the debt without their help.

I headed upstairs stripping into pyjamas. I pulled the quilt closer to me as I felt myself begin to shake.

God, I was cold.

Alex and his polo game had a lot to answer for. If I was getting sick because of it, I really was going to kill him. I found myself almost falling asleep until I heard a voice.

"Oh good, you're home."

I cracked open an eye and flinched from the light, "mum?"

"You're never home anymore, Mel. I'm missing you. I know we have our differences," she said.

I tried to sit up, but I felt too weak.

I stood up, wincing in pain. The room spun, and I blinked a few times, trying to focus on my mum.

Everything was blurry.

I blinked again trying to focus.

Then, I dropped to the floor as everything went black.

# Chapter Twenty-Six

## ALEXANDER

I had never driven so fast before, not even at the tracks.

I was just thankful I hadn't even gotten halfway to London before I got the call from Elena that Ella had passed out and was heading to the hospital.

I tapped my fingers on the steering wheel, trying to think.

She looked fine today, tired but fine. She hadn't said anything about feeling poorly.

I pulled up at the hospital, jumping out of the car. "I'll call you," I told Jones.

I really admired Jones for one reason, and he knew when to not get in my way. And for that, he was always going to be my number one guard.

I ran into the hospital, heading to the accident and emergency department. I knew many people were turning to look, but I didn't care or that mattered was Ella. "Hi, where can I find Melinda Brown?"

"You can visit—" the woman looked up from the computer, and her eyes widened. "Oh my God. Erm, your Highness. I apologise. Erm, what was the name again?"

"Melinda Brown." I had no bother about using my title and privilege to get me in to see her. I wouldn't be able to concentrate without knowing she was okay.

"Follow me."

I followed the lady. and she brought me to a room, I opened the door and walked in. Ella was lying on the bed and throwing up into a bowl. "Ella." I rushed to her side holding her hair as she threw up.

She finished throwing up, and a nurse came and took the bowl away from her.

"Are you okay?"

She crinkled her eyebrows in confusion. "What are you doing here?"

"Ella, you got rushed to hospital. There is nowhere else I'd rather be," I told her, sitting on the bed. "What happened? You seemed fine all day."

"I had a headache. I blame Megan's ridiculous early wake up call," she shrugged. "The room started spinning, and my vision went a little blurry. The next thing I know, I wake up here with the worst headache ever. I felt like a hippo sat on me."

"A hippo?" Elena said.

"Yeah, I feel like it's quite a heavy animal, and you'd get a headache if they sat on you," she said.

I took a deep breath in, shaking my head slightly. I had to wonder where Ella's mind was sometimes. "What has the doctor said?"

"I don't know. I was asleep," Ella said in a duh tone.

"They're running some tests to see what the cause of her passing out was," Elena said. "They've just taken her blood. They are making sure she has no concussion, and then I'm pretty sure they'll let us go home."

I nodded. "You didn't feel sick last night?" I asked her again.

"Nope." She shook my head. "The only thing that made me feel sick was that horse giving birth, still scarred for life."

I laughed. "Miracle of life, Ella." I couldn't get the picture of her face out of my head. It made me wish I had a camera that I could have taken a photo of that moment.

"Potato, potato," she said with a small grin.

The door to the hospital room opened again, and I looked to see the doctor enter. "Melinda, we are just waiting for your blood test results to come back, but we're pretty confident that the lack of fluids is running you down. I'd recommend rest and drink plenty of water."

"Thank you," Ella said.

"You can be discharged, and you can go home," he said.

The doctor left the room, and I pulled my phone out of my pocket, checking the time. It was 2:00 a.m. and I knew that meant waking up for meetings tomorrow well today would kill me.

"Alex, you should go," Ella said.

I frowned. "Ella no—"

"Alex, you have meetings in a few hours. You still have to get back to London. You're going to be way too tired. I'm fine, I promise," she said.

I shook my head.

"Mum, can you give us a minute?" Ella asked, looking at her mum.

The door opened and shut again. I never took my eyes off her. She climbed onto my lap wrapping her arms around my neck. "I'm fine, Alex."

I rested my head on her forehead. "You worried me, Ella. I hated getting that phone call."

"I didn't mean to worry you," she said softly. "Also, I need you to take care of yourself, too. Are you driving back or is Jones driving you?"

"Jones is driving us back. I mean, I'd say if he's finished throwing up," I said sheepishly.

"Throwing up?" She asked, confused.

"I may have broken several if not most road laws to get here," I said quietly.

She shook her head. "Well good job. You're royal and probably will never get arrested for it. Seriously Alex, I am fine, but you need to go home. You're going to be so tired, you need to take care of yourself."

I snorted. "Pot, kettle, black."

"Point taken."

I pressed my lips to hers, kissing her. "I love you, Ella."

"I love you, too. Seriously go. Message me when you get home please." I nodded, giving her one more kiss.

God, I was addicted to her.

I stood up, pressing another kiss to her lips.

"Go." She pushed me away.

"Message me if you need anything, ok? I will get you whatever you need," I told her.

She nodded and waved goodbye to me as I walked out the room.

I found Elena talking to a man, and the conversation looked intense. I bypassed her, not bothering to say bye.

I headed towards the front of the hospital. It took me five minutes before I found Jones waiting by the car.

"How is she, Sir?"

"She's okay. Apparently, she's dehydrated and overworked. Hopefully she will take it as a warning to slow down," I said, biting my lip.

Jones let out a sigh. "Oh, Sir. You have much to learn when it comes to females."

I got into the car, ignoring his comment, because deep down he was right.

I also knew Ella would have no intention of resting. I also couldn't force her to stay rested. I wasn't sure how well she would take to kidnapping. Probably not well. I mean, I could try.

I shook my head.

*No Alex, that wasn't the answer.*

I looked at my phone seeing the photo of Ella and I from the ball. I loved how we looked at each other in these photos. I was fighting every part of me to not go back and stay by Ella's side.

The trip back home was faster than normal. Although, I suppose it helped that it was the middle of the night. Jones pulled up, and he got out of the car, opening the door, "Thank you, Jones."

"Good night, Sir."

I entered the palace.

"Alexander?"

"Mother," I said, following her voice into one of the many living areas. "Why are you still awake?"

"You were meant to be back a few hours ago. "Have you been racing?"

"No."

"Alexander, what have I said about racing?"

"Mother, I haven't been racing. Ella got rushed into hospital. I went back to see her," I said. "She passed out and 999 said to take her to the hospital."

"Is she okay?" Mother asked, standing up and rushing to my side.

I let out a yawn. "Yeah, apparently she was just dehydrated, so she needs rest. They took some blood, and she'll get her test results soon. I'm going to sleep. I'm beat."

"I love you, Alexander."

"Love you, too."

---

My alarm was blaring way too early for my liking.

I groaned, turning it off. I slipped out of bed, getting ready.

And before I knew it, I was back in parliament listening to their agenda for today. I pulled my phone out of my pocket, sending a text to Ella to see how she was feeling.

I stared at the message, waiting for a response, but it still said delivered.

"So, we'll stay for an hour and discuss what to add to the next meeting, and then we're done for the day," John said.

I couldn't help but roll my eyes.

What a waste of a day.

I could have stayed in bed or gone to the farm again. I wanted to check on the foal that was born last night.

I felt my phone buzz and looked at the message.

It was from Ella.

I'm good. Do some work, baby xx

I rolled my eyes.

The fact she thought I could focus on work right now instead of her really blew my mind.

I looked at the people in front of me. "I'm really sorry, but I'm going to have to leave right now. Something has come up. Thank you so much," I said, standing up. I walked out of the building, going straight to Jones and getting into the car. "To the farm, Jones. I need a day away from all this."

"Certainly, sir."

"Wake me up when we get there," I said, putting the belt on and reaching for the blanket.

I closed my eyes.

I needed to catch up on sleep because I was too tired.

Far too quick, we had arrived at the farm and Jones had woken me up.

I headed over to the stables, walking in and picking up a brush instantly to brush the horses.

If I wasn't a prince, I think I'd become a vet or work with animals. There was something so peaceful about animals. They were beautiful, honest creatures and in their world, there were no worries, and that was what I loved about them the most.

# Chapter Twenty-Seven

## MELINDA

A week had passed by since I passed out.

I still hadn't heard back from the doctors about my blood test, so I was assuming no news was good news.

I had blurred vision every so often, but I just put it down to being tired.

I snuggled into Alex.

We were currently lying in a pick up truck and looking at the stars. It was such a simple perfect date, and I loved him for that. Snacks, drinks, and him. It was what I needed.

"This is perfect," I told him.

"You think time can just stop?" He asked.

"I wish," I whispered. "If time could stop, I would love to hold some of our bubble moments."

"Hmm, does slapping me count as a bubble moment?" He asked with a chuckle.

I laughed. "The first one you did and didn't deserve," I

admitted. "You shouldn't have kissed me during a freak out. I was rambling and getting my head round the boy I liked being a Prince. What did you think it was going to be like Cinderella? If so, you picked the wrong girl. I'm not Cinderella."

"No, you're better," he said.

He kissed me sweetly, and I couldn't help but smile. He rolled me on my back gently and deepened the kiss. His lips left my mouth, and he started kissing down my neck.

I was breathing heavily, I could feel his erection pressed against the top of my thigh.

I couldn't help but laugh. I loved feeling how turned on he was. This would be the first time we had been intimate since I had discovered the truth about who he was.

"Not here. Not now."

I rolled my eyes.

He narrowed his eyes. "Maybe I should start spanking you every time you roll your eyes at me."

"Ooo, I'm scared," I mocked.

He reached over, pushing me down gently and turning me over before. He gave me a small smack on my bum.

I bit my lip trying to keep from laughing, and this was the man that wanted to wait for us to sleep together again.

"Maybe you'll think twice before rolling your eyes at me again."

I scoffed. "Catch me if you can." I looked him directly in the eye and rolled my eyes at him.

Now I knew it would annoy him. I was only going to do it even more.

He reached over, pressing his hands into my sides.

I squealed as he began to tickle me. I tried to get away.

"Not so cocky now are you, baby?" He whispered in my ear.

I pressed my lips to his and deepened the kiss, I pulled away biting his lip gently and he let out a moan. "You sure you don't want us to have sex?"

"Ella, we are not having sex outside in the cold," he said flatly.

I rolled my eyes and a few moments later I felt a smack on my bottom. He climbed out the truck and held his hand out for me. "Where are we going?"

"It's cold, so I'm thinking a drive thru is calling our name," he laughed.

I took his hand as he helped me off. I could get behind that. We got into the car heading straight for McDonalds. We sat in the car park as we both ate our Big Macs and shared a box of chicken nuggets.

If this is how love was going to be for the rest of my life, I could get behind it.

Alex drove us back home, and I looked to see the house in darkness.

Mum was probably with him again.

We got out of the car and headed straight upstairs. After I locked the door, he sat on my bed as I did a quick look to see if anyone else was in the house.

"Mum?" I called out.

I knocked on her door, pushing it open seeing she wasn't there. So it meant she was with him.

I headed back into the bedroom, shutting the door and turning to look at Alex who was sitting up on my bed.

I crawled towards him, my lips coming into contact with his.

Alex took over the kiss, making it rougher as I rested on his legs. He let out a moan, and it was the hottest sound ever. It brought me back to our first night together before the whole truth spilled about who he was.

I pulled away, resting my forehead against his.

"Ella," Alex said, brushing my hair out of my face.

"Do I need to beg for you to fuck me?" I asked pouting.

He rolled his eyes.

"You're allowed to roll your eyes, but I get spanked," I said flatly.

"The last time we slept together shit blew up, Ella," he said softly. "You know it was a good night and morning and then blew up because you discovered who I was."

"Well, you have no more secrets that could blow it up, so I think we'd be okay," I told him softly. I pressed small kisses to his neck. "Please."

He grabbed me by the waist and flipped us over, lying me down on the bed, "How can I refuse you?"

I let out a laugh as he began to undress me. He slipped a finger inside my pussy, and I moaned. He gently sucked my clit as I gripped onto his hair and pulled on it. He pressed small kisses down my body as he reached my pussy. I could feel my orgasm building. His fingers moved faster and harder.

"Alex." I moaned.

I wrapped my legs around his neck. I stiffened as I felt myself coming.

He pressed little kisses up my stomach and chest, my

legs loosened dropping to his waist as his lips finally touched mine. "You taste delicious, Ella."

I giggled. "My turn, Prince," I whispered, kissing his lips. I pushed him back on the bed, climbing on top of him. "I like this position. But you, my Prince, are far too dressed for my liking." I began to undress him, throwing all of his clothes on the floor. I shimmied down his body as my pussy glided over his dick.

He groaned, holding my arms. "Oh, no."

I shook my head.

"You teased me. My turn." I moved down, taking his dick into my mouth and sucking on it gently.

He gripped my hair and pulled my head further down taking his dick all the way into my mouth as it touched the back of my throat. I tapped his leg, and he pulled me back up.

I took a breath and stared at him.

"You have no gag reflex, interesting." He chuckled.

He pushed me to lay down and climbed on top of me. His dick entered me, and I moaned. He felt so big.

"Fuck." I wrapped my arms around his neck and kissed him. I had expected him to go hard and fast, but instead, he was going slow.

"Look at me, Ella," he ordered.

I did as he said. Once my eyes met his, I couldn't look away. I was falling deep and fast. I stroked his face and kissed him again. I felt my orgasm coming, so I gripped him tightly.

I stiffened as I came on his dick. I let go of him and looked at him. "This feels so right."

"Do you think you can orgasm a third time?"

I moved my hips grinding on his dick.

He groaned.

"I want you to fuck me hard, Alex."

"With pleasure baby," he said. He held onto me as he kneeled and pressed me down onto the bed. He pulled his cock out slowly, and I moaned. As he reached my opening, he pushed all the way back into me, making me moan loudly. "You feel so good, Ella," He pressed his lips to mine and kissed me again. "I'm going to fuck you, so hold onto me."

I wrapped my arms around his neck. He began to move his dick inside me going hard and fast as he did. I clutched onto him, moaning.

Alex was groaning in my ear, and it made me hornier. I was beginning to thrust with him, meeting him halfway. I crashed my lips onto his as I raked my hands through his hair, pulling it. I could feel my orgasm building. "Alex, *fuck*."

"Ella," he groaned out.

He pressed small kisses on my lips, and I smiled against his lips. I threw my head back as I felt a rush. My toes began to curl as I felt myself coming.

I held onto Alex tightly as I came apart around him. I could feel him still moving inside me. I rested my head on his chest as I felt him begin to move inside me again. I wrapped my arms around his neck. "I love you, Alex," I whispered in his ear.

As soon as I said the words, he began to stiffen inside me. I felt the intense rushing feeling come to me as we came together. He picked me up and turned us around. I fell onto his chest, and he wrapped his arms around me.

He still hadn't pulled out of me, and I had to admit, it felt nice just to lie there.

"I love you, too." He kissed me softly. "We better get you cleaned up. Wrap your arms around me." I did as he said.

He picked me up. As he did, he slipped out of me, and I giggled.

"What?"

"It feels funny." I chuckled.

He pushed open a door to the bathroom, and he switched on the shower. We stepped under it.

The hot water felt nice against my skin.

He grabbed a flannel and began to wash my body. He grabbed a shampoo bottle, handing it to me. I squirted it into my hand and began to wash my hair. As I was washing my hair, I began to watch Alex cleaning himself. I noticed that he was also hard again. Eventually, he realised I was watching him.

"You make me horny," he shrugged.

I washed the shampoo and conditioner out. I watched the soap suds fall down the drain. I bit my lip as I knelt on the shower floor.

Alex looked down at me, raising an eyebrow.

"It's my turn to play," I teased.

I dragged my nails down his chest as I moved to lay down in between his legs, I looked up at him as I wrapped my hand around his cock.

"Fuck, Ella," he moaned.

I wrapped my mouth around his cock and sucked him gently. Then, began to lick up and down his cock.

I heard him groan and saw him smile. He wrapped his

hands in my hand and pushed me further down his cock. "Take me in your throat, baby."

I took him further and further in before I felt him at the back of my throat. I loved the feeling of him. He held my head as he began to thrust into my mouth, I was pretty sure I could come without him even touching me. I could feel his thrusts getting shorter and more rapid, and eventually, he stiffened, coming in my mouth.

I pulled away, swallowing. He pulled me up, kissing me. I deepened the kiss.

"Fuck," he muttered.

I smiled against his lips.

I loved making him feel like this, the way he lost control. I loved it.

I stepped out of the shower and grabbed a towel, wrapping it around my body. I got another one for my hair.

He turned off the shower, stepping out and wrapping a towel around the lower half of his body. He held his hand out for me to take, and I did.

We made our way back to the bedroom.

He laid us on the bed as his hand caressed my back.

I laid there, enjoying the feeling of us finally being together with no secrets between us. I looked into his eyes as he stared at me and I smiled a little. "I love you, Alex."

"I love you, Ella."

# Chapter Twenty-Eight

## ALEXANDER

I thought nothing could beat waking up next to Ella, but waking up next to her after making love to her a few times during the night was a whole different feeling.

I pulled her to my chest, not wanting to let her go.

I could just imagine her rolling her eyes and calling me a caveman.

She was still fast asleep. I watched her, taking all of her in. She was beautiful, and she was mine.

I was surprised I hadn't heard anything from my father over her background check. I could only guess that meant there was nothing to find.

As I said, there wouldn't be.

My whole trust was put in Ella, and I believed she hadn't kept anything from me.

I reached for my phone, scrolling through TikTok making sure to keep the volume on low, so I didn't wake her up.

I felt her begin to stir after half an hour of scrolling.

She turned around in my arms.

"Good morning," I said, pressing a kiss on her forehead. "How are you feeling?"

"Good," she mumbled.

"Are you feeling sore?" I asked softly. "Do you need me to run you a bath?"

"A little sore, but nothing too unmanageable. I loved last night. It was much needed."

"Me too, Ella." I pressed my lips onto hers, and she deepened the kiss.

Almost instantly, my dick had started to get hard against her thigh. Her hand reached down between us, and I let out a groan as I felt her hand wrap around me. "Fuck."

She giggled as she slid down the bed. I pulled the covers off us as her tongue touched the tip of my dick. Her tongue swirled around the tip, teasing as she moved her hand up and down my length. She lowered her mouth down my length, taking the full thing I moaned her throat felt so fucking good.

She pulled back as she coughed. "Fuck." She took a breath before taking down to the base again as her hand wrapped gently around my balls, stroking them. I moaned and began to fuck her face, moving my hips to meet her, sucking my dick up and down.

I could feel my orgasm building. "Ella, I'm going to come. If you don't want me to come down your throat, you need to move," I warned her.

This only seemed to spur her on more, and she bobbed her head up and down.

I grabbed onto her hair, and she moaned against my dick.

"Fuck." I moaned as I felt myself coming.

I watched Ella swallow down every drop.

She pulled her head off my dick and slid up my body. I pulled her in for a kiss, and she deepened it immediately. "You're perfect."

She shook her head. "I'm not, but that was fun." She laid down next to me, breathing heavily.

"I think it's time I return the favour," I grinned, hovering over her.

She shook her head. "I'm feeling sore," she admitted. "I could really use that bath you offered to run."

I nodded, getting out of bed and pulling my pyjama bottoms. I headed to the bathroom and began running the bath. I squirted some bubble bath in and mixed the bubbles with the water. I walked back into her room, and she was covered in a towel. "Your bath is running." I bent down, kissing her head. "I'm going to make you some breakfast."

"Are you sure? My mum might be downstairs. She still dislikes you a little," she said, wincing.

I laughed. "Ella, you're in my life hopefully forever. I'll win your mum over, either that or die trying."

"It's your funeral," she said, rolling her eyes.

"Hopefully not." I kissed her once more before grabbing my phone and heading downstairs.

I may need Chef just in case.

I think I could remember all the lessons, but I wasn't sure.

I walked into the kitchen and began to look through

the fridge and cupboards. I pulled out tins of beans, tomatoes, sausage, bacon, and eggs. I placed them all on the side.

*I could make breakfast. This was going to be easy.*

I hoped.

I potted around the kitchen as I began to put the sausages into the oven letting them cook before I started to cook anything else.

"Who knew the prince actually knew how to cook?"

I turned around jumping slightly and saw Elena dressed for work leaning against the wall looking at me with a frown. "Erm, I learned recently, ma'am," I said. "I wanted to surprise Ella."

"Ella?"

"It's the nickname I have for your daughter," I explained.

Had Ella not told her mum much about us? It seemed like she was close with her mum.

"As in Cinderella?" She scoffed.

"No," I said, shaking my head. "My sister is called Elizabeth and I call her El, so it feels wrong to call Ella El, so she got Ella instead."

"Did you treat my daughter respectfully?" Elena asked.

"I always treat her respectfully," I said, my brows furrowing in confusion. "I'm sure if you would like any more information, you could ask your daughter, but for the respect of our relationship that is all I'm going to say on the matter," I said, shrugging.

I couldn't put my finger on this woman. For some reason, she hated me with a passion, which don't get me wrong I was used to, but it seemed like it was more than just the normal playboy Prince thing that was often shared in the media. No this hatred seemed deeper down and I couldn't put my finger on why. Forget the background check on Ella, maybe I needed one on her mother. "What's your problem?"

"I don't like you," she said, walking away from the kitchen.

I turned around checking on the sausages.

"Melinda, I'm going to work!" I heard the front door open, and she mumbled something before it closed again.

"Who shit in her cornflakes this morning?" Megan asked.

I jumped, spinning around.

Megan was doubled over in laughter.

"You fucking scared me," I said letting out a breath.

"Wow you scare easily." Megan laughed. She sat on the kitchen table resting her feet on the chair, "Ooo, you know how to cook, that's surprising."

"I learned recently. I wanted to make Ella breakfast in bed one morning," I said.

"Cute. Where is she anyway?"

"In the bath. She's sore," I said.

Megan squealed and my eyes widened as I realised what I had just said. "You slept together?!" She jumped off the table, running up the stairs. I heard her slam the door open.

Well so much for Ella having a relaxing bath.

*Did Melinda forget to tell Megan this was not the first time we slept together?*

I potted around the kitchen, preparing breakfast.

I guess for the three of us now, I would have to get used to Megan being around if I wanted to be with Ella.

I heard footsteps coming down the stairs just as I began to plate breakfast and they both entered the kitchen.

"How are you feeling, Ella?"

"Better, thank you," she said. I felt her come over, wrapping her arms around my waist and patting my chest. "Could have done without the Spanish Inquisition."

"I just said you were sore. Did you not tell her about our first time?" I asked with a chuckle. I turned around and pressed a kiss to her lips.

"Hmm, you're lucky I love you," she whispered against my lips.

"Ugh, I'm so single," I heard Megan groan.

"I made breakfast for us all," I told her.

"I'm doing a good job training you," she teased. She let me go and went for the forks and knives, lying them down on the table.

I placed a plate in front of Megan. "Ooo, we're being served by a Prince." She grinned. "Not everyone can say that."

I rolled my eyes and placed Ella's plate down before walking over and getting mine. I sat with them. "How many people can say the Prince is annoyed at them?" I retorted.

"Probably loads. I could see you being annoying," Megan said matter of factly.

I looked at Ella who was laughing. "I'm sorry that was fast for her."

Megan nodded. "It really was, usually I'm a little slower."

"Truth." She dove into breakfast.

For the next fifteen minutes, it was silent. And man did I enjoy that silence. But soon enough it was over, and then started Megan's inquisition.

"So, now down to the dirty details," Megan said with a grin.

I let out a groan which Ella seemed to echo. "Megan, I already told you I am not telling you how big his dick is."

"Well, it must be pretty big if you're sore, or are you just tight?" Megan said.

"Megan!"

"Did he treat you right? Did he make you come?"

"Megan!" Ella shouted.

"Surely, this is the question you ask when she's alone?" I asked, raising an eyebrow.

"But she won't answer me, and it's fun to see her embarrassed. May as well go to the source," Megan shrugged like it was obvious.

"What if I said I was really good in bed, and then Ella said the opposite when I left?" I questioned.

Megan cocked her head to the side. "Didn't think of that. Someone just tell me. My life is boring." She turned to look at Ella. "We're besties ride until we die. You should tell me."

"Fine. He was amazing in bed. Yes, he's big. No, I'm not telling the exact size. I didn't pull out a ruler and measuring tape. Yes, he made me come. It was special, perfect, and everything a first and second time should be. Happy?" Ella said.

"Extremely," Megan grinned. "The majority of my curiosity has been squandered." She paused. "For now."

I shook my head.

I looked at my phone and saw a text from Jeremy about races. I replied back saying I would be there.

I hadn't raced in a while and I needed to feel the adrenaline of going far too fast.

"Right, I'm going to leave you girls to the girly chat," I told them. I stood up and headed upstairs to get dressed. I came back down, kissing Ella. "I love you. I'll see you soon."

"I love you, too."

# Chapter Twenty-Nine

## MELINDA

Daisy's seemed louder and brighter before, either that or maybe I had begun to suffer from migraines, which would be a first.

After morning breakfast, I ended up heading over to Daisy's with Megan for my shift.

I needed to refocus.

Alex was taking all my attention away from trying to clear the debt and actually working. Daisy didn't mind me not doing as many shifts as I used to. She was loving the fact that I was having a life.

I walked into the kitchen and rubbed my head. "Chef, do you have any paracetamol?"

"In the locker. You know which one is mine, so just take it," he said.

"Thanks Dave, love you!" I called out.

I headed into the staff area opening his locker and popped two tablets into my hand before heading back into the diner and pouring myself a glass of lemonade and took two of the tablets.

"Melinda, could I have a word in my office?" I looked to see Daisy appearing at the door.

I nodded and headed to the office with her. I sat in the chair, rubbing my temples and sighing.

I could handle most things but headache or an earache turned me into the world's biggest baby. I was okay admitting that, too.

"What's up?"

"Are you okay?"

I looked at Daisy in confusion. "Fine, why?"

"Melinda, you're looking awfully thin. Have you been eating?"

"More than usual," I said honestly. "If you had asked me this back in August, I would have said no. Is something wrong? Am I not doing a good job?"

"Melinda, this chat has nothing to do with your work. I am worried about your health. You look like you're losing a lot of weight. This has nothing to do with the Prince, does it?"

I looked down at myself, I didn't think I looked awfully thin, clothes seemed to still be fitting the same. "No, Alex isn't making me do anything I don't want to do. He loves me the way I am. I've been a little sick but nothing major. The hospital took blood tests, but I haven't heard anything, so I assumed no news is good news."

"What did you take the tablets for today?"

"Headache. I think I'm suffering from migraines," I said with a shrug. "Look Daisy, I appreciate the concern more than you know, but I promise I'm good. I'm healthy as far as I know."

"How's the debt repayment going?" She asked softly.

I had broken down to Daisy a year ago when I first discovered the debt that mum had wracked up in my name. If I was going to claim it was fraud, it would've meant that I'd have to go to the police and the chance of my mum getting arrested was very high. As much as it pissed me off, the whole situation I loved her. I wouldn't want to see anything bad happen to her. You only had one mum and as questionable as mine was, I loved her. "Still a good few grand left. Every pay here helps, I'll get there."

"Melinda I wish you would let me help you." Daisy sighed.

"Daisy, I appreciate it, but I can't just take money from you. It wouldn't feel right," I told her. "You already do enough by giving me this job."

"You say me giving you money doesn't feel right, but you using the hard-earned money to get rid of the debt doesn't feel right either," she said, shaking her head. "You should make your mum pay for it."

"Accept their guilt money? No thanks." I scoffed.

Did I have too much pride? Probably.

Did I care? No.

"I'll be fine Daisy. Thanks."

Daisy nodded, not saying anything else.

I left the office heading back into the diner and focused on working.

A few hours later, my shift finally finished.

I headed straight home. I walked into the house and slumped on the sofa.

I was way too tired.

My headache didn't go away and tablets weren't doing anything to help. I squinted as it started to blur. I blinked a few times trying to focus my eyes. It wasn't helping the room was getting blurrier. My heart started to beat faster.

*Why wasn't it getting clearer?*

"Mum!" I yelled. I screamed, blinking faster and faster. "Mum!"

I heard footsteps running down the stairs and I felt the breeze as she ran into the room. "Melinda, what's wrong?"

I blinked even more. My mum was blurry. "I can't see." I could feel the tears starting to fall down my cheeks.

"Blink a few times, honey. Nice and slow," she ordered.

I had no idea how she was so calm right now. I couldn't fucking see. I was breathing heavily and could feel my leg bouncing.

"Calm down," she snapped.

"I am!" I screamed.

I heard my mum sigh as I cried harder.

"Baby Boo, I need you to breathe. Nice and slow, you're safe here. I know you're worried. You need to try and calm down."

*Baby Boo.*

God, it had been so long since I heard my mum call me that.

I did as she said, breathing nice and slow. "Mummy, why can't I see?"

"Tell me what you can see."

"Everything is blurry, but bright," I said. "I've had

really bad headaches all day. Daisy said she thinks I'm too thin."

"I kind of agree with Daisy, and I know you've been eating more than you used to Baby Boo," mum said softly. "This is what we're going to do. I'm going to get you in the car, and we are going to the closest A&E department. We are not leaving until we have answers."

"We already tried that when I passed out," I mumbled.

"I don't care. If I have to go full mama bear, I will," mum said. "You're going to keep those eyes closed and try not to panic. I know it's scary, but we will get through it."

I nodded, and she grabbed my hand pulling me off the sofa. She led me out of the house and towards the car.

Every instinct made me want to open my eyes, but for a change, I listened to my mum. I had a little bit of faith that she wouldn't let me walk into a door or trip over. I heard the door open, "Bend and sit. You're in the front seat."

I did as she asked. I reached around for my seatbelt, clicking it in place. I heard the other side of the car open and she climbed in starting the car. "It'll be ok, right?"

"Baby Boo, I know we've had our differences the last year, but let me tell you no matter what I am your mother. I will fight whoever I need to," she said. "I'm not leaving until I know what is wrong with you. They did a blood test a week ago, and we heard nothing. I want answers."

The car started moving.

I sighed. "Mum, why don't you like Alex? Even from the first meeting you were very standoffish."

"Oh baby boo, it's complicated. It comes down to that

I don't want to see you hurt. You don't belong in his world, and pretty soon, he'll toss you aside."

"He loves me, mum," I whispered. "And I love him."

"Baby Boo, sometimes love isn't enough," she said.

I opened my eyes slightly and shut them immediately as it was still blurry.

I didn't want to believe my mum. I felt like right now Alex and I could get through anything.

"I'd like to believe it is," I admitted.

"Did he take care of you when you had sex?" She asked.

I choked on air and coughed, slapping my chest a few times. "Mum!"

"What? We're both adults. Also, I tried asking him. He was respectful of his answers," she mused.

"You did what?" I asked in disbelief.

"Yeah, did he not tell you?"

I shook my head. "No."

"So, did he?"

"Yes, mum. He was the perfect gentleman," I said. "He made it special. I felt loved and cared for."

"Were you safe?" She asked.

I pursed my lips as I tried to think of that night, "I think so. I'm like seventy percent sure we were safe."

I heard mum sigh. "God, I hope so."

I didn't say anything else because my sex life was not something I wanted to keep discussing with her.

It didn't take long before we arrived at the hospital, and she got me out of the car, leading me into A&E. She sat me down before walking off to the reception desk. I opened my eyes, blinking a few times trying to adjust to the brightness. The blur was getting a little less. I could at least make out shapes of people and things.

*I would be okay. I had to be.*

It was just migraines. With some medicine and relaxation, I should be okay. I looked to see what I hoped was the outline of my mother walking towards me. She sat down next to me. "We'll be seen soon."

I heard my phone ding and pulled it out of my pocket handing it to mum. "Can you read it?"

"Megan says, 'why did she choose law? Lectures suck ass, and so does the work,'" she said. I heard another ding, and mum snorted with laughter. "'Maybe I should quit and become a stripper. Ugh, saying that I'm too lazy and that sounds far too people-y.'"

I smiled, letting out a little laugh.

"Do you want me to tell her you're at the hospital?" Mum asked.

"No, I don't want anyone to know until we know," I admitted. "That includes Alex. Just don't reply yet. I will figure something out later. Maybe pretend I fell asleep early."

"How are your eyes? Are they still completely blurry?"

"Erm, they're a little better. It kind of feels like I need glasses, but obviously we know my last eye test was fine, but it's a minus four," I said.

I laid my head down on my mum's shoulder, and she stroked my hair.

I couldn't help but smile. It felt like I was a baby again. Much easier and simpler times, that was for sure.

I lost track of time as we waited, but my mum never stopped playing with my hair. I loved it.

"Melinda Brown?" Someone finally called.

I stood up with mum as she led us through the hospital until we got to the hospital room. She let me sit down on the chair. "So, what can I help you with today, Miss Brown?"

"I've had a horrendous headache all day, and then, my vision went blurry," I said.

"This is our second hospital trip. The last time my daughter passed out, they said they took some blood. We never heard anything," mum said. "I am not allowing my daughter to be fobbed off again."

"Let me look up and see if anything has been added in your file," she said.

I told her my date of birth as she tapped away at the computer not saying anything but focusing on the computer her brows furrowing as she read every now and then and that did not fill me with confidence at all. "Nobody gave you a follow up about your blood test results?"

"No. Why what's wrong with me?" I asked wide eyed.

"Your blood came back a little abnormal, and they've asked you to be referred to a specialist for another blood test to test for certain things," she explained. "So, let's do another blood test, and I'll put a rush on it. Hopefully, it won't be too long until you get results."

"What is she to do in the meantime if her vision keeps going blurry?"

"Relax and don't panic."

I rolled my eyes.

*That was shitty advice.*

As if I couldn't help panic when I couldn't see.

Would it be a case of I could lose my sight permanently? I didn't want to go blind. Things around me started to come into focus once more. I looked at my mum who was biting her nails and bouncing her leg. She was worried.

I reached for her hand, squeezing it tightly.

"It will be okay."

I had no idea if my mum was saying it to convince me or her, either one it wasn't working.

I tried to think back to when I was last feeling shitty. I just assumed it was a lack of tiredness or not eating properly.

What if it was something more?

What if I had ignored important signs?

What if they were going to tell me I was going to die in like three to five business days.

Okay that was a little dramatic but, had I ignored my health just because I wanted to be stubborn.

## Chapter Thirty

# ALEXANDER

Something seemed off, and I couldn't figure out why.

Ever since Ella and I had slept together again, she had been distant. I was terrified I had done something wrong.

Most of my texts were met with one word answers or a meme.

It felt like she was hiding something but I didn't know what. I was letting my father's paranoia get into my head and the last thing I needed was his paranoia.

I walked into Elizabeth's room and slumped down onto her bean bag.

She was currently reading her stuffed teddies a story.

I laid back and enjoyed her story, trying to forget everything else. Although. I wasn't successful because my mind drifted back to Ella. I pulled my phone out of my pocket, seeing if I had any messages from her or TikToks that she had sent me.

Nothing.

I heard the door open and turned to see Henry walking in and slumping down on the bean bag next to me with a loud sigh.

I let out a little laugh. “I know why I’m in a mood, but why are you in a mood?”

“Mum and dad are making me get a tutor,” he said.

“A tutor? For what? You’re not even in high school yet,” I said confused. “Surely you don’t need a tutor for anything important just yet.”

“That was my argument too!” Henry said, his hands in the air clenching as if he was trying to strangle someone. “Apparently, it’s not normal that words jump around the page. The letters and numbers get muddled.”

I sat up and looked at Henry. “That’s not normal. How long has this been happening? Is this why you don’t like to read.”

He buried his head into the bean bag.

“Henry, mum and dad might be right on this. It sounds like you have a learning disability,” I told him gently.

“I’m not disabled!” He snapped.

“Henry, that isn’t what a learning disability means. It just means your brain works a little differently than mine, Arthur’s, our parents, or even Elizabeth’s,” I told him. “We have to find a way that your brain can learn and absorb the information. It’s not a bad thing.”

“It’s not?”

I pulled him off the bean bag into a hug and squeezed him tightly. “It just makes you more special Henry. We love you whether you have a learning disability or not. So go back to mother and father, and tell them you’ll accept the tutor.”

He nodded, getting up and leaving the room. "Thanks, Alex."

I smiled to myself.

Maybe I should be a therapist instead of a Prince. Or maybe it could be a side hustle.

I stood up, leaving Elizabeth to her tea party and walking throughout the Palace.

For a place so big, I did feel bored a lot. It was the weekend, which meant no duties for a change.

Ella said she was working, and I was procrastinating my butt off not doing university work. Maybe I should have taken a leaf out of my own book and did some work, but I couldn't focus.

"Alexander, your father is looking for you," a butler said.

I groaned, "Can't you just pretend you didn't see me?" I asked.

"Afraid not, Sir," he said with a small smile.

I groaned, heading towards the office. The door was open as I reached and I could hear whispering. "Nicely," I heard someone mutter sharply.

I walked into the office and saw my father and mother standing by the fireplace. "You called?" I asked sarcastically.

"Hello Alexander, could you sit down?" My father asked, pointing to the chair as they both took a seat on the sofa.

I shook my head. "I don't want to. This seems like bad news. I don't want bad news or vibes."

"Baby boy, sit down," Mother said gently.

Dread filled my stomach. My mother only called me

baby boy when she had bad news. It was the same nickname she used when my grandfather and grandmother died.

I sat down and looked at them concerned. "What's wrong? Who died?"

"Nobody, honey," mother said.

"You only call me baby boy when there's bad news," I told her. "So, what's the bad news?"

"The background check Miss Brown agreed to has come through," Father said.

He handed me some papers, and I looked at him confused.

"She didn't come back clean, Alexander."

"What do you mean?" I asked, confused. "Ella would tell me anything I needed to know. How do I know you haven't fixed it? You haven't exactly been quiet about your hatred for her."

"Alexander, I am concerned that is all," Father said, shaking his head.

"Baby boy, your dad hasn't made it up. Open it," mum said.

I slumped back on the sofa and opened the envelope. I flipped up the paper, and my eyes laid on the envelope. My eyes widened as I read her finances. "Holy fuck, how does someone get into that much debt?"

"You didn't know?" Mother asked softly.

I shook my head and continued to read.

Her father, Roman Brown, was arrested for murder and assault. There was still a warrant out for his arrest.

My eyes widened as I saw the name. "How?" I looked at my father. "How did he attempt to kill you? If this was true how did she even step into the Palace with our security?"

"We used to be close, the name rang a bell. When she appeared that's why I was so standoffish, Alexander. Roman Brown used to be a close friend of the family, his mother was my father's P.A. We grew up together. And then one day, it all changed. He tried to kill me, and I never did find out why."

"You're sure it was him?" I asked.

My father nodded. "He left a note."

"She's never mentioned her father before," I whispered.

I read the rest of the background check.

Ella was receiving money from him.

Why would she hide this?

Why hide the relationship with her father?

Some of the other things were things I already knew.

"No. This can't be true."

"I'm sorry, but it is."

I shook my head, "No, I love her!" I stood up, running a hand through my hair. "There's got to be an answer for this. She wouldn't—"

"Alexander, how well do you know this girl? Forget about your feelings, think practically. Was she with you for access to money? Have you slept together?" Mother asked.

"I really don't want to discuss my sex life with you," I said. "It's not any of your business if we have."

"It is, if she cries assault."

"She wouldn't!" I snapped.

"How do you know?"

"Our relationship is on record. The public knows we are together."

My father scoffed. "You can still assault someone in a relationship, Alexander."

I walked out the room, slamming the door behind me.

She wouldn't do this.

She loved me.

I slammed my fist into the wall next to me and screamed. "Fuck!" My fist went straight through, and I pulled it out, ignoring the pain. It didn't compare to the pain I was feeling over her betrayal.

I walked over to the garage and grabbed my keys off the hook, getting into the car. I opened the garage and sped out until I got to the gates, and they were opened. I pressed my foot down on the accelerator. I had no idea where I was driving to, but I needed to clear my head.

I pressed the button to roll down the window and enjoyed the breeze in my face. I finally stopped driving as I reached the River Thames.

Something about watching the river go by was peaceful.

I looked at the time, seeing it was only 3:00 p.m. I pulled my phone out and clicked Ella's face to open the messages. She still hadn't replied to my messages. I pressed the call button and it began to ring almost immediately I got sent to voicemail.

*Why the fuck was she ignoring my calls?*

I slammed my hand on the steering wheel.

It couldn't be true. I pray to God it's not true. I love her, and I can't lose her. I rang her once more, hoping this would be the time she answered, but it went to voicemail.

I needed to see her.

I reversed away from where I parked and headed to her.

A couple of hours later, I was parked outside of her house.

I had seen a man enter her house and as I focused I noticed it was her father.

*Fuck.*

They were right.

I pressed her caller ID again, giving it a ring. It rang three times before I was sent to voicemail again. I got out of the car, walking over and knocking on the door.

The door opened and Ella stood there with surprise etched on her face.

"We need to talk."

She frowned and nodded letting me into the house, I pulled the envelope out of my pocket as she sat in the living room. "What's wrong? I'm sorry for dodging your calls."

"You lied to me, Melinda," I said.

Her mouth dropped open, "What?"

"Why didn't you tell me the truth? What was the point of lying?"

"What the fuck are you talking about you?" She asked, taking a step closer to me.

"Your fucking father!" I shouted.

She flinched. "I don't have anything to do with him."

"So, he gives you money for shits and giggles?" I asked, shaking my head. "Melinda, you're in debt, and he gives you money."

"If you would let me explain, I don't accept his guilt

money," she snapped. "The debt isn't something easy I can explain—"

"He tried to kill my father, too. I mean I kind of don't blame him too much on that front. You lied to me.."

She flinched slightly. "You don't know the full story, Alex."

"Don't call me that," I snapped. "You've lost that privilege. I trusted you. I fell in love with you."

She reached forward, pushing me away from her.

"Then, you don't get to touch me. Let me explain."

I could feel myself shutting down. "You can't be trusted. Did you sleep with me just to accuse me of assault to try and blackmail me?"

Her eyes widened. "What the actual fuck? Did you seriously just ask me that after having sex with you?"

As I looked at her, I knew I struck a chord, most normal people would back down, but I didn't care she was destroying my heart. "Well."

She stepped closer. Before I could react, she reached up and slapped me hard across the face. "Get out. I can't believe you even just fucking suggested that. You fucking arsehole!"

I handed her the envelope, "You lied, and I'm the arsehole?" I laughed, shaking my head and walking out of the room.

"Alex, stop! We need to talk about this!"

I opened the front door staring at her. "No, the time to talk about it would have been when you told me the truth. We're done, Melinda."

"Please," she begged. "Let's talk about this."

"You broke my heart," I whispered.

I turned around, heading towards the car and ignoring the swarm of paparazzi who were trying to surround me. I got into the car and sped off immediately and dialled Jeremy's number.

He answered immediately. "What's up, dude?"

"Get me a race as soon as possible," I said. "Some good stuff, too."

"Did something happen?"

"She fucking broke my heart man. She lied."

"Oh, fuck. Forget the race. Come to my house. I have the antidote," he said.

"Be there soon." I ended the call pressing my foot on the accelerator, heading straight to Jeremy.

If anyone could make me forget all this bullshit, it was him.

## Chapter Thirty-One

# MELINDA

I stared at the empty space Alex had just left.

*What the fuck had happened?*

I looked at the envelope he placed in my hand, ripping it open. I scanned it.

*Are you fucking kidding me?*

I stormed into the kitchen and came face to face with mum. "Get the sperm donor here."

Mum walked over to the backdoor, and the sperm donor entered. "You tried to kill Alex's dad?!" I screamed.

"What?"

I threw the paper at them. "How could you not tell me? Either of you. I told him there was nothing I was hiding!"

"Melinda, calm down," mum said.

I shook my head and started to bounce my leg, "You've ruined everything! I hate you both! Why did you do this?"

"Ugh, rude. How come I got blamed for his attempted

murder?" The sperm donor said with a roll of his eyes. "Melinda, he's just a boy."

"There you go mum, he's just a boy," I snapped.

I spun around, storming out the house. I entered the park, walking around the small pond before sitting down.

I pulled out my phone and looked at the call log. I shouldn't have dodged his calls.

*God, how much had he spiralled with me not answering my phone?*

I should have just answered them. I sent Megan a pin drop of my location, knowing that she would come.

My phone began to buzz with messages.

I opened it up, seeing some of the people from my course talking. I opened them up and my heart sank. The break-up had already hit everywhere. I opened my social media apps and saw videos had been posted as well as comments. People were making suggestions of why we would have broken up. Hate comments and death threats were beginning to enter my inbox.

I shut my phone off as tears slid down my cheeks. I sniffled trying to keep silent whilst crying.

*How did everything go so wrong?*

I ran a hand through my hair and started playing with the ends.

I couldn't understand how the sperm donor tried to kill his dad?

I couldn't wrap my head around it.

The debt I could understand because I should have been honest with Alex about it. It had blown up in my face. But the father card, he should know any time he tried to mention it I would just push away or change the subject.

Had I created all of this?

I heard a crunch in the grass and turned to see Megan wrapped up in a coat and another one in hand, she walked over placing it on my shoulders. "Your mum rang and said you didn't take a coat or shoes."

I looked down at my feet and realised she was right. I had left the house barefooted.

Megan sat next to me and reached over, squeezing my hand.

The tears began to fall harder as she squeezed onto me tighter.

"What happened, Mel?"

"He broke up with me," I whispered, sniffling. "I didn't tell him about something, and then my sperm donor tried to kill his father. I didn't know."

"What was it?" Megan asked, confused. "You two were so wrapped up in each other, I thought he knew everything."

"My secret," I mumbled.

Megan looked at me confused, "I don't understand, Mel. What secret could be bad enough that he would dump you."

"I have debt."

Megan snorted. "Don't we all? The joys of university."

I looked at my best friend.

She was so innocent in her thinking and I loved that for her.

"No," I admitted. "When the sperm donor left my mother, things got bad. My mother racked up a lot of debt in my name. She committed fraud, and I owe shit ton of debt."

"What the fuck?"

I sniffled. "I was eight the first time I picked my drunk mum up off the floor. I used to worry she'd vomit and die. She lost her job, and that's when she stole my identity, wracking up a load of debt in my name. I couldn't get a maintenance loan or much help from university, because to them, I look like we have loads of money. They tried to give me guilt money, but I can't accept it. I know the easiest thing is to accept it, and a lot of my problems would go away, but it feels like it would just be sweeping everything under the rug."

"El, how much do you have left to pay?"

"Eight grand," I whispered.

"That's why you were working so hard, and why you didn't always eat," Megan whispered. She pulled me into a tight hug and I burst into tears, it felt so good to say it out loud. A weight had lifted off my shoulders. "Hey, what was it you said before? Ride or die, remember? When we're together, no judgement. You can get that from anyone else."

I sniffled and let out a little laugh. "You do listen to me."

"You can say some insightful things." She laughed. "A problem shared is a problem halved. Did you try to claim fraud?"

"They wanted me to report it to the police, but they would know it was mum. And as much as I'm pissed, she's my mum," I said.

"Maybe you should talk to my dad. He might be able to help from a law perspective," she said. "You can talk to him and know he won't do anything without your permission or report your mum."

"Thanks, Megan. You're the best friend anyone could ask for, you know that?"

"I know. Right, the next problem is Jeremy Kyle," she grinned. "I really do miss that show."

"Alex asked me if I slept with him to claim assault and then blackmail him," I whispered, my heart breaking with each word.

I couldn't help but replay the way he flinched, and the way he shut down. Our conversation started with Alex, and it ended with Prince Alexander.

He had rushed back to public persona.

His armour and protection.

"The fuck is wrong with him? What would you gain out of blackmailing him?"

"Money, to pay the debt," I said.

"Fucking idiot. Does he not realise you are obsessed with him."

"I don't know how this is going to be fixed. He hated me, Megan. I let him in and fell for him. Now, he hates me," I cried. "I can't. He called me a liar. How did they think the sperm donor who tried to kill his dad wouldn't affect my relationship?"

"He has no right to call you a liar. Did he forget he kept a massive secret of being a fucking prince from you? Hello pot, meet kettle."

I snorted a little.

This is why I love my best friend.

"You know what this therapy session needs," Megan said, raising an eyebrow.

"What?"

"Warmth for a start because how the fuck are you not freezing? It's nearly December man," she shook her head in disgust.

"You always were dramatic."

"And alcohol, let's add some fun to this little pity party."

I looked at her, it probably wasn't a good idea considering I needed referring to a specialist but on another note I didn't fucking care. "Oh, also, I needed another blood test. I lost my vision the other day. Yay for trauma!" I jumped up and held a hand out for Megan who looked stumped. "Let's go get drunk."

She reached for my hand standing up and we began to make the slow walk out the park, now Megan had mentioned the fact I wore no shoes I finally felt the cold on my feet. I shivered slightly. The quicker we got out the cold the better, because I was feeling it now.

I blinked as my vision went a little blurry, although it had happened a few times since the hospital trip I still paid no mind to it.

I stopped as the world began to spin.

"El, are you okay?"

I shook my head, I placed my hands on my waist as I struggled to breathe. It was like I had run a marathon without actually running one. "I think I need to—" I squeezed my eyes shut trying to focus. "I need—" The world tipped as I found myself falling to the ground.

"El!" Megan shouted.

I sat up trying to find balance. "I don't feel—" I slumped into the grass as the world went dark around me.

# REVIEWS

Reviews mean the world to indie and self published authors like me. It would really mean the world if you left a review at your chosen retailer, or any of your social media.

Thank you so much for taking your time reading mine book it means the world.

# ACKNOWLEDGMENTS

I'd like to start by thanking my readers, without you guys reading and supporting this book would not be possible without you. I'd also like to thank you guys for being so patient as it has taken me a few years to release another book.

I would like to thank Kirsty from the PrettyLittle-DesignCo for the absolute stunning cover she made. I love working with her and she blows me away every time.

I'd like to thank Jade Church and Jessica Sydney for all the hard work both of them have done by getting this book ready for readers and I have loved working with you both.

I'd like to thank Wings & Words community, they have been amazing with their support the readers as well as Beth and the team, thank you so much for all you do for me! You guys do amazing work when it comes to getting my book into reader's hands.

Giselle from Xpresso Tours for her help in getting this book out and into readers hands.

Chloe thank you for all your support in the early days when it came to this book I remember so many of our random chats about it and you making me covers and listening to me rambling so thank you.

My parents thank you for always believing in me and supporting my dreams.

Alex thank you for showing me what love feels like, and that once you have the right person nothing is ever too much. I love you.

# ABOUT THE AUTHOR

Samantha Jayne Grubey is an author of new adult romance.

When she's not writing or reading you can find her probably procrastinating life away and playing sims, or wasting so much time on TikTok.

If you would like to stay up to date on any new releases, sign up to the newsletter at www.samanthajaynegrubey.com

# ALSO BY SAMANTHA JAYNE GRUBEY

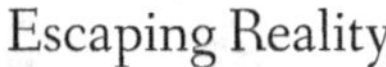

Escaping Reality

Nobody wants to live without their best friend, but when Holly is murdered, Chlo has no choice.

Chlo is the only person who has the answers - too bad she can't remember when she wakes up two weeks later.

Chlo is sent to a rehabilitation centre where she has to learn to grieve, along the way of trying to access her memories she has to deal with her feelings for Corey, her best friend's brother.

For Holly was always a reason to stay away, now it's their reason to try.

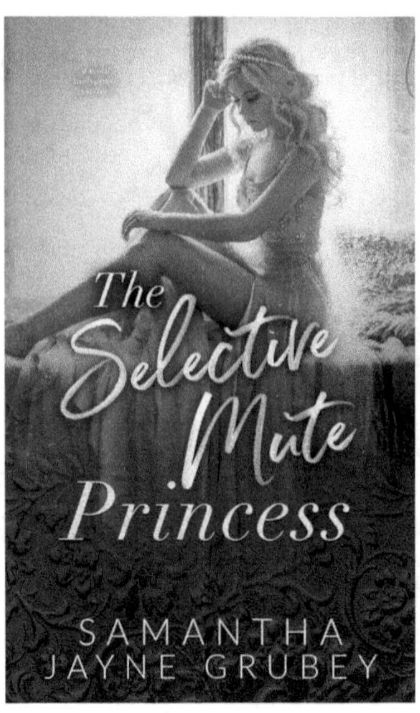


Princess Amelia has been silent for ten years, ever since Amelia and Ava were kidnapped. One returned home the other did not. Amelia has always kept herself guarded with her twenty-first birthday approaching things are going to be changing.

Ethan Sparks is on his first assignment, guard the Princess in the Palace. The longer he's there the more he finds himself being drawn to Princess Amelia, he can see she's drowning and he wants to help.

Romantic interests stirs in a mixing pot of emotions as Amelia and her family recover from the kidnapping and murder of her sister. Unsure what to feel or who to believe, Amelia needs to find her truth, as she deals with her trauma and finally brings her family to mend. Along the way they find themselves hitting challenges at every wall. So many questions left unanswered by the kidnapping and murder, can she finally find the answers she's searching for? Can Amelia finally allow herself to live and be freed from the guilt she feels? Can Ethan survive the challenges that come with falling for a Princess in line for the throne?

www.ingramcontent.com/pod-product-compliance
Lightning Source LLC
LaVergne TN
LVHW010604100826
845148LV00014B/2835

* 9 7 8 1 7 3 9 8 8 3 6 5 2 *